The Forgotten Prince

THE FORGOTTEN PRINCE

The Wedding Series
Book 7

Patricia McLinn

CHAPTER ONE

She was going to pretend she didn't remember him.

Karl saw that even as he approached the knot of officials and onlookers surrounding her.

He'd spotted her the second she'd walked in to this VIP lounge at Marco Polo Airport outside Venice, Italy. Narrow black skirt that should have been understated, but wasn't on her. Simple white blouse unbuttoned just enough to catch attention, not enough to demand it.

Harmon Reed.

The woman of his dreams. Or nightmares, depending on how you looked at it.

All these years and she shows up in his life here, of all places. And now, of all times.

He'd been surprised—and a few other things—as he'd watched her breeze in, connect a device, and begin tapping away at it without the slightest hesitation.

Hesitation had never been her style.

He'd been deciding between catching her eye and the far, far smarter course of raising the newspaper in front of his face so she wouldn't see him, when the stir began. More accurately, he was wondering why the hell he hadn't already raised the newspaper.

The disturbance didn't start right away. Even when it did, it started small.

One of the women who worked behind the desk approached where Harmon sat and asked a quiet question. Harmon tried to carry it off with a high-handed wave before she resumed typing rapidly. The woman didn't buy it, taking out her phone and hitting numbers while standing right beside Harmon's shoulder, like a dog who'd found a coyote in among the herd.

If she got herself out of this, he decided, he would strategically retreat behind the newspaper—no more debating—and figure it was all good.

The incident escalated, voices in Italian and English rising, words coming faster.

Uniformed airport security arrived. Passport demanded and supplied. In between, she kept typing. Then came this official in civilian clothes who wrapped a hand around her arm and drew her upright out of her chair, even as she strained to reach her device.

That's when Karl stood and started forward.

He was still some distance away when the ring of spectators parted for an instant and their eyes met. The flicker in her hazel eyes disappeared almost before it happened.

But he'd seen it. And he knew.

She'd seen him coming toward her and had decided in that instant to play the I-don't-remember-you game.

If that wasn't just like her.

The never-need-a-hand-even-if-I'm-drowning, stubborn as a mule female.

He should turn and walk away.

It would be the smarter thing to do. Far, far smarter. On so many levels, from international relations to his personal sanity.

He reached the group.

"What's the problem here?" he asked the official who still had a hand wrapped around her arm.

Karl didn't like that hold on her arm. But he wasn't going to let that interfere with accomplishing what needed to be accomplished. He kept his tone mild enough not to ruffle feathers yet firm enough to make it clear he expected to be answered.

"Nothing to concern you, sir."

His assigned handler hurried forward from wherever he'd discreetly disappeared to when they'd arrived at the lounge. "Your—Sir. What problem have you? What may I do to assist you?"

Handler wasn't the title this guy used—this guy or any of the others he'd been assigned over the past year or so. Here the official term translated to something like host, guide, and easer of all things. But Karl figured handler covered it. One of them always appeared when he hit Europe, no matter where. He could have shaken them, but that would have made a lot of people unhappy, from this guy expecting a good tip, on up. Way up.

Hey, if they wanted this guy to walk him from his arriving flight to the VIP lounge and then on to his departing flight, fine. He'd go along. As long as they didn't bother him at home.

"I asked this gentleman what the problem was." Karl nodded toward the official in the suit.

His handler frowned at the man. "You must—"

"This does not concern you," the official repeated. This time he barely tacked on the "sir." Possibly because he was annoyed at the interference. More likely because his charge kept shifting her weight unexpectedly, causing him to jerk forward and back, and side to side. Looked uncomfortable.

What was she up to?

"Afraid it does concern me," Karl said without emotion, "since this lady is a member of my party."

"*Your* party?" she muttered low enough that the official didn't hear.

But she'd given herself away. There'd be no cause to mock a stranger with that question or that tone. Especially a stranger in the VIP lounge, being treated with obvious deference. It only made sense because she *did* recognize him.

"Your party?" said his handler in confusion. "But…?"

"Yes." He'd learned long ago not to volunteer unnecessary details. No phrases about forgetting to mention she was coming. No explanations about arranging to meet her here. One flat word.

"Ms. Reed is in your party?" the official asked with not quite a sneer.

"Yes."

So she was using her real name. Someone up to real trouble wouldn't use their real name. He had to bank on that, and hope like hell he was right, since it wasn't just himself he was putting on the line here. With Harmon, though…

And it could be she still used Reed, while her legal name was her husband's. But he'd have heard if she—He shut off that line of thought. Needed to keep his attention on this situation, not get distracted.

"Why does she not say—?"

The official's question was drowned out by a spate of animated Italian from the handler. Karl caught enough words here and there to know it was about him and his position. The official wasn't silent, not by a long shot, but after four or five exchanges he seemed to be winding down.

Then a new woman from behind the desk came over and gave a curt nod to the first woman, who retreated quietly. This woman had more clout. Body language proclaimed that all around—hers, the first woman's, the handler's, even the security official's.

More rapid Italian. He thought the phrase she kept repeating translated to "ready for departure." His handler started saying it, too.

The official was done for, though not ready to submit. He said something insistent to the handler, who argued back.

Reluctantly, the handler turned to him. "I am most sorry, sir. This … this man you see here of a name I will discover asks if you will please verify your responsibility for this—the lady. Ms. Reed."

At that moment, she plunged sideways, freed herself from the official's hold, reached a fingertip to the device, tapped it decisively, then relaxed.

The official had the opposite reaction. His now-empty hand balled into a fist as he stumbled after her.

Karl stepped between them, looking down at the official. "Yes. I verify my responsibility."

The official wasn't stupid. His eyes showed that he recognized that he stood on the threshold of real trouble.

The handler and the woman from behind the desk broke into more rapid Italian. The official pivoted on his heel to start away, but the handler proved his worth by holding on to him and demanding "*passaporto.*" The official half tossed it to him as if it were of no consequence, leaving without a backward glance.

The handler caught it on the fly. "Your flight is prepared, Your Hi—sir. Now. We must go now. I will—" He darted back to where Karl had been sitting.

Karl said a quiet "*grazie*" to the woman, who smiled, bowed her head, and returned behind the desk.

The addition to what had been his party of one busied herself with turning off her device and slipping it into a cross between a duffel bag and a purse.

Before she'd finished, the handler was back, indicating with gestures and bows that they should precede him.

She raised her eyebrows at the cowboy hat the handler presented him.

Those arches hiked a bit higher when he put the hat on, but she said nothing. Even fell in step as they exited the VIP lounge and started along a hallway.

He knew it wouldn't be that easy.

Neither of them said a word or looked toward the other until a sign overhead indicated the hallway would branch off soon.

"Thanks, but I can take it from here, uh, cowboy." Looking straight ahead, she spoke too low to be overheard by the handler behind them.

He replied at the same volume. "Don't be stupid as well as stubborn, Harmon."

"Do I know you?"

Another mistake. She didn't look at him. That would have been the natural reaction of a surprised person.

"Yes."

He tightened his hold on her arm. From the corner of his eye he saw her wince. He was pretty sure he hadn't put his hand in the same place the official had held, but just in case, he released that hold.

On the other hand he knew who he was dealing with, so he shifted his hand to the small of her back and reached across with his other hand to hold her wrist. It would appear solicitous to an observer, but it gave him even better control.

"Really, I can—"

"I don't care what you think you can do. What you're going to do is walk quietly beside me and get on an airplane. We're being watched and soon we'll be watched *and* listened to. Don't blow this."

"I can't—"

"You can."

"I don't want—"

"Tough."

She tried to pull away as they reached the intersecting hallway. He held on.

"I have to get to—"

"You're making this side trip first. You're not making a liar out of me this time, Harmon."

Her only reaction after that was a slight bobble in her step when she saw the Bariavak royal seal.

Not bad since he still felt like falling flat on his face when he saw it, and he'd been dealing with this for more than a year.

"Welcome, Prince Karl," the attendant named Raya said with a smile.

Harmon didn't even blink. So, not only had she recognized him, she knew his present circumstances.

He greeted Raya, quietly asked her to double the tip for the handler, and said Ms. Reed was joining them today.

He shook hands with the handler, who turned pink with either delight or embarrassment.

While Raya dealt with the tip and welcomed the unexpected guest, he said hello to the two pilots and had confirmation that it should be as smooth a trip as it could be over the mountains that surrounded Bariavak.

Strapped in across the aisle from where Raya had guided Harmon, he settled back, adjusted the brim of his cowboy hat so it covered his eyes and went to sleep.

CHAPTER TWO

Asleep.

Not pretending. Not faking.

Truly asleep.

She used to watch him sleep. Sure and solid and reliable. He'd always been able to sleep—

Nope. No memories. Not that far back, anyway.

Back to the scene in the VIP lounge was okay.

She'd had it handled. Or she would have in the end. It's why she'd changed out of her flats and slacks into these heels and skirt. Bad for some places, perfect for Italy. She hadn't even started to use the weapons in her arsenal when he'd strode in.

She didn't appreciate being claimed that way, like a piece of lost luggage, or being shanghaied away from her destination for this entirely unnecessary detour.

She *really* didn't appreciate not being able to tell him that she didn't appreciate it.

She wanted to put a dent in that cowboy hat. Possibly in the head below it.

Instead, she smiled at the attendant pretending not to study her.

She buttoned the next higher button on her blouse, then settled herself into the comfortable seat, hoping for some sleep herself.

"No," Karl ordered. "Don't say anything."

She'd barely opened her mouth. Besides, they were outside the tiny airport for heavens' sake, well away from the royal jet, out of earshot of anyone else. Walking across a small parking lot that could be anywhere in the world, at least anywhere that boasted a backdrop of erratic mountain peaks jostling each other for their piece of the sky.

The guy with the luggage cart—all Karl's, since her bag was on its way to London and she never let anyone handle her tote—had already reached an ordinary pickup truck and was putting the luggage in the back.

"This is Bariavak's idea of royal transportation?" She had to say something, since he'd told her not to.

"No. This is my buddy, Mirche, leaving me a truck to drive."

"Mirche? Army nickname?"

"Nope. What his parents named him when he was born here in Bariavak. Means world peace." There was a twist in his voice that made her suspect Mirche wasn't the most peaceful guy.

Without releasing her elbow, he tried to tip the guy, who'd finished stowing the two bags and intersected with them a few yards from the truck.

"No, no, no." The man held up protesting hands.

"For Mina's birthday," Karl said.

The man smiled all over his face. "You remember, Prince Karl? You remember such a thing?"

"I do. And you better remember it, too, Franc."

They chuckled as comrades. The man accepted the tip and trundled away with his cart.

Karl escorted her to the passenger door, opened it, waited for her to climb in—not easy in these heels and skirt—closed the door, locking it with the key pad as he went around the front to get in the driver's side.

"Really? Locking the door?" she said as soon as he got in.

"No telling with you. Didn't want you high-tailing it down the street."

"I still could have unlocked it and—"

"Fine. I wanted to cut down your head start."

She sighed. "You wouldn't have had much trouble catching up.

Not with these shoes and skirt."

He gave her a look from the corner of his eye that she couldn't read. Was he remembering the time they'd raced back to her car after—No, no remembering. Especially that.

He started the engine and backed out of the parking spot.

"Hey," she protested. "Why are we leaving the airport? I thought you just wanted a private place to yell. We can't leave. I need to get on the first plane to—"

"No planes until tomorrow. You'll have to stay overnight at the hotel."

"Look, whoever you are—"

He made a noise that an optimist might take for amusement. She doubted she'd ever been that optimistic.

"Give it up, Harmon. You gave yourself away back at Marco Polo."

She released a mildly exasperated breath. "How?" It might be useful information for the future. In case she ran into anyone else from her past whom she'd—

Maybe not so useful, since this scenario wasn't likely to be repeated.

Ever.

"First, eye contact," he said, jerking her thoughts back to her question. "Smart mouth to a supposed stranger. Not surprised enough about my knowing your name. Couple other things. All of it said you knew damned right well who I am. Then 'Bariavak's idea of royal transportation' said you knew my circumstances."

Interesting that he separated who he was and his *circumstances.*

Each moment he listed ran back through her mind. How she'd felt at those moments didn't matter. Not then and certainly not now, so she pushed the thoughts away.

He helped with that effort—surely without knowing it—by asking, "What was that about? Back at Marco Polo."

"I needed a charge."

He looked over at her.

"All the spots out in the main area were taken," she said. "There must have been a convention or something, because I checked up and down the terminal. I was going to lose power before I finished. And I was running out of time."

"You caused a riot in the VIP lounge to get your device charged?"

"A riot? That? Boy, you're still that kid from the sticks, aren't you?" she scoffed.

He looked at her. She was sorry she'd said that last bit. Not because it wasn't true—at least, it had been true and it might still be, no matter what his "circumstances." But why say it at all?

"And now you're Prince Karl of Bariavak," she added, as if there'd been no pause in her comments.

"Not exactly."

"That's what King Jozef of Bariavak wants. For Karl Wethers, born an American, veteran of the U.S. Army, and now the owner of a ranch in Wyoming, to become his heir to the throne of Bariavak."

Instead of pointing out that she must have been paying attention to the media stories about his "circumstances" to know all that, as she expected, he said, "You missed the part about the ranch being small, tiny, or struggling, depending on which report you saw or read."

"Modest was the term used."

"Huh. Don't recall that one."

"Is this ranch of yours worth giving up a crown?"

"You should see it."

He drove skillfully through narrow streets designed for horses, not pickups. Now and then he raised a hand in greeting to another driver or a pedestrian. Some responded in kind and some removed hats or bowed their heads.

His concentration on his driving and the interactions with others gave her an opportunity to look at him more closely than she'd been able to before.

The young face she'd first known had pared down to the essentials of bone, muscle, flesh. That one time since—What was wrong with her? The past stayed in the past.

His build had changed, too. He'd been rangy, almost gangly. He'd filled out, broadened.

His hair still showed some red, but it had darkened considerably from the last time she'd seen him.

No. The last time she hadn't seen his hair because—

"You've changed more than I have," she said abruptly.

"Still impatient, huh?"

"What does impatience have to do with—"

"Cuts out a lot of time fishing for compliments about the years being good to you when you land your own like you just did."

She waved that off as unimportant. "You were a boy."

"And you weren't a girl?"

"No, I wasn't. Hadn't been for a long time. Maybe never. Not the way you mean."

"What way is that?" He braked to a stop at a traffic sign.

She waved that off, too. "But you were definitely a boy. A boy from the country with wide eyes and a wide-open heart."

He turned his head toward her. They looked at each for a moment. The memories and the defenses shifting and moving, but never aligning to allow passage from her to him or him to her.

She blinked away first. Only then did he say, "Whether I was or wasn't back then, I'm not a boy anymore."

No. Not a boy anymore.

She shifted, went for light. "Since we agree I haven't changed, why'd it take you so long to spot me?"

"It didn't."

"I'd been in there ten, fifteen minutes easy before you—"

"I saw you when you walked in."

"I'd be touched except for the fact that if you'd gotten up and come over to say hello at the start I'd have been accepted, so none of the rest of it would have happened, and I wouldn't be stuck here now."

He tilted his head slightly, staring through the windshield. "Probably an instinct for survival that warns of nearby danger—that's why I spotted you and that's what kept telling me to stay in my seat."

"Then why didn't you?" That came out too sharp. It threatened to slice through layers she never let slide. Quickly, she added in a lighter tone. "Or you could have left me on my own. I'd have handled it. I *was* handling it."

He continued to stare into space as he mused, "Why didn't I stay seated? Let whatever was going to happen to you happen?" He slowly turned his head to make eye contact. "Your father."

CHAPTER THREE

He pulled the truck into a narrow curved drive in front of a small hotel that probably started its life as a house. A big house with a grand entry, but a house all the same.

"This is where you'll stay tonight," Karl said.

Two young men tumbled out of the building, calling hellos and taking Karl's bags from the bed of the truck without instruction. It had the ease of habit. Clearly, he'd stayed here before and was going to stay here now.

But he didn't say that. Which you'd think he would if he had any thought of their spending time together. Dinner, perhaps. Catching up on old times. Sharing laughs at old memories…

Right.

"They'll take good care of you here," he said. "They know your luggage was lost."

"Do they? Then they know wrong. My luggage isn't lost. My luggage is where it's supposed to be. Which is where *I'm* supposed to be."

He ignored that. "They'll get you what you need. If you want something else, ask. They're nice people. Don't take anything out on them that's meant for me."

She let out a long breath. "I won't. I could have handled it, Karl. That doesn't mean I don't recognize … You didn't have to do all this."

"I said you were in my party. I was responsible for you."

There was a pause, as if he expected her to say something to that. She didn't.

She was too busy hearing the echo of what he'd said in that airport hallway. *You're not going to make a liar of me again.*

He got out, went around the truck and held the door for her. As she climbed down, tugging at the skirt hem that seemed determined to reach her waist, he didn't look away.

Not that she could flatter herself any about that. Because his voice was unaffected when he said, "There's an early afternoon flight tomorrow that will take you to Frankfurt. The people here at the hotel will get you there at the right time. From Frankfurt, you should be able to get a flight to wherever you need to be. Goodbye, Harmon."

"Goodbye." She started toward the building. She stopped. Still with her back to him, she said, "Karl."

Turning, she saw he was at the front of the truck, heading toward the driver's side. He paused, but turned only his head.

"Thank you," she said, then went inside.

The next day, from his favorite overlook high up on the mountain above the castle, Karl watched the royal plane take off, climbing hard to get over the ring of peaks that had protected this country for centuries.

She was gone.

Out of Bariavak.

Good.

This would be tricky enough as it was without Harmon Reed throwing Molotov cocktails into the mix.

That's why he'd arranged everything indirectly and so he wouldn't see her again.

Not that there would have been much time left over from the unofficial meetings he'd held, last night with one man, this morning with a handful of people.

He just wished she hadn't looked at him that way when she'd said thank you yesterday. That mix of firebrand and vulnerability that had bowled him over long before he'd acquired the survival skills to deal with her.

Twelve Years Ago

She was sitting on a waist-high wall at the side entrance to the Officers' Club, swinging her legs side to side, the motion edging up the hem of her dress.

Now he'd see it as a female trick meant to call attention to the shapeliness of her legs. Then he'd just seen her legs.

"Hey there, Corporal."

He knew she was teasing. Her ease said she belonged here on the base, so she darned well knew rank insignia.

"I'm a private."

Her eyes widened. "Are you? Even better. How about giving me a ride." Behind her, in the room beside the officers' club that was rented out for events, a party was going on.

"I don't have a vehicle."

"I do. Can you drive anything smaller than a tank?"

"Yes. But why don't you drive yourself?"

"That's not very *gallant*." She'd pronounced it the French way. It seemed to come naturally to her. "Don't you want to drive me?"

"Where to?"

"Anywhere that's not here." She'd meant that to sound light, flippant. He caught darker currents in it.

"How old are you?" he'd asked abruptly.

"Again, not *gallant*. But I'll tell you anyway—twenty-one."

"I'm nineteen."

"That's old enough to drive. Unless you don't want to." That was the first time he heard it, that firebrand vulnerability.

Looking back, she'd probably meant to goad him. She never knew he'd responded to the vulnerability.

"Can I help you down?"

It took a second for her to get what he was saying, as if she'd expected to be turned down. Then her eyes sparked and she grinned. "I'll jump."

An instantly recognizable sound accompanied her motion.

"You've—"

She laughed over his concern. "I've ripped my dress. That's a good omen. A great omen. Let's go, Corporal."

"I'm—"

"I know. You're a private."

"I'm Karl Wethers."

They made love that night in her little convertible. At least he'd made love. She might have been having sex.

Though in the weeks that followed he was sure…

Nearly sure.

Not that it had made any difference in the end.

The end.

He couldn't say it was unexpected.

Not since the morning after they met, when he discovered she was the daughter of Major Brooks Reed. And that she'd skipped out on the combination college graduation and twenty-first birthday party he'd been throwing her.

But when the end came it wasn't from the direction he'd expected.

Not from the major. Not from his own commanding officer.

It all came from her.

Stark and sure and brutal.

It should have prepared him for their next encounter.

CHAPTER FOUR

"It is a pleasant surprise to see you here, Prince Karl," said the man who opened the side door of the castle for him. "His Majesty has asked that you join him immediately upon your arrival."

In other words, it was a surprise—pleasant or not was debatable—that he'd driven himself to the castle and self-parked, which was why he came in this door instead of the entrance used when an official car delivered someone to the castle.

There were enough entrances to this place to qualify it as Swiss cheese. And enough rules about when to use which entry that it should have been a video game.

The rest of the message conveyed that King Jozef of Bariavak was not pleased that Karl hadn't already checked in. It had likely been left with every doorkeeper to be sure Karl got it.

Saved time for the king when his displeasure had been pre-administered to the transgressor.

Karl was later than he'd planned to be, starting with the detour up the mountain to watch the takeoff. When he'd finally checked his watch, he'd lost a major chunk of the afternoon.

So the king had a point.

All he said to the man at the door was, "In his office?"

"The Brocade Room, Your Highness."

Karl stifled a sigh.

Not only at that form of address, but also because the Brocade Room meant a social gathering was in progress.

He'd far have preferred a work session in the office, even though it was guaranteed to include the king's ongoing pressure—subtle or not—to accept the position as heir.

Delaying the moment that pressure resumed was why he'd sat so long up at the overlook above the castle. Yeah, he'd wanted to be sure her plane departed, but the hours after that had been preparing for re-immersion into this bizarre world where he was addressed as a prince.

That was the only reason. Getting ready to shift from rancher to supposed royalty. Had nothing to do with her. Not after her plane took off. Everything else was all in the past. Done and buried.

As it had been for years.

"May I take your hat, Your Highness?"

"No, thanks. I'm fine." He'd learned early on not to let go of his cowboy hat. Took too darned long to get it back so he could leave. But he did take the hint and remove it, leaving it in the sitting room off the king's office. He even dragged his hand back through his hair to ease the hat dent as he made his way to the Brocade Room.

Before he'd left home, he'd been tempted to go into the town closest to his ranch and get his hair buzzed again.

But King Jozef had a point. It did make him look like a military man. That was fine with him, but might not hit the right note with the people of Bariavak. Some of them were already pretty edgy and they didn't even know his true goal.

The usher or guard or whatever they called him recognized him and opened the door before he reached it. Like he'd suddenly lost the ability to open a door himself because somebody traced his family tree back to the King of Gelicia. Neither the king nor the country had lasted long.

The Brocade Room was not the most cheerful in the place, and that was going some, considering it had been built as a fortification against invaders several hundred years ago. Bright, open, and airy had not been on the agenda. Subsequent updates had gone for grand over cheerful.

Still, he felt cheered when he saw that Katie and her husband, Brad, were there amid a gaggle of government officials.

Katie—or more formally, Princess Josephine-Augusta Katrina

Mariana Sofia of Bariavak—should have been next in line for the throne. She was King Jozef's granddaughter, as confirmed by DNA tests.

During a failed rebellion, her father had died and she had been kidnapped as a baby by rebels determined to land another blow to the royal family. Katie had grown to adulthood in a small town in Wisconsin with no idea she held the title Princess Royal.

Now she didn't want it.

Didn't want the throne. Didn't want any of the royal trappings.

All she did want was a relationship with her grandfather.

Otherwise, she insisted on being Katie Spencer, living most of the year in Wisconsin with her basketball coach husband, then coming here for the summer to run basketball camps and other activities for Bariavak's youth.

She had stood firm on those points—with her husband and her grandfather. Now she had the life and marriage she wanted.

Karl was glad for Katie. They'd hit it off when they'd met a little over a year ago, as if they were cousins who'd grown up together instead of being connected only by a thread of a distant ancestor in common.

He even liked Brad, now that the other man had gotten past wanting to punch him out because King Jozef had thrown Katie and Karl together in hopes of a match.

The trouble was, with Katie and Brad sticking to their guns about the life and future they wanted, King Jozef was increasing the pressure on Karl to officially become heir to the throne.

He didn't want it any more than Katie did.

The only one who did want it was Prince Vatche, King Jozef's nephew by marriage. But nobody wanted him anywhere near the throne, especially the people of Bariavak.

Karl scanned the room. No sign of Prince Vatche, who always placed himself in a spot where he couldn't be missed. Things were looking up.

He exchanged hellos and handshakes with a number of people as he worked his way toward the clot around King Jozef, which obscured the room beyond them.

"Ah, Karl. You have arrived."

There was a definite thread of complaint in the king's greeting. Karl grinned as they shook hands. "I have, Your Majesty. You look well."

"Should bow," muttered the austerely handsome older woman just behind the king's shoulder.

"You also look well, Madame." Karl didn't address her complaint. They'd covered that ground. He was not King Jozef's subject. He was not going to bow to him.

He gave Katie a quick hug and shook hands with Brad Spencer. Other people began to melt away, as if to give them privacy for this reunion.

"We expected you last week." King Jozef wasn't letting this go.

"Branding was delayed. Like I said when I told you I couldn't get here until this week," Karl said evenly.

"And then yesterday," the king continued, as if he hadn't spoken. "The plane arrived, but you did not."

"I was bushed after the trip."

"If you would use the royal jet for the complete journey…"

King Jozef let the comment die uncompleted as he met Karl's eyes. But Karl didn't fool himself that he was the reason the king let it go. He'd spotted the nudge Madame had delivered to the king's arm.

Madame Sabdoka was the king's staunchest defender and sharpest critic. What else she was to him—in the past or now—was nobody's business but theirs.

"We're so glad you're here, Karl." Katie patted his arm.

"Yeah," Brad agreed. "I could use help at the camp tomorrow. My main assistant's out with a sprained ankle."

Karl perked up. "You need a skilled basketball player to show them how it's done?"

"I need a good-sized body to block out under the basket to teach them how to outmaneuver mountains. Will you be there?"

"I'll be there just to make you eat those words."

Brad chuckled, clearly not worried. "Usual place. Ready to go at nine."

"I had an hour on my schedule for you tomorrow morning, Karl," King Jozef said.

"Oh, but Grandfather, we can't disappoint the kids." Katie took his arm. "And this leaves you an hour to walk in the gardens as you promised you would do every day and so seldom do."

King Jozef looked into his granddaughter's eyes and that was that.

Too bad he didn't melt that way for Karl.

"Madame," Katie said, "will you see to it that…"

Katie kept talking, but Karl didn't hear her words.

A broad-backed man had moved aside, revealing a woman in a simple white blouse and a narrow black skirt. The kind of skirt that would ride up with certain movements, like trying to step down from a pickup's high seat, revealing legs that could invade a man's dreams. Old dreams … and dreams from just last night.

"What the hell."

Madame sucked in a breath at his muttered words. Katie and Brad went silent. He didn't know what the king did because he didn't make a sound, and hearing was the only one of his senses that wasn't completely trained on Harmon Reed.

Who was in Frankfurt.

Damn it. She was in *Frankfurt*.

He frowned at her.

The corners of her mouth rose, her chin lifted. Was he imagining that her eyes held a hint of uncertainty? Had to be. Uncertainty wasn't any more a part of Harmon Reed than patience was.

What was she up to? Why would she finagle her way—?

It didn't matter why. She shouldn't be here. She *couldn't* be here.

He frowned more deeply at her. She raised her shoulders slightly…

"Who draws such a ferocious expression?" The king turned as he asked the question. "Ah, Ms. Reed, yes, yes, please do join us. I wish to introduce you to my granddaughter and her husband." He did so, drawing smiles and handshakes. "You met Madame Sabdoka earlier and I believe you know Prince Karl."

Karl looked sharply at the king, who was beaming innocently at Harmon.

"Good evening, Your Majesty. Madame. Prince Karl," she said to him with the slightest nod of her head.

"Ms. Reed." It was a bit curt. But that was a big improvement over wanting to grab her arms and shake her until she let loose why she wasn't hundreds of miles away instead of standing here in the Brocade Room of Bariavak Castle looking totally at ease and—

"We had a most productive meeting today," King Jozef said.

Meeting? She'd had a *meeting* with the king?

What he wanted to say to that was a lot stronger than *What the hell.* If he said it aloud Madame might keel over. Or, more likely, icily disapprove him into oblivion.

"But we will talk no more of such matters until after dinner, when we can discuss in comfort," the king concluded. In other words, not amid a crowd of people trying their best to overhear. "For now, I desire to introduce you, Ms. Reed, to my First Minister."

He slid a hand under her elbow, but before he departed with her, he looked back at Karl, Katie, and Brad. "You should circulate and say your hellos."

It was a royal command. Not a suggestion.

They obeyed. But even as he made the rounds, Karl kept a lookout for his opportunity.

It came when he and Katie crossed paths inside the dining room door.

"Who told him?" he demanded of her.

"Him? Grandfather, you mean? Told him what?"

He studied her face. Katie wasn't much of a liar, so she probably didn't know what he was talking about.

"Yes, the king. About—" He stopped himself from jerking his head toward Harmon. A gesture everyone could see. A gesture a few definitely *would* see because they missed nothing. "Her."

"You mean Harmon? I have no idea who talked to Grandfather about her. Is there a reason somebody would? What would they tell him about her? How do you know her? Was there something between you?"

There wasn't a question in there he wanted to answer.

He grunted. Wished he'd kept his mouth shut. He'd need to give Katie some kind of an explanation. Eventually.

First, he would get through this so-called informal dinner—ah, yes, he saw he had been assigned a seat across the table and far enough away that he could not query King Jozef. Or her, because she sat beside the king as an honored guest.

She'd once more unbuttoned that button she'd had undone at Marco Polo Airport, but had fastened on the plane. The blouse had looked a little worse for wear when she said goodbye last night. It had been freshened up since then.

Throughout the meal he tried not to watch her while he fended off questions from his dinner companions—some oblique, some direct— about his future in Bariavak.

After dinner, King Jozef separated his guests with a combination of speed, decision, and deftness that would be the envy of a topnotch cutting horse.

Karl found himself now maneuvered into a spot beside the king, bidding official good nights to the main group of departing guests, while Madame escorted a small group that included Harmon to the sitting room beside the king's office. He felt an unexpected kinship with cattle that were worked by top-notch cutting horses into going in a direction not of their choosing or liking. Damned frustrating to be blocked at every turn.

Karl had helped an elderly lady to the stately car drawn up for her at the base of the broad steps. He returned to the top as the last guest bowed to the king and departed.

With deliberation, he used the formal address rather than the more casual "sir" that the king had long ago insisted on. "Your Majesty—"

"Ah, that was well-done, Karl. Personally escorting the widowed mother of the First Minister was an adroit maneuver."

"It was not a maneuver. It was a courtesy to an elderly lady who didn't look too steady on her feet. And if she'd gone down she'd have taken that young usher with her," he said of the member of the household staff he'd replaced. "Your Majesty—"

"Brandy has always been her weakness. Now, our duty well done, we shall join the others." The king took his arm and turned him toward the sitting room.

"Right. The others. Including Harmon Reed." Karl emphasized her name. "I don't understand why she's here. If she has led you to believe—I haven't seen her for years. I brought her to Bariavak only because it was the best solution at the moment and I owed her father. I should have asked your permission before bringing a passenger on to your jet, but—"

"You should not. You have full use of that and all else," the king said. "Now, we shall join the others.

"Sir—"

"Now, we shall join the others," King Jozef repeated firmly.

CHAPTER FIVE

Harmon studied the few people assembled in the room that was the closest thing to cozy she'd seen in the castle.

Madame had brought her, Katie, and Brad here directly from the dining room. King Jozef and Karl entered a moment ago, after escorting out the departing guests.

"Ah, now that we are all comfortable," King Jozef said once they were seated at his direction and Madame had offered him and Karl the coffee she'd already provided to the early arrivers, "I can share with you here, you who are most directly affected, that I have contracted with Ms. Reed for the benefit of her services."

"*Services?*"

Karl's sharp word drew a quick, surprised look from Katie.

His tone could have been construed as casting aspersions on her virtue, but Harmon figured it more likely stemmed from his doubt that she could be of service to anybody.

"Yes," King Jozef said, unperturbed. "They will be most beneficial as we negotiate the correct course for the future of Bariavak."

Karl faced the king directly. "Is it your desire to open this discussion to her?"

She had a sudden impression of two boxers standing their ground, delivering blows they'd landed before. Neither backing down.

"Do you have any cause not to?"

Her breath hitched. Karl could tell plenty of tales—

"That is not my call." He didn't pause or look away from King Jozef.

Though, really, why should she worry if he told tales? She hadn't sought this job—whatever the heck it was, which wasn't at all clear, since the king had asked her a whole lot of questions without answering any of hers. In fact, she'd told him several times that she wasn't available. He'd sailed on as if she hadn't spoken and somehow it became understood that she would remain in Bariavak for an unspecified period, to do unspecified work for him.

She wished she had a recording of that conversation. She could definitely learn from his technique. Once she figured out what it was.

His strategy in the lead-up to the meeting was clearer.

First, walking out of the hotel expecting to go to the airport, but instead encountering a driver delivering the out-of-the blue news that the king of Bariavak requested her presence. The impressive mountain-climbing drive in the official car up to the castle that seemed to grow out of rock. Being escorted to the history-soaked anteroom … and left to wait long enough for nerves to take hold if she'd been so inclined.

She wasn't so inclined, so, instead, she'd thought back over everything Karl had said since Venice.

There wasn't that much and she'd already reviewed it during the night, but this time she pushed away the intersection with their past and focused on what might connect with the king.

That's what King Jozef wants. For Karl Wethers, born an American, veteran of the U.S. Army, and now owner of a ranch in Wyoming, to become his heir to the throne of Bariavak.

That's what she'd said to him.

And he'd detoured into a discussion of ranch size.

There it was, big as life. Yet she'd missed it at the time.

What the king of Bariavak wanted of him. And his reluctance to comply.

She'd tucked away that observation for later consideration because that was when she'd been escorted in to see the king. She'd certainly had no attention to spare while undergoing his discreet yet expert grilling.

King Jozef was wily. Definitely wily. She would need to keep that in mind.

Also determined. She'd told him that what he wanted—from what she'd gathered from his vague phrases—was not the sort of work she did. He overrode that, saying she had more than enough expertise and that her background added another dimension that a more traditional candidate could not offer.

Traditional candidate to do exactly what, she *still* didn't know.

"It could and should be your rightful decision," the king said now to Karl.

The overt topic was whether she would be involved. Harmon had the feeling the subtext was much broader, including Karl's role. His life. His future.

"It's not my call," he said.

Was he saying he'd let King Jozef decide his future? That seemed unlike him. Could he have changed so much over the years?

He'd never been a pushover. She should know, because she'd poked at him all the time, trying to get him to do what she wanted as those before him had. He hadn't.

If anything, she would have expected him to become even more of a non-pushover, what with his years in the Army and now running his own ranch.

A knock sounded. At King Jozef's command, the door opened and the guard announced, "Mr. and Mrs. Pierce."

The others stood with expressions of pleasure, even Madame's face softened. Though Harmon thought she caught a hint of wariness in Karl's eyes.

A young woman rushed to give the king a hug, which he returned with pleasure.

When the hug ended and the woman stepped back, Harmon forced herself not to gape. The woman's resemblance to Katie—whom she was hugging now, after having kissed Madame on the cheek—was remarkable.

"Hello, Harmon."

She turned quickly at the male voice behind her. "Hunter Pierce. Good to see you."

Boy, she was off her game to have missed the cue of "Mr. Pierce." She knew about his connection to Bariavak's ruler, both because she liked to stay up on things and because she'd encountered Hunter Pierce before. Yet she'd been so caught up in the resemblance of the two women that she'd let him slip up behind her unseen.

Interesting that he didn't seem surprised.

"And you," he said. They shook hands. "I'd like to introduce my wife, April Gareaux Pierce. April, this is Harmon Reed."

"Hunter is my liaison with your Department of State," King Jozef said. "April and Hunter are our dear friends."

After she shared a handshake and a smile with April, she addressed Hunter. "I'd read about that Christmas you two spent with King Jozef in D.C., how you'd married and been transformed. And now I can see it for myself. A smile. An actual smile. I don't know that I ever saw you smile before. I'm very happy for you both. Congratulations." She turned to the king. "I quit, Your Majesty."

Everyone—everyone except Hunter—looked startled.

Karl's surprise, she noticed, faded immediately. His concentrated gaze went from her to Hunter.

"Why?" the king demanded.

"Because, assuming that the services of mine that you want involve getting media attention of any sort, Hunter Pierce will not let me do my job."

April Gareaux Pierce's eyes kindled to full-blown wrath. "Hunter is the best and most wonderful employee the Department of State or any other arm of the government of the United States could—"

Hunter appeared prepared to sit back and let this play out. Even, perhaps, pleased by his wife's response.

Karl talked over April ruthlessly. "What do you mean, Harmon?"

"He won't let me say what I need to say. I have to have freedom to work. He'll quash, squash, and silence. He's done it before and no matter how happy he is with married life, he'll do it again."

"When did he do it before?" April's wrath wasn't gone, but curiosity had banked the fire.

"That's not important—" started Hunter not liking this so much anymore.

April put a hand on his arm. "Go ahead, Harmon."

She did. "You know he'd been promoted into criminal investigations then got sent back to security? That would have been before you met." April nodded. "Well, I was there when it happened. It's long and complicated—"

"And telling details would still breach security," Hunter said sternly.

"Details schmetails. The gist of it is some idiot in Washington was willing to risk the safety of—yeah, yeah, I know, Hunter. No details—a member of the armed services and his or her family because the idiot thought it was easier to advance an investigation by using them as bait and he ordered Hunter to operate that way. Instead, Hunter kept the military family safe *and* advanced the investigation. And they demoted him."

"I disobeyed an order—"

"That wasn't why you were demoted and you know it. It was because you showed up that Washington jackass. Between us, the local reporter and I had it all. Great stuff. *Great.* We could have made him a hero. It would have made that State jackass and his stuffed-shirt cronies not only back down but beg Hunter if they could pretty-please eat their own shirts. And what did I get instead? Quashed, squashed, and silenced. *That's* what I got from Hunter Pierce."

April had undergone an amazing transformation, from wrath to glowing. "Thank you, Harmon. I knew it must have been something like that because he wouldn't tell me a thing about it." She wrapped both hands around Hunter's arm and smiled up at him. "Of course, now I'll have to track down that idiot and—"

King Jozef interrupted with an amused click of his tongue. "Thank him, my dear April. Because if he had not returned Hunter to Washington someone else would have been in charge of the operation that brought us together and you would not have met Hunter."

"Did you have something to do with me getting yanked back to

Washington, sir?" Hunter demanded, clearly suspicious.

King Jozef clapped both hands to his chest. "I? As you said, you disobeyed an order. Purely an internal matter for your Department of State. And one for which you, too, should be thankful."

Hunter's sharp gaze stayed on the king a breath longer, then fell to April's hands on his arm. His free hand covered hers. "I am."

"And now," King Jozef said briskly, "we must consider the matter at hand and the purpose for which I have engaged your services, Ms. Harmon Reed."

"I'm dying to hear," she muttered.

The king ignored that. "Your expertise is precisely what we require."

"Her expertise?" Karl frowned.

"Media," King Jozef said.

"That's not exactly—"

King Jozef's wave silenced her. "The issue, Ms. Reed, is the future of my country."

"Bariavak will be fine, Grandfather," Katie started. "It's the crown that—"

"The crown *is* Bariavak. The royal family is Bariavak. That is the past and the future of Bariavak." From that exclamatory height, the king's voice dropped. "That is how it should be."

Harmon caught a slight movement and shifted enough to see Brad Spencer cover Katie's hand in the space between them on the sofa. His wife turned her hand to grasp his and squeezed.

In contrast, Madame's movement was overt. She walked to a narrow window, leaving her back to the room. But from this angle Harmon could see her impassive reflection.

The king was continuing, "When our neighbors were conquered from this direction, then the next direction, then the other, over and over, we stood solid. We, the royal family of Bariavak, and thus our country as well."

"Mountains kept out invaders," murmured Hunter.

King Jozef grandly failed to hear what was audible to everyone else. "Now, what shall happen? I had one daughter only and no other—"

From the corner of her eye, Harmon caught a flicker in the window that held Madame's reflection. But the woman was still when Harmon looked in her direction, so she returned her focus to the king.

"—children. My dear Sofia died after her husband was killed by rebels, having had one child only themselves, the Princess Josephine-Augusta. When the rebels took her..." He stilled.

Harmon felt a surge of sympathy for the man behind the crown.

As she was meant to, she realized.

Not that his emotions weren't genuine. They were. That's what made it powerful.

Wily, definitely wily.

The King of Bariavak sighed. "But now my granddaughter refuses the prerogatives and duties of her birthright, leaving—" Brad stirred. Harmon had the impression King Jozef altered course mid-sentence. "—us to find a different path for the throne of Bariavak."

The only change in Karl she could detect was a slight pulling back of his already straight shoulders.

"Your Majesty, may I ask a question?" Harmon asked.

He inclined his head graciously. "You may, Ms. Reed."

"If an heir to the throne was your concern, you could have remarried at any point in all these years, couldn't you?"

The only person who didn't turn to stare at her was Madame, who continued her vigil at the window.

"I hoped to find my granddaughter."

"No, you didn't," Hunter said.

King Jozef glowered at him.

He didn't back down. "You went along, but you never believed we'd find your granddaughter."

"Pah, of course I did. I was certain of it. And so it happened."

Harmon looked directly at the king. "But you couldn't have counted on that. Not for nearly three decades. Far safer to marry again. You might have had a dozen more children by now. In fact, it's not too late to marry now."

CHAPTER SIX

"Good night. See you tomorrow," Karl said to Katie.

She touched his arm to stop him. "Wait a second."

He'd known this was coming from the moment she'd said she'd walk him out to his truck. Didn't mean he had to welcome it with open arms.

"I've got to rest up for the basketball camp—"

She ignored that. "What's with you and Harmon Reed?"

"Nothing."

She ignored that, too. "You're usually so easy-going, Karl. Not tonight. Not with her. You were this close to being downright rude."

"I'm not going to mince words when it comes to someone getting close to King Jozef."

Her face softened. "I know you're protective of him and I am so grateful for that. But, Karl, you're nicer to Prince Vatche than you were to Harmon Reed tonight."

"Aw, c'mon." He grinned, hoping to tease her out of these questions. "I wasn't that bad."

"You were," she said earnestly. "I know you think it's good, uh, policy not to be on open terms of enmity with Prince Vatche, so you're more cordial to him than the rest of us, but still … You were so cool to Harmon. You clearly knew each other before—"

"Yeah. Which means I'm in the best position to know she's not a good fit here."

"Grandfather thinks she is."

"Based on what? That's the mystery. How he even knew she was here—"

"When you were busy driving her out of the country as fast you could, you mean?"

He raised then dropped his hands. "That's the rumor going around already, huh? Did she start it?"

A concerned frown drew her brows down. "Karl, you know I'm on your side. We all are. If she bothers you that much, I can talk to Grandfather and—"

"Don't, Katie." Far better if King Jozef didn't take any more interest in his activities than he already did. "I'll take care of it. Your whispers in the king's ear should be saved for important things like the basketball camps. Which reminds me…"

"I know, I know. You have to be up early. I can take a hint—"

Right, after she'd had her say she could take a hint. Katie Spencer was a lot tougher than she looked.

"—but remember, if you need backup, or someone to talk to—"

He leaned down and kissed her on the cheek. "I've got Cousin Katie."

He heard something then. Or sensed it. Sensed *her*.

"Seriously, Karl, I know you had a history and it must have ended badly, because—"

"Hey, I was one of the lucky ones. I didn't get a Dear John letter while I was deployed in a war zone. I know guys who did. Too many of them. A Dear John letter or a Dear John email or a Dear John phone call. Or, worse, returning from deployment to find the house and bank account cleared out." He focused over Katie's shoulder. "So I should consider myself damned lucky you severed the ties well before I was deployed. Right, Harmon?"

Katie spun around as Harmon stepped forward out of a shadow between the entryway lights.

"Right," she confirmed steadily.

"Suppose I should have thanked you for that," he said. "A little late, but thanks."

Katie pulled in a breath. "Karl, don't be cruel—"

"Cruel? Me? I'm just telling the truth. Again we'll ask the other person who was there. Harmon?"

"Actually, he's being soft on me." She held her head high and her voice was steady. There might have been a slight sheen in her eyes. Or it might have been light reflecting on the surface. "I wanted out and I accomplished that in the fastest and easiest way for me. I wrote him a letter."

"More of a note than a letter," he said, as if that mattered.

Looking directly at him she said, "You judge, Katie. What I wrote was, *Karl, I know you love me, but be realistic. It was never going to work out long term. HR.*"

Katie's hand still resting on his arm tightened.

"Have to give you credit, Harmon," he said evenly. "You were right. It was never going to work out long term. Good night, Katie. I can only hope this is good-bye, Harmon."

He turned and left.

He thought about that conversation as he drove down the narrow, twisting road that gave some of the mountain tracks back home in Wyoming a run for their money.

It had felt good in the moment, but he shouldn't have been so blatant.

Wishing her gone wouldn't make it happen.

Not any more than wishing she'd stay with him had made that happen. Or—He shut off the memories.

If there was a worse time to have Harmon Reed dropped into the castle inner circle he couldn't imagine when it could be. It was a delicate point and it wasn't going to get any less delicate for a year, maybe more, according to the plan sketched out at this morning's meeting.

Just what they needed, the grown up version of a girl who'd liked to juggle lit sticks of dynamite.

Just what he needed, the grown up version of the girl who'd exploded that dynamite in his face. More than once.

Now, of all times.

But that's the way it was. So what he had to do was suck it up and stop letting his feelings about their history be so clear that Katie and everybody else got curious.

Calm.

Smooth.

That's what was needed now. No matter what.

The walk as Katie Spencer escorted Harmon to where she should have gone to be driven back to town was silent and awkward.

"The car and driver are waiting here, Harmon," said the woman who refused to be a princess, indicating the door to a paved area.

Harmon thanked her and took a step.

A light touch on her arm stopped her.

"Harmon, whatever happened between you two, Karl's a good man."

"No argument from me there. He is. And he's also right. The fact that it ended and how it ended was all my doing."

Katie frowned. "When something like that happens, both people—"

"Nope," she interrupted ruthlessly. "All me. And if I could go back to that moment, I'd do the same thing again. Perhaps more tactfully, but the same result. It never would have worked for us."

Having left the other woman nothing more to say—which was precisely what she'd intended—they said goodnight and Harmon left.

The driver who returned her to the hotel—at a pace that made a turtle look madly impulsive—also informed her she would be picked up at ten the next morning. Royal decree by proxy.

The small lobby was empty except for a man at the front desk who handed her the room key without asking her identity.

Amused voices rose from the back. She thought she heard Karl's laugh. She took half a step toward the door behind the desk. The man moved to block her.

He said a word and gestured to a discreet sign on the door. Neither was in English, but "private" seemed likely.

As if Karl hadn't been clear enough, now strangers and signs were telling her she wasn't welcomed.

She didn't blame him one bit.

That did not mean she would accept it.

"Ah, an enjoyable evening, don't you agree, Therese?" The king of Bariavak opened the pendant clasp at the back of her neck, then kissed her briefly above the collar of her dress. "To have April and Hunter join Katie and Brad. And Karl, of course. With this young lady Harmon Reed a captivating addition. Tomorrow you will please to tell her she need not be so formal in addressing me."

"What scheme is in your mind now, Jozef?" Only between the two of them did they use first names.

"Scheme? No scheme."

"You learn Prince Karl has had a companion on his flight from Venice, an unexpected companion, and you break appointments, delay meetings, and put all your attention to discovering who this companion is."

"A most curious circumstance is it not? That Karl steps into a scene at the airport. That he claims to know this woman. Escorts her onto the royal jet. And then, without talking with her, firmly goes to sleep for the entire journey. Is that not curious?"

"He was tired."

He gave a small hoot. "Not even you believe such a thing, Therese. A woman he does not know yet has put himself forward to aid, he talks to in the airplane. A woman he knows, perhaps casually, he talks to in the airplane. A woman he knows well and has a fondness for, he talks to in the airplane. A woman he knows well and does not like, he does not act for at all. No, it is only a woman he knows well and with whom there is strong emotion—strong, but not comfortable—then, only then does he not talk to her in the airplane. Did you see his face when he saw her there in the Brocade Room?"

"I saw."

"And through dinner. The looks, trying to discover with his eyes only how she came to be there."

"He did not use his eyes alone in questioning you after dinner."

"No, no he did not. I had to be firm." He chuckled. "He is wondering still—now, this very moment—how she came to remain in Bariavak when he expected that she had flown away. It will not come fast, but we shall weaken his closed mouth and we shall discover what import has this woman from his past."

"What does it matter now if there is such a woman in his past? When you hoped for a marriage between him and Katie, I understood, but now?"

"Do you not think it important that the future king of Bariavak has the right woman by his side?" He kissed her, then went around to his side of the bed.

"He will not be king," she said when they were settled side by side. "He will not do it."

"We shall see."

She clicked her tongue. "You say you desire to settle the future of your country, yet you spend your time like a meddlesome matchmaker."

"I did well with Hunter and April."

"So you claim. But with your own granddaughter, you cannot make such a claim. You tried to end her love with Brad and to bring her together with Karl. No match you made there."

"Perhaps I do more than you think for my Katie, since now she and Brad know their hearts."

She clicked her tongue again. Not buying it for a second.

Until a few years ago, when these American youngsters entered his life and his Therese came back into it, it had been many, many years that he had never once been questioned this way. It was, at times, the only thing he missed in all the changes made since he had traveled to Washington, D.C., more than eighteen months ago now.

"Why you are even thinking of such things I do not understand. Not when you say over and over that it is Bariavak's future that is your first cause."

"Ah, Therese. Perhaps I do both. Make these matches and make the preparations necessary for the future of Bariavak."

"They won't do it," said his stubborn Therese. "Not one of them will take the crown when you no longer wear it. Harmon Reed was right. You should have married again, Jozef."

That treaded close to a past they so rarely discussed. He did not answer.

"You could marry again now," she said. "A bride from a royal family of childbearing age."

He put his arms around her. "Ah, Therese, how could I hope to find a bride so understanding as to accept your role in my life. And mine in yours."

"For the sake of Bariavak—"

"I will not sacrifice you again. Ever." In a milder tone, he continued, "We will find a way that does not require such a sacrifice, of this mythical bride, of us. I will not have that for you. Never again."

King Jozef was at it again.

If Karl hadn't been certain of that yesterday, he sure was the instant Harmon walked into the castle gym.

She stopped after one step inside. Turned back to the unseen person holding the door for her, who apparently confirmed that she was where she belonged.

She'd been expecting a meeting with the king, no doubt. That's probably what she'd been told, too. A meeting or a working session or a consultation.

With the king in his usual form, she certainly wouldn't have been told she'd be ushered in to a gym to watch a basketball camp drill on driving to the basket that Brad was explaining to twenty kids while Karl stood in as a defender. The whole process took a while, with the translator repeating everything for the young Bariavak players.

Karl saw April spot Harmon and wave her over to where she and Katie were sitting on the new bleachers. The decrepit gym had gotten a facelift in the past year. There were plans for a facility that—unlike this one—couldn't have previously been used as a dungeon, but that would take a couple more years.

"Then you drive to the basket," Brad said.

Used to the delay for translation, Karl didn't transfer his attention from Harmon back to the court in time.

Brad drove to the basket all right, leaving tire marks all over him, knocking him on his butt, and dropping the ball in the hoop as gently as an egg.

"Distraction is the enemy." Brad kept a straight face as he gave voice to the lesson. The translator and kids didn't, laughing uproariously.

Distraction wasn't the only danger…

CHAPTER SEVEN

"Harmon. Over here."

April Pierce waved to her from the bleachers. Katie gestured to come sit with them.

Harmon started toward them.

Karl went down—hard—and she stopped involuntarily.

Above the amusement of the young players, his laugh came as Brad hauled him up. That same laugh she'd heard last night from behind the closed door.

Absently, she continued toward the two other women.

"Good morning. Great to see you," they greeted her.

"Good morning to you both, too. I was told to expect a meeting with the king this morning, then when I arrived, I was sent here and my escort said to stay with you all until the king summons me."

"That sounds about right." April scooched over and patted the now open area between her and Katie. "Come sit down and tell us all about yourself. Where's home?"

"Everywhere. That's what happens when you're an Army brat. All us Army brats say home isn't a place, it's where the people you love are." It came out with ease, since it was her standard answer.

"Who are the people you love?" Katie asked with an openness that robbed it of any sense of prying. "You and Karl—"

Uh-oh. Too late, Harmon realized the potential danger hidden in her answer. No one had asked her that before.

Under the theory that a good offense was the best defense, she started talking before her companion could finish the second question. "I've been dying to ask, Katie, how are you and Karl related?"

"We're sort of cousins, both tracing our ancestors back to the three-times great-grandfather of King Jozef's mother. We figured that out when we met last year. When did you and Karl meet?"

"So, the three-times great-grandfather of King Jozef would be your five-times great-grandfather, right, Katie?"

"I suppose it is. Though they aren't in the direct royal lineage. Not for Karl, either. But since you know Karl, maybe you already know—"

"You're sure you're not related to the royal family?" she asked April.

"Sure. But that's not what we want to talk to you about. What—"

"That's amazing, because you certainly have such a strong resemblance to so many of the royal family portraits I saw yesterday. You know the ones outside the king's office? On top of that, you two look so much alike you could be twins."

She directed the last part at Katie, who took that bait. "Not really, April's much prettier."

"I am not, Katie, and she's trying to change the subject."

Katie faced Harmon. "Why would you want to change the subject? Unless you don't want to talk to us about Karl. But why would that be?"

April laughed. "The direct approach."

"It saves a lot of time. One of the many reasons I don't want to be a princess. All the time you have to spend working around to expressing what you could say flat out in a few words."

"Is that why Karl doesn't want to be a prince and the heir, either?" Harmon asked.

"That's—" Katie started.

April cut in. "Karl has an admirable respect for the people of Bariavak, which has made him concerned about them accepting him, when every indication is that they already have."

Harmon had the feeling that response came straight from the Department of State, by way of Hunter.

She supposed it was unlikely that Hunter and April would be staying here if they didn't back the king's position.

That meant Karl was getting pressure from two sides to become the heir to the throne of Bariavak: King Jozef and the United States government. It could explain his slight tension when Hunter arrived last night.

Was anyone pressuring him from the other direction? Besides himself.

A faint worried frown pulled at Katie's forehead, but she sounded at ease when she asked, "So how did you and Karl meet, Harmon?"

"Oh, it was ages ago. Ten, twelve years. We only knew each other a short time. Ships passing in the night."

Neither of the other women looked convinced.

"Must have been pretty intense ships passing in the night," April said with emphasis. "For you both to remember each other after all these years, I mean."

She didn't mean that, but it suited Harmon's purposes to pretend she did.

"Circumstances, what was going on in our lives. You know how those can make a memory stick with you. I was just out of college and he was launching his Army career when our paths crossed. So it was a transition period for each of us. He was under the command of the Colonel's best friend—"

"The Colonel?" April asked.

Her mouth twisted. "Lieutenant Colonel Brooks Reed to be specific."

"Reed? Is that your father?"

"Yeah. His best friend is Colonel John Griffith Jr. Have you heard stories about him from Karl?" Each woman shook her head. "You should get him to tell you. At least what he can tell you. A lot of it is classified. Grif sort of took Karl under his wing. And since he and my father were friends that threw us together. That's all."

That's all...

No, that wasn't all.

Karl's mouth on hers. Then lower. And lower. Making her pulse beat faster and shatter. Then stroking inside her. Joined. Pulsing together. Until—

"And then he left for other duty and I left to start being a grownup."

Her grin felt tight and stiff. She might have given up on the attempt if Hunter hadn't arrived then. That distracted April and seemed to remind Katie of her husband down on the court.

So the rest of the conversation, with Hunter joining them to watch the final drill of the day's session, was about basketball.

Harmon had never been partial to the sport. Until now.

The guide who'd brought her to the gym this morning had said the king would summon her when she was required.

With the camp session over and no summons so far, Harmon remained chatting with the others in the bleachers, then trailed along when they left.

They didn't go far.

Apparently with the ease of familiarity, Katie had timed it perfectly so they reached a narrow hallway outside the locker room as Brad and Karl, hair still damp, but dressed in street clothes, emerged.

The swinging door caught Karl in the hip and he groaned elaborately.

"Are you okay, Karl?" Katie asked.

"You did spend a lot of time on the floor," April added with a twinkle.

He gave her a dour look. "I'll live. No thanks to you," he added to Brad. "I should start a rodeo camp and use you as a roping dummy."

As general laughter died out, Brad, with one arm around Katie, said, "Good to see you again, Harmon. We all got the bum's rush last night before I could say I thought you made interesting points. Got me thinking."

"Like what?" April asked.

"Like why did King Jozef go along with pretending you might have been his granddaughter over Christmas the year before last if he didn't believe it?"

"To make things right with Hunter," she said immediately. "Hunter's father had been on the king's staff. Only Hunter survived the rebellion. King Jozef wanted to be sure he was okay, that he had what he needed. He felt responsible. He wanted to—"

"Maneuver me." Hunter's tone was even. He glanced at his wife, then Katie. "Harmon needs to know what she's dealing with. *Who* she's dealing with. He looks like a trimmed down Santa, but he could have given Machiavelli pointers."

"Hunter," protested his wife.

He didn't relent. "He tried to get you to join his household. He tried to push me into coming to work for him. He tried to push Katie into a life she doesn't want. He tried to push Brad out. Now he's on Karl."

"Don't worry about me."

"But he's accepted my wishes and our decisions on how we're going to live our lives," Katie said.

"Because Madame persuaded him that if he didn't he'd lose you," Brad said.

Hunter nodded. "Exactly."

"And that brings us back to what Harmon was saying last night. Since he didn't think he'd find his granddaughter and he's never liked Prince Vatche or the guy before Karl—"

"Prince Stephan Carlos," Hunter supplied.

"Right, him." Brad kept going, "He'd known for years that Vatche and Stephan Carlos were the closest in line for the throne, so why *didn't* he get married again? It's what royalty's been doing for centuries. Sometimes marrying a bunch of times trying to get an heir."

"You wanted him to be a latter day Henry the Eighth, killing off wives when they didn't bear sons, Brad?" protested April.

"It makes as much sense as waiting all those years, then suddenly looking around and deciding he needs an heir, pronto."

April said, "He devoted himself so exclusively to the welfare of Bariavak that I think it was only when he faced serious surgery a year and half ago that he considered what would happen when he's no longer here."

Brad looked doubtful, but didn't argue further.

Especially not when a woman they called Elisabeta came down the corridor and said they were expected upstairs for lunch, though the king wished to see Prince Karl and Ms. Reed for a moment first in his office.

CHAPTER EIGHT

Accompanied by Elisabeta, the others took a different route from the locker room.

Harmon followed along beside Karl, trusting he would lead them to the king's office.

If he ditched her—not outside the realm of possibility, considering his reaction to her presence so far—she'd have to find her own way. Maybe call for directions. Did they have cell service inside—

Karl interrupted her thoughts. "What made you go frozen faced when you were talking with Katie and April?"

"I do not go frozen faced." She tried to ease her clenched jaw.

"If you say so. Brad was right. You had an interesting point last night."

"One among my many excellent points."

He ignored that and said, "About why King Jozef hasn't remarried."

"Ah." She slanted a look up at him. "So you're going to be reasonable and fair today? Change of strategy? Or change of heart?"

She wished she hadn't used that last phrase. Really, really wished she hadn't.

It didn't appear to affect him, however.

"I always go for reasonable and fair," he said coolly.

She decided on a change of strategy herself. To stop prodding him and accept his comments at face value. It had nothing to do with the phrase she wished she hadn't used. Nothing. "Did you notice anything about Madame's reaction to that discussion after dinner?"

"Madame showed a reaction? Better get out a news alert."

"It was a flicker. When she was looking out the window. I could see her reflection. At least I thought I caught a flicker..."

"Probably your imagination. Or the light in the old glass."

That was a likely enough explanation—the old glass, not her imagination—that it stopped her for a moment.

"But I suspect Brad and Hunter are right," Karl continued. "King Jozef thought he could orchestrate a succession of his choice. It's only recently that he's begun to understand that his plans aren't going to turn out."

"What plans of his do you think he understands aren't going to turn out?" Because from her observations—admittedly limited—the king was a long way from giving up on the idea that Karl would succeed him.

"For starters, the king was gung-ho about Katie and me getting married. In fact, we gave it a shot."

"Did you?" she said coolly.

"Not getting married," he explained kindly. "But seeing if there was anything between us. Would have solved a lot of problems. Not that Brad would agree." His brief chuckle was dry. "Not even while he was busy arguing that Katie should fulfill her royal destiny. Besides, Katie had a different destiny in mind. Took a while for the two of them to straighten that out, then persuade King Jozef that they weren't going to budge. But they did. And he accepted it. It helped that they were already married."

"What? They were already married?"

"Before they came to Bariavak. But they got twisted up the way people can sometimes and took a while to untangle it. You can't spread that around."

"Like I would. Though it is hard to believe you'd have considered an arranged marriage just to please somebody else, even if he is a king."

"It wouldn't have been to please the king."

She shot him a look. His face was impassive. "You and Katie do seem to get along well."

"We do. Wouldn't have been any trouble at all to fall in love with Katie."

Karl bending down to kiss Katie last night. On the cheek, but still … Was that because she was married while his own feelings…

She felt a twinge.

Not jealousy over him and Katie. Absolutely not. It was this other thing that had been biting her lately.

She'd first noticed it with the Colonel and Ann-Elise, his wife. It wasn't that she minded him remarrying. They'd never been close—to put it mildly—and she'd been prepared for him to remarry since her mother's death when she was thirteen.

No, it wasn't anything to do with the Colonel … except the way Ann-Elise looked at him. And the way he looked at her.

That had taken her breath away.

It had also been the first time she'd recognized this twinge, though she'd had it several times since, including a couple instances last night, watching Hunter and April together. Katie and Brad, too. Heck, there'd even been a moment between King Jozef and Madame.

It wasn't jealousy of the people. It was love-jealousy.

Jealousy that they had love. That kind of love.

So that's what the twinge was about when Karl said it would have been easy for him to fall in love with Katie.

Nothing to do with him specifically. Instead, it was this generic and totally idiotic love-jealousy twinge.

"Certainly it appears it wasn't any trouble for her and Brad to fall in love," she said.

"I wouldn't go that far." He gestured for her to precede him around yet another corner. These corridors made a maze seem like an Interstate across Kansas. "They had their ups and downs. Anyway, that's when King Jozef zeroed in on me. Something else you can't spread around."

She stopped, hands on hips, facing him. "Stop treating me like a gossip columnist. You have no idea what I do, do you?"

"From what King Jozef said about services, PR."

"No."

"Journalist."

"No. Rather than have you go on futilely guessing, let me ask, have you heard of a media fixer?"

"People who translate when a journalist comes in from another country?"

She snorted. "Translate, arrange, secure, investigate, dig, keep out of trouble, hold their hands, and everything else you can imagine. Without good fixers, ninety percent of the foreign correspondents would land on their faces—or worse."

"What about the other ten percent?"

"They're no good even with great fixers. All things can be made better by a good fixer—that's rule number one. Rule number two is some things can't be fixed. Rule number three is to know which is which."

"You're a media fixer."

"More like I'm a fixer of fixers. Think of it as a matchmaker—I match the right fixer with the right journalist or company or film crew."

"And get a percentage for your trouble from the fixers you find work for."

She tilted her head to look at him from a different angle. "Cynicism? From Karl Wethers? My, oh my. Actually the fixer-seeker pays the fee. That's where others who've tried what I do have screwed up, because their loyalty shifts to whoever's paying."

"Yours doesn't."

"Mine's with the fixer. Always with the fixer. There'll always be someone else who needs their services and mine. But the great fixers? Can't replace them."

"What do you do for them?"

"Get them jobs, get them paid, get them respect, get them credit. I take care of them the way they take care of journalists or film crews or whoever."

His eyes narrowed. "How does that fit in with King Jozef?"

"I have no idea."

"Did he tell you he needs a fixer or a fixer's fixer," he added when she started to protest.

"No."

A hint of frustration came through when he demanded, "What *has* he said he wants you to do?"

"He hasn't."

"He's offered you a job without saying what the job is?"

She grimaced. "When you put it that way, it sounds crazy. I should be in London. I've handled a lot of my work from here, but, yeah, I should be in London. Yet, here I am. He hasn't even actually offered me a job. He's made assumptions and issued orders thinly veiled as invitations."

"Welcome to my world," he said dryly. He nodded his head toward a door with a man in a suit standing outside it. "The king's office."

It was a warning to watch what she said, as if she'd needed it.

Karl spoke to the man, who reached for the door.

As he opened it for them, Karl said, "Damn." And shook his head.

"What?" she asked.

"Should have known that if there was anyone who could manage to find—or create—a job where you can bite the hand that feeds you it would be Harmon Reed."

It surprised a laugh out of her that she carried with her as Karl gestured her to precede him into the room.

Karl stopped for an instant at the threshold.

Reacting to Harmon's laugh—God, he'd forgotten what a great laugh she had—or to the presence of the other man with the king, he didn't know.

He didn't bother hoping the king didn't know which either, because having him zero in on either one was bad.

Very bad.

"Harmon, Karl, come in, come in. So good to hear you two enjoying each other's company." Before either of them could deny the king's implication—and how could they without being utterly rude, he added, "Come and let me introduce you to Andrej Skala. He is to have lunch with us. He knows the others who will dine with us, so I wanted a chance to make you known to each other. Prince Karl, may I introduce Andrej Skala."

The man was taller than the king, shorter than Karl. His regular features were dominated by fiercely intelligent eyes that promised humor from the creases at their corners.

He wore a beautifully fitted suit quite different from the jeans and sweater he'd worn during their meeting in the hotel's kitchen last night and again this morning with a slightly larger group.

"He has been reminding me that I declined his services as my private secretary at the start of his career," the king was saying. "Instead, he has served in varied capacities in business and in the government, including the embassies in Tokyo, Washington, and London. Now he has returned to Bariavak to agitate for democracy."

Karl strode forward and extended his hand. "A man after my own heart."

"It is a pleasure, Your Highness," the man said, meeting his handshake with a slight squeeze of reassurance.

"Harmon, I believe you do not know Andrej Skala." King Jozef added enough edge to the pronoun to let it be known that he knew Karl and Andrej Skala did know each other.

Damn.

Though Karl supposed it was to be expected. They'd have to be even more careful.

Harmon flicked a look at him he didn't catch.

The king introduced Harmon to Andrej Skala with his usual charm, finishing up with, "Shall we join the others in the dining room now?"

"If I might have a word with you alone, sir," Karl said. "It won't delay us long."

Before the king could respond, Harmon put her arm through Andrej Skala's and said cheerfully to him, "Don't worry. It's not about you. He wants to tell the king to throw me out on my ear. Again."

"He must wait then," the king declared in the same cheerful tone. He took Harmon's other arm. "We shall enjoy the meal Madame has arranged for us at the appropriate temperature and Prince Karl may try his best at such argument during it. But he will not succeed, even should he rant and rave as befits the image of one of his coloring."

"Don't let the red in his hair fool you. He's more stubborn than fiery," Harmon said.

Even before King Jozef responded, Karl saw that Harmon felt she'd made a slip. He could have told her to forget it—the king had known they knew each other all along.

"Ah, you have come to know him well so quickly." For all the mildness of the king's tone, he'd roused Harmon's suspicion.

Good. Maybe realizing the king was more dangerous than he seemed would make her decide to leave on her own.

The three of them started off.

Karl followed. Biding his time.

CHAPTER NINE

"Where are you, Harmon?" Ann-Elise said as soon as she answered her phone. Harmon tucked the phone between her shoulder and ear as she unlocked and entered her hotel room. "Aren't you supposed to be in London for R&R? That's why you said you couldn't come see us in South Carolina."

"Being married to the Colonel is affecting your vocabulary, Ann-Elise. You used to say vacation like a civilian."

Inside, she fished out her earpiece so she had both hands available to bring in her tote filled with books. Katie had taken her to the castle library after lunch, recommending books on Bariavak's history and culture, letting her borrow a few of the less-rare ones to expand on what she could find online.

"Vacation? I can only dream you'd go on a vacation. The military's rest and recuperation is the best I can hope for with you. And the only way you'll do that is if you come here to visit so we can both sit on you. When are you coming?"

"I can't now, Ann-Elise. I'm even farther—"

"Behind. I know. Anyway, it doesn't take being married to your father for me to notice that you're not where you said you were going, you're not taking the break you said you were going to take, and you haven't answered my question. I thought you were going to be in London this week."

"You know that sometimes I can't tell you—"

"This isn't one of those times."

"How do you know it isn't? Never mind," she said fatalistically, kicking off her shoes. "I can tell by your voice that you already know where I am. Sally spilled it? I'm going to have to have a serious conversation with my assistant about confidentiality."

"Delay and diversion, Harmon. Where are you?"

"You already know I'm in Bariavak."

"Yes, I do," the Colonel's wife said calmly. "But it's so good for you to say it. Now, tell me why?"

"A job."

"Came up awfully suddenly, didn't it?"

"That happens."

"Anything to do with the successor to the crown?"

Harmon stopped "How do you know that?" before it could escape. "That's a good guess since all the coverage in other countries about Bariavak for the past year and half has been about princesses—lost and found, real and unreal."

"Also about an unexpected prince. One I understand you've known for a long time and, ah, well."

"I knew him once upon a time. Not—"

"How appropriate for a prince."

"—anymore." Harmon dropped the prince issue, feeling she'd been bested in that round. "Even with all that interest in princesses, it doesn't mean that's the only thing going on here. You'd be astonished, but they manage to fill their newspapers and news reports here without every word being about a princess."

"Or prince."

If she'd been talking to just about anyone else, Harmon would have answered with something flip or sidetracking. But Ann-Elise picked up on way more than was comfortable when she did that. Silence was her best response.

After a moment, the other woman gave a short sigh. Harmon had the feeling she knew exactly what was going on.

Not for the first time, Harmon felt torn about whether marrying Ann-Elise was the best thing the Colonel had done or the worst. All from her perspective, of course. From his it was clearly the best.

"How's the pregnancy coming, Ann-Elise? How are you feeling?"

This sigh was gustier. "I'm told I'm blooming. I can only vouch for that being true when it comes to my middle and my ankles. With twins, it all happens at warp speed. Any day now I expect my ankles to become merely a rumor."

"Swollen?"

"Swollen now. Soon to be eclipsed by my belly."

Harmon chuckled. Then she said seriously, "Take it easy."

"You sound like your father."

"That's—There's somebody at the door. Gotta go."

"While you're looking out for all your fixers and this king and your old flame, you take care of yourself, too, Harmon."

"I always do."

King Jozef had insisted Karl needed to catch up, despite receiving daily reports from Bariavak when he was in Wyoming.

After a round of afternoon meetings with various ministers, he was ushered into the king's office.

"So how do you find the state of our state, Karl?" the king asked with a bit of a twinkle.

"My state is Wyoming. Particularly the bit of it that my ranch covers. And the ranch suffers from me not being there."

The king's twinkle died. "Bah. You have those hired men."

"Not hired. Friends who are filling in for me. And by doing that, they're not available to work for their home ranch. So that ranch is short-handed, too. Domino effect."

"Sell this ranch and it will no longer be an issue."

"I'm not selling. I am returning home soon. As I've told you before, sir, this will not be an extended stay. Being away during the summer is difficult."

"You said the same of the spring."

"Right. That's calving season. Summer's dawn to dark, too, with moving cattle, haying, irrigating, and the rest. Fall is roundup. Winter's the only time it lets up. I gave you two months last winter and can return this winter if you want me."

"Better that you remain here all year."

The king's grumble sounded pro forma, so Karl moved on. "This afternoon's meetings informed me that the status here is the same as what I read in the reports the day before I left home." He considered that. "Same as what I read while I was traveling, too."

"Ah, yes, your travels, when you returned with the charming Ms. Reed."

"Don't view that as an endorsement of her skills, sir. I had no idea what business she's in. I stepped in to help her solely out of respect for her father. I knew him when I was in the Army."

"Of course, of course. I understand. Though it is fortunate that she does have such skills."

"What do you have in mind for using those skills, sir? I don't see—"

"Ah, time shall determine that. Now, as to these reports, what is your view on the Minister of Education?"

"My view remains that he's an idiot. We've talked about this. You should replace him."

From experience, he didn't try to fight King Jozef's change of subject. Though he sure wished he knew what the king was up to with keeping Harmon around.

It could knock his plans off the rails completely if he wasn't careful—his plans regarding Bariavak, he meant. Nothing to do with her personally.

"Better to keep him occupied in my government—even poorly—than to be outside my government with too many hours to cause trouble for me, for Bariavak. I have thought to put Andrej Skala in as the deputy minister."

The old fox was probing. He did it well, too. Delivered that line as if it couldn't possibly have ramifications.

Yet it made Karl sure that the king did have at least an inkling of what was going on. But an inkling was a far cry from knowing for sure. Or officially.

He intended to keep it that way.

He paused, hoping to project an air of considering the proposal. "He would be wasted in that position. The minister would feel challenged and block every move he tried to make."

"What would you recommend?"

"Dalia Beralokza."

"Indeed?"

"She's been around long enough to know how to get around the Minister when she can or how to butter him up when she needs to. She is entirely devoted to improving education for the kids. That's her only ambition."

He sat calmly under the king's searching regard.

After a moment, King Jozef tapped his desk. "You are right. That is the best decision."

"One you'd already reached," Karl said dryly.

The twinkle was back. "Perhaps, perhaps."

"A test, sir?"

"You don't fault me for that, do you? It is natural in this circumstance."

"I'm not auditioning for the job."

"You believe you do not need to audition?"

"You know otherwise, sir. I do not want the job."

"I need a successor. A worthy successor. Someone with honor and brains, who understands duty, who will love Bariavak as it deserves, will look after it in the future when I am gone. You see that. You understand that."

"Yes, I see that Bariavak needs a plan for its future. I understand that."

"Then you agree that Vatche is not worthy—"

"Agreed."

"—and that you are the logical choice."

"I've told you. Neither logical nor available, Your Majesty."

"Bah. You will see. When the future becomes the present."

Karl just hoped that what he saw then wasn't the view from the throne of Bariavak.

CHAPTER TEN

The knock had given Harmon the excuse to wrap up the call with Ann-Elise.

"Who is it?"

"Karl."

There were no peepholes in this historic building. If she wanted to know what he wanted, she had to open the door.

She opened it with the earpiece in place.

Karl inquired if she was still on the phone by cocking one eyebrow under the brim of his hat.

She shook her head. "Just finished."

"You going to let me in?"

That first instant of opening the door to find him standing there in his cowboy hat had thrown her. He'd worn it that summer they were together when he was out of uniform. Seeing it now, it was as if she were seeing both the boy she'd known so long ago and the man who stood here now, but also with dark shadows thrown in that—

This was not the time. Or the place. If she was lucky it would never be the time or the place.

But a good deep breath and her mind was working again.

He might be here to tell her to get lost—again. Or to try to find out what she knew—nothing. Or ... well, she wasn't going to find out unless she let the man in.

She stepped back into the doorway of the bathroom so he could pass, leaving plenty of room.

He eyed her as he went by. "You look ... harried. One of your fixers get broken?"

"Not this time." Perhaps she let too much relief into that, because his focus tightened on her and he stopped.

"But they can?"

She answered seriously. "Yeah. They can."

"I've heard about western journalists being murdered…"

"That's the tip of the iceberg. The part you see, with a mass hiding below the water. There are regimes that round up journalists, sometimes systematically, sometimes in spasms. Sometimes enough pressure can be brought to let the foreign journalists out, but the natives … They're often not as fortunate."

She turned away from his scrutiny. The corner of her eye caught something in the bathroom mirror. A dribble down the front of her blouse from lunch. Great. Her only alternative was a crumpled, not-clean t-shirt, which she needed to get washed. Even then, it wasn't exactly castle attire.

And in the meantime … "Whatever you've come about is going to have to wait while I clean this. I just discovered a spot on my blouse. My only blouse."

She swung the bathroom door nearly closed, dampened the washcloth and dabbed at the spot. It wasn't coming off.

"So, you go to bat for these broken fixers?" he asked from beyond the door. From his voice, he was prowling around the room.

"As much as I can."

"How'd you get started doing this? Doesn't sound like there's a school for learning the ropes."

She redampened, using more water this time, and tried again. Better.

"There's not. Definitely on-the-job training and that's when you're not making it up as you go."

"How'd you get started?" he asked again.

She drew a breath. Adding water, dabbing and turning, adding water, dabbing and turning.

"A friend needed help. Hey, I've been meaning to ask you—why are you staying at this hotel?"

"It's a nice place. People are nice. Food—"

"Is nice. I got it. But why not the castle?"

Finally, the spot was about gone. She draped the washcloth over the edge of the sink with something like triumph.

"Turns out I'm not the castle type," he drawled.

"You're not trying to tell me it intimidates you, because I wouldn't buy that. Anyone who wears his cowboy hat at Marco Polo Airport, not to mention in Bariavak Castle is not intimidated."

She glanced in the mirror as she pushed her hair back—

"Wear my hat *to* the castle. Not *in* it," he said mildly. "Important to know the protocol."

—and saw that a wide swath of her blouse had gone transparent.

So had the bra under it.

Damn.

"So Army protocol was a warm-up for you, huh. You should tell the Colonel about it. He loves that sh—stuff, too."

She was not going back out there when she was the next-best thing—or next-worst thing—to bare-breasted.

"So you haven't given up being hard on your father. He was always fair and—"

"How would you know? You weren't in his command." She looked around the bathroom.

"—well-respected by his soldiers."

She ignored that. "You were always Grif's pet, though."

"Colonel Griffin had no pets."

She ignored that, too. "Did you know he's in Wyoming now?" She put a dry washcloth between her bra and the shirt. It slipped with her first step. That wasn't going to work. "Grif, I mean."

"Yes."

"Ah. You get together, swap old war stories, huh?"

"You could say that."

She returned to the room with a bath towel folded to a narrow band slung over her shoulder and coming down well over her breast.

He was leaning back against the desk, hat still in place. Had he been looking at her screen? Her papers? Wherever he had been looking, his gaze now rested on her towel accessory.

"Strategic," he muttered.

"Necessary. I'm so sick of wearing these clothes. Can't wait to get them off."

As the words left her mouth, she recognized them as a mistake of the open mouth, insert foot variety.

But he would ignore her accidental double entendre. No way Karl Wethers wanted to be reminded of what had once been between them. And she couldn't blame him.

He cocked the same eyebrow at her. Not looking away. "Don't let me stop you."

She went still an instant, then deflected with a short, sharp, "Ha" of laughter. "So Prince Karl of Bariavak isn't the saint I've been hearing about."

"Not a saint. As you know." He looked at her and she met the look, not allowing herself any hesitation. There was heat there. Not the open, flaring heat from that summer. This was far from that uncontrolled range fire of youth and passion.

Not that she wanted that. It would be a nuisance. A complication.

This heat was well-banked. Fully under the control of a man who had no intention of letting it get out of hand. So she could relax. And be glad that fire would not enter into their dealings. Because he wouldn't let it.

Something else crossed his face then, pushing the heat farther back.

"Not a prince of Bariavak, either," he said.

She laughed despite herself. Perhaps in relief. Perhaps not. "That's right. You're a prince of Gelicia."

"Which no longer exists."

"Did you have any inkling about your royal roots beforehand?"

"None. There were family stories that my paternal great-grandfather was something vaguely aristocratic somewhere or other in Europe before he made his way to Wyoming. But since he was prone to tall tales no one put any credence in them."

"How'd you find out?"

"Your friend Hunter Pierce. Showed up as a representative of the Department of State at a hotel where some Army buddies and I were taking it easy for a weekend."

Army buddies. Any of the ones who'd been with him when—?

"So Hunter ended your fun?"

He grunted a yes. "Told me my family tree, took DNA, and gave me a headache that hasn't gone away."

"Your father—"

"Dad died three years back."

"I'm so sorry, Karl. I know you were close."

He'd talked about his father, so often. All his family, actually. His parents, his sisters. And the friends he'd made at the ranch where he'd worked before joining the Army.

She'd never met them. Any of them.

She turned away abruptly, moving the tote out of the pathway.

"Thanks," he said shortly. "Gelicia's inheritance law was strictly oldest son, so that left me."

She looked up. "If you don't want to be involved, why don't you sign a paper, abdicate, or something?"

"Wait until you meet Prince Vatche—the Prince Karl alternative— then we'll see what you say." He used that dry tone a lot more than he used to.

"You always were prone to taking on all the responsibilities of the world."

"Not of the world. Only for the people I care about."

She'd once been one of those people … Her heart jerked with an erratic thud. That tote must have weighed more than she thought.

"In other words, the king. But it's not like he's your grandfather. Especially since Katie's living her own life and not buckling under to King Jozef."

"Nice way to talk about your employer."

"I'm serious, Karl. You've only know the man, what? A year?

Are—"

"A little more than that."

"—you going to let him run your life?"

"You knew him only a few hours before you let him turn your life upside down."

"That's different. It's a job. Not the rest of my life."

"That's what I want to talk to you about—the job, not the rest of your life," he clarified with aloof mildness.

She was beginning to hate that tone.

"There are cross-currents under the surface here in Bariavak that could easily trip up an outsider. Especially a newcomer."

"You're worried about an outsider getting hurt from tripping or about the impact of any tripping done by outsiders on those cross-currents?"

"Does it matter? Better that it all stays within Bariavak."

"Are you trying to say what happens in Bariavak stays in Bariavak?" she asked with a chuckle.

His stern expression didn't change. "That about covers it."

She flipped over a hand. "Confidentiality's part of the package anyway. But I do have a question."

He said nothing. Wasn't going to invite the question, but wasn't blocking it, either.

"What are you doing here, Karl? *Really* doing here."

"You know."

"I know what the papers have said and the line you just gave me, but I know yo—I used to know you and it doesn't match. Prince? Heir to the royal throne of Bariavak?"

He shrugged. "As you've experienced, King Jozef can be persuasive."

She tilted her head, studying him from that angle. "Or are you being swayed by the strategic value to the United States? That's Hunter Pierce's role, isn't it? To remind you that being able to fly over Bariavak is the most direct route for a lot of our military. Saves hours, could save lives."

"King Jozef signed the renewal of that agreement a year and a half ago."

"There'll be another renewal eventually. Not to mention other interests in this region. Hunter's bosses at State will be much happier with you on the throne than any other future for Bariavak. How much pressure is he putting on you?"

He said nothing.

"You could tell him to go … uh, jump off a cliff."

He chuckled, and sounded genuinely amused. "Not a wise move with April around. Remember the old rule: Never drop your gun to hug a grizzly."

"Remember it?" she repeated dryly. "Can't remember what I've never heard before. In fact, I suspect you just made it up."

"Thought for sure you were about to have that rule demonstrated last night," he went on with no indication he'd heard her protest, "when you said you were quitting because of Hunter. Thought April was going to leave your body parts spread around for the crows to feast on."

"Nice way to talk about that nice woman. And you don't need to sound so enthusiastic about the prospect."

"Uh-huh. Usually very nice. Leave it to you to rouse her inner grizzly."

Karl Wethers was lying to her. Lying by change-of-subject omission, rather than commission, true, but lying nonetheless.

She might not argue too strenuously if he said she deserved it. What she didn't deserve was the direction he changed the subject to with his next words.

"Heard your father's going to make full colonel."

"So I'm told."

"There's that frozen face again."

"I do not—."

"How is he?"

"Fine." Snapping that wasn't the way to handle this anymore than that knee-jerk response to the accusation of going frozen-faced. She spread her arms in an expansive gesture indicating openness and honesty in multiple cultures. "More than fine. Ecstatic. He's going to be full colonel and he's going to be a father. At his time of life. Can you imagine? A dream come true."

"He remarried?" There, that surprised Mr. Cool. "Grif never said anything. Does he know?"

It was no surprise Karl had stayed in touch with his former commanding officer. There'd been a true connection there, despite the gap in their ages and ranks. They had similar outlooks on doing the right thing.

"Oh, yes," she said airily. "Grif was best man at the wedding. A year ago this fall. Her name's Ann-Elise. That's who was on the phone earlier. She's an artist. Illustrations, book covers, all sorts of projects. Self-employed and doing well. Younger than him, but thank God older than me. It all happened fast. They essentially eloped."

"You like her."

Yes, damn him, she did. Though how he'd reached that conclusion from what she'd said...

Liking Ann-Elise had been as much of a shock as the woman herself. If there had been anyone less like the delicate, retiring woman she remembered her mother as it was hard to imagine.

"I like that she doesn't put up with any orders or other military crap from him," she said, not confirming or denying his conclusion.

"Huh."

That sounded like it had a whole lot of subtext to it that she couldn't translate. And no sense guessing. "Huh, what?" she demanded.

"Interesting is all. And they're going to have a baby? How do you feel about that?"

How *did* she feel about it?

Hell if she knew.

When they'd called her last month she'd been in a country that wasn't particularly friendly to women or westerners or media. Not the worst she'd been in by any means.

She'd slipped in to the country to check if her fixer, who'd had a confrontation with some of his countrymen who strongly preferred the Fourteenth Century to the Twenty-First, truly was okay. Her guy was weary and concerned about his family, but committed to continuing his work.

She'd arranged for additional unobtrusive security measures for his home when her phone said a call was coming in from TC/AE—the Colonel and Ann-Elise.

It was there in their voices with the first hellos.

"What's up?" she'd asked.

The Colonel sounded like his throat was a little raw. "We have news."

Then he stopped.

"Tell her, Brooks," said Ann-Elise.

A less patient person—like her—would have spilled whatever there was to spill. A more laidback person would have let the Colonel get to it in his own time. She respected the middle ground staked out by her father's second wife—impossible to call her a step-mother.

"We're having a baby," he said in a rush.

"You're going to be a sister, Harmon." From her voice, Ann-Elise was smiling. "Twice."

"We're having two babies. Twins," he said.

"I think she can figure that out, Brooks," Ann-Elise said with a chuckle.

Don't be so sure. At that instant, Harmon hadn't been sure she could figure out anything.

She'd done her best with the usual words of congratulations. Which probably hadn't been all that good. It had felt stiff and awkward. Except for when Ann-Elise spoke.

They'd kept the news to themselves until the doctor said it appeared to be a normal pregnancy, Ann-Elise had said.

"Your family must be excited," Harmon had gotten out.

"They will be when we tell them. We wanted to tell you first," Ann-Elise said.

She'd sat on a crumbling concrete wall. Harder than she'd intended.

"I, uh … I'm happy for you and we can talk, uh, later, but I'm not confident about this connection."

"We can hear you fine," Ann-Elise said.

"Security?" the Colonel demanded.

All she had to do then was hesitate. Wham, bam, end of call.

There'd been a few calls since then. The more successful ones were when it was just her and Ann-Elise talking.

Every phone call one or both of them asked her to come see them in Columbia, S.C., where the Colonel was posted to Fort Jackson. There was always a good reason she couldn't.

All that flashed through her mind from Karl's "*How do you feel about that?*"

Looking up to find Karl watching her, she felt as if her thoughts and memories had projected on a screen for his viewing enjoyment. Frozen-faced her a—.

"Actually they're going to have twins. So, he's going to be a father—father of two—in a few more months," she said.

"Father of three. He's already a father. Has been for years. Good thing he has that experience behind him with twins coming."

"This is one of those instances when experience is a detriment."

"Bull."

"Now you sound like Ann-Elise. But the Colonel agrees with me. He even said at their wedding—"

"Said at their wedding? So Grif was best man and you were at their wedding, too? You said they eloped. That doesn't sound like an elopement."

"I said 'essentially'."

She wasn't telling him about Ann-Elise's family and Grif's family being there, too. She especially wasn't telling him that she'd been maid of honor, at Ann-Elise's insistence, and had helped the bride pick a dress—at her own insistence.

He'd make way too much of that.

"So you're saying that having you at their wedding was essential for them."

We're not getting married without you there, Harmon. Ann-Elise had said that and made it stick.

Another thing she wasn't telling Karl.

She flipped one hand to wave off the memory and his words. "Ann-Elise is big into mending fences."

He leaned back. "Why do you and your father still need fences mended? I'd think you would have outgrown that a long time ago."

"*Me?* He—"

"Nope. It was you. Giving him a hard time. Turning a cold shoulder to him. Acting like he was a sadistic—"

"I never—"

"—dictator. Hurting him every chance you got. Leaving that party he gave for you."

"*He* didn't give it for me. He got some non-com's wife to do it."

"You hold that against him? All it says to me is that his party-giving experience was getting beer and pizza for a group of his pals. But he wanted that one to be nice for you, so he went to someone who knew about those things. And you left in the middle of it."

"With you," she shot back.

"I didn't know you were ditching the party your father was giving you."

"You wouldn't have gone with me if you'd known?" She made it a challenge. Remembering what had happened that night. How he had felt against her, inside her ... how he had made her feel...

"No, I don't think I would have," he said after consideration. "I'd still have wanted to, but I don't think I would have."

Then I'm glad you didn't know. The words were right there, trying to pop out. She held them in.

Instead, she said lightly, "That would have changed things. We probably never would have seen each other again."

"Yes," he said seriously, "that would have changed things."

CHAPTER ELEVEN

Karl Wethers wished he'd never met her that night.

Too bad. He had. And she'd met him.

And because of that, he'd charged in to her rescue—

In Venice. Her *supposed* rescue at Marco Polo Airport. The sequence that had brought her here.

That's what she meant.

She shimmied her shoulders, shaking off thoughts of the past, the Colonel, and especially Pvt. Karl Wethers.

The knock on her door the next morning jittered Harmon's heartbeat for no reason at all.

It wasn't like she was expecting anyone.

Or like Bariavak was a dangerous country, she added quickly, even though there was no one to convince other than herself.

"Who is it?"

"Ms. Reed?" said a young female voice.

"Yes." She opened the door.

The person facing her matched the voice. Young, female, fresh-faced … and loaded down with enough shopping bags to be moving in.

"I am Ruzena. May I come in? I have a few items for you to try on from Jitkas', my parents' shop."

"To try on? I didn't request any—"

"On orders from the castle," the young woman said with a mix of briskness and awe. As she spoke in barely accented English, she started in. Harmon had to back into the bathroom to avoid being sideswiped by bags. "If these do not satisfy, we have many more, which we can bring to you at your convenience."

"I could come to your store, you know."

"But the castle said … It is for your convenience."

"Who at the castle?"

"I was instructed not to divulge…"

"But it was someone actually at the castle?" She held the other woman's gaze.

Dimples appeared and Ruzena said with the air of a conspirator, "In a manner of speaking."

In other words, Karl.

The only one she'd complained to about the state of her wardrobe.

Was this his way of saying he didn't want her to mistake his "Don't let me stop you" as enthusiasm about her taking her clothes off? When a man tried to get you *in* to clothes instead of out of them…

Nope. Didn't matter. Did. Not. Matter

Besides, she did need clothes and it was nice to have the things brought to her. "Okay, let's take a look."

As the young woman began to remove clothes from the bags and hang them from doorknobs and the top edges of doors in an impromptu display, Harmon asked casually, "What time did Prince Karl call you this morning?"

"There was a message from him waiting when we opened."

The skirts were long. The tops were high-necked and dark. Not one of them would cling. Certainly none would go transparent when wet.

So the first thing on his mind this morning had been to see her attired in a collection that would suit a nun headed for a funeral.

Interesting.

She promised Ruzena she'd look through the selection, but first she called April and Katie, who enthusiastically agreed to meet her for shopping at Jitkas' followed by lunch.

She then picked out enough basics from the nun-heading-to-a-funeral theme Karl had dictated to get her dressed for the day, letting her send her clothes off to be cleaned.

She felt downright lighthearted as she and Ruzena walked between stone buildings in the oldest part of the city. She felt even better when they entered the plain, narrow store to discover wonders inside.

Katie and April were equally enthusiastic. They entered into the spirit of replenishing her wardrobe, helping her find several more items—none suited to a funeral or a nun.

Especially the shimmery cobalt blue number she'd just put on, with a slit in the long skirt up to here and a drapey back that made you immediately imagine what it would look like turned around.

"Now *that* is a dress," April said with a whistle as Harmon exited the dressing room.

"That's *fabulous* on you," Katie said. "Too bad you can't wear that to the reception."

"What reception and why can't I wear it?" Harmon was looking at the back of the dress in the mirror, so she caught the exchange of looks between the other two women.

"No one's told you about the reception the day after tomorrow?" April asked. "It's a semi-regular gathering, not like the gala at the end of next week—"

"What gala?"

Katie groaned. "They haven't told you about that, either?"

"We'll fill you in over lunch," April promised.

"Maybe I'm not invited—I don't mean for lunch, since I did the inviting for that. But to the reception and gala."

"You're invited," they said in unison.

"In that case, don't you think I *should* take this dress? For one or the other—the reception or the gala."

She had every intention of getting the dress, but she hoped to nudge a little more information out of these two.

"It's not..." Katie paused. "Bariavak."

"It's for sale in a Bariavak store."

"Of course, and it's beautiful, but some feel the country's being overrun by us—Americans—and that it's pushing aside the native influence. So to wear a dress like that—"

"But I designed and made the dress," Ruzena blurted out.

All three of them turned to her. Harmon recovered first. "You did? That's fabulous, Ruzena. That settles it. I have to get this dress and tell everyone where I got it and who created it."

Ruzena's cheeks went rosy. "I would be so honored."

Harmon turned in the dress, taking another look in the mirror. "I'm the one who's honored. While I get changed, you better start adding up my bill, Ruzena. This might take a while."

"Oh, but the castle said—"

"No way. I pay for my own clothes. Don't worry. I'll explain to the castle."

Returning to the dressing room she caught an exchange of looks between April and Katie that had her thinking they knew exactly who "the castle" was in this instance.

They ate at a nearby restaurant Ruzena suggested after Harmon asked for ideas. Harmon thought she'd meant to recommend somewhere else until her mother interrupted in their native language. After a short, rapid exchange Ruzena named this restaurant. She'd also called ahead for them.

There was a private room waiting.

"Tell me about this reception," Harmon said when they were alone.

"The king holds them regularly," Katie said. "He mixes in ministers, other government officials, senior staff members, any visiting dignitaries, and regular citizens. They're popular with his subjects."

"But not with you." It required no acumen to figure that out.

"They're not my favorite thing, but I understand the benefits."

"He used to invite his subjects in once a year—at Christmas. But after he had one of those open days at the Embassy in Washington, he recognized how powerful they could be. He says they let him get the pulse of his people," April said.

"In that case, I have to go, even if it means gate-crashing."

Katie chuckled. "No need to gate-crash. For that or the gala."

"Are Carolyn and C.J. coming for the gala?" April asked her friend.

"They can't make it this year—they were here last year for the Ashton basketball team's tour." She'd added that explanation for Harmon. "You know C.J.'s the head coach at Ashton. Most of the year Brad's one of his assistants and I run the office. Carolyn's his wife and our dear friend. Grandfather combined the annual gala with an event for the team last year. It was gorgeous."

"Then why do you sound so glum?"

"She and Brad were in a bumpy spell at the time of last year's gala," April said in a conspiratorial whisper. "Which is like saying those mountains on the horizon are slight hills."

Katie simultaneously sighed and smiled. Harmon had a feeling she knew which was for the past and which was for the present.

"That and they made me wear a tiara last year."

"Whoa. That tone sounds like a serious hate for headgear."

"It's heavy and it hurts. I am looking forward to this year's without it, although I wish Carolyn and C.J. ... but Brad's grandmother's coming. Wait until you meet Andy. You'll love her."

A phalanx of wait staff appeared at that moment. Only after they swept through did Harmon have the opportunity to ask, "How about you, April? Any family coming in for the gala?"

"We're hoping next year. It takes a lot of organizing with that big crew."

"They're wonderful people," Katie said. "I met them last year when Grandfather and I first met, well, met as adults, I mean. Then April's family—"

"Mostly not blood, but family nonetheless," April inserted.

"—took me under their wing at April and Hunter's wedding."

That led to more details about how April had first connected with

King Jozef and the tale of how Katie had discovered a history—and family—she'd had no inkling of.

"The only downside is some of the people," she concluded morosely.

Harmon raised one eyebrow.

"Prince Vatche," April said wisely.

"He's the worst, but he's not the only one," Katie said. "I swear some of those stuffed shirts in Grandfather's government would only be happy if they made me miserable."

"By forcing her to be Princess Royal and the heir apparent," April explained in an aside to Harmon.

"Fate worse than death."

Harmon's clearly fake sympathy drew a smile from Katie. "Well, it would be for me. I've got the life I want. I don't know why they can't understand that."

"Because a number of them would kill to have the position you've said you don't want."

Harmon thought April regretted saying those words. Especially when Katie added. "I know. Always slinking around and wheedling, trying to get their candidate named as the heir because they have him in their pocket. Of all of them, Vatche is the worst. Of course he wants the crown for himself. He's so blatant about it. Wants it for the power. Not to help the people of Bariavak, not to preserve the good traditions, not to bring beneficial advances. Just because he wants everything for himself. He's so … so … slimy. I know that's not nice, but he is. Wait until you meet him, Harmon."

"I think I'll stick with Brad's grandmother. I have another question."

She sensed them both put up their guard.

"Tell me about Madame. I'm dying to know something that makes her more human. She scares the stuffing out of me."

They both relaxed.

"You and me both," Katie said.

"You're kidding. She adores you, Katie," April said. "And you wouldn't believe how much she's loosened up from when I first met her in Washington. She'd been running Bariavak's Embassy there for ages. It was a year and a half ago, the Christmas before the king's surgery when Hunter introduced me to him…"

April told about her early encounters with Madame, then Katie added hers.

Aided by a few adroit questions, Harmon put together Madame Sabdoka's history.

Therese and Jozef had been childhood friends, then teenage sweethearts. Until the king's father cut off the relationship abruptly, announcing the royal bride he had selected for his son, then immediately sending the then-prince off to a series of foreign assignments.

A year later, Therese married and became Madame.

"Then came the rebellion."

The mood at their little table shifted. Katie's father had been killed in that uprising before she was born. Rebels kidnapped her, then raised her with no knowledge of her heritage, and her mother had died, broken hearted, months after she was taken.

"Madame's brother was head of the king's guard. Her son was his second in command. Both were killed," April said.

"How awful," Harmon said.

April nodded. "Her brother, Laurentz, was Hunter's father. Laurentz had married late and Hunter was just a boy…"

"Whoa. Madame is Hunter's aunt?"

April and Katie smiled slightly, lightening the mood. "She is," April said. "He ran away after his father's death, right into the fighting. Soldiers rescued him. They and aid workers helped get him to the United States. Afterward, Madame and the king secretly did a lot behind the scenes to help Hunter."

"What a story," Harmon said. "If he let me get this story out, he could be a star."

"He will never go public. It's not him."

That clearly was fine with April.

She cleared her throat and returned to narrator mode. "Not long after the rebellion, Madame's husband also died. Though from everything I gather that was not the tragedy the other events were. He was a gambler. And not one of those mythical successful ones. Madame went to work at Bariavak's embassy in Washington. I suspect the king had something to do with that."

"I'm sure he did," Katie said. "Did you know she was offered an ambassador's post, someplace where it would have been ceremonial? Elisabeta told me that. Madame refused, saying she wanted to earn her way. That's when she went to Washington."

"Where she ruled the embassy for years," April picked up. "I suppose she and the king must have been in formal situations together, but it wasn't until the Christmas before last that they had a chance to be together just as people after all that time. She never left his side during his surgery and recuperation that winter."

"You did all that, April, bringing them together," Katie said.

"No. It was circumstances. Though I did help get her to unbend a bit over making Christmas cookies."

"Elisabeta says everyone says it was you and they're all grateful, because both Madame and Grandfather are so much happier than they were," Katie insisted.

Harmon smiled. "Strange to think of King Jozef and Madame as wild young things. And scary to think of her any less unbent than she is now."

"Oh, she was," Katie said with emphasis.

"And she was even worse when I first went to the embassy," April said. "Still, there was something when she and the king were in the same room … I told Hunter there was something between them. Of course he didn't believe me. Not at first, anyway. It's sweet to see them together now."

"It is," Katie agreed. "It's also sad that they spent so many years apart. I have the feeling that it was a true and great love they had as youngsters, ruined by—"

Her sentence died with the opening of the door and the arrival of more staff.

It was time to leave then. And there had never been an opportunity to bring the conversation back around to ask the question she'd hoped to slip in about whether Karl had anyone near and dear to him coming for the gala.

CHAPTER TWELVE

Prince Karl of Gelicia was nowhere to be seen that day or the day after.

King Jozef was too busy to have a meeting with her.

Hunter Pierce might have been hiding out with Karl, because she didn't see anything of him, either.

April and Katie were busy with preparations for both the reception and the gala and—knowing herself and her lack of experience hosting such things—she cut them a break by not asking to be involved.

She didn't even consider trying to see Madame.

One morning she wandered into the basketball camp, thinking pumping Brad for information might pay off. But other than a quick wave and smile, he concentrated on the young players.

That didn't mean Harmon wasted her time.

She and her assistant, Sally, had only a couple issues to thrash out—which was as good as it ever got. She talked to a prospective client—and eliminated him. A second one who wanted a film crew in Argentina advanced to having Sally line up the background check. She worked through a hiccup with one fixer and a stubborn knot with another. She okayed the final agreement that would keep three more of her people working through the summer.

"If you have to disappear," Sally said grudgingly, "this isn't the worst time for you to do it."

"I haven't disappeared. Besides, you wouldn't have seen me until my U.S. swing in the fall anyway. I'm just in a different hotel room."

"Doing something weird."

"Not weird. At least not yet. More like undefined."

"Does that mean doing nothing?" Sally asked hopefully.

"No. It means I'm self-directed."

"Uh-oh. You know what my mother says."

Sally's mother trained dogs. She'd said more than once that Harmon was like certain breeds—if you didn't give them a job that kept them busy, they'd find their own job and then, watch out.

"Yes, I do know what she says," Harmon cut in quickly to avoid hearing it again. "Gotta go now."

Satisfied that her business was in good shape for the moment, she turned to the final job left to tackle.

The one that King Jozef said he'd given her but refused to define.

Harmon wondered if she should warn King Jozef about what Sally's mother said about her and give him one last chance to define this job.

Nah.

He'd had plenty of time.

She was about to find her own job to do.

She started by developing connections with journalists here in Bariavak. Especially freelance journalists with no ties to the existing government or anyone else.

She already had a mental list from reading newspapers and magazines translated to English online and from talking to everyone she met at the castle, in the hotel, around town.

Now, she set up meetings, coffee, breakfasts, lunches, teas—no dinners yet—putting faces with names. She also mined her other connections to see who knew anybody in Bariavak.

She picked up quite a few scraps to start sorting into mental piles in connection with Katie's talk about ministers maneuvering to become kingmakers. Unfortunately the largest pile comprised distasteful tidbits about Prince Vatche.

Nobody in Bariavak wanted him as their king. Nobody. And considering all the factions trying to inch ahead, it took someone, uh, remarkable to unite them.

She also dug into Andrej Skala, intrigued by the dynamics of that meeting in the king's office.

What she quickly learned was that he was considered the one person who might be able to unite the squabbling groups who wanted democracy. Every other possible leader was fatally divisive.

For that and other reasons, she dug discreetly.

She was somewhat hampered because she couldn't ask anyone at the hotel about him. Karl had friends on the staff. Surely not all of them, but she couldn't risk asking the wrong one something that would zing right back to him.

On the other hand, he had unwittingly given her another resource by sending Ruzena. At her parents' shop and others spots that Ruzena recommended for necessities and not-so-necessities, Harmon cultivated wide-ranging conversations, picking up bits and pieces that seldom connected ... at the start.

Katie called receiving line duty Royal Torture.

Karl was inclined to agree with her. Receiving the guests for these receptions was certainly one of his least favorite things about being a prince. And since that was a long list that was saying something.

As the first in the royal line, an official Karl only saw at these functions pronounced the names of the visitors as they reached him. It was then his duty to pass them on to Katie, with Brad remaining protectively at her elbow. Katie, in turn, handed them over to the king, with introductions when necessary.

It was like loading cattle through a chute, only you had to remember every name, say something polite to them, make them like you, and you couldn't wave your hat at them or slap them on the rump.

And the line kept coming. He looked up in hopes the end was in sight and...

Those legs.

Guests being adroitly corralled into the receiving line shifted, opening his sight line to those farther back, and he recognized her legs.

Hell, he recognized one leg. Because when she walked, the slit in that half a dress showed her left leg from the heel, resting on an impossibly tall spike, up to almost … where it wasn't leg anymore.

The right leg only showed in brief flashes and that was from the knee down. But he hadn't even needed that to know it was Harmon.

He'd managed to avoid her for nearly three days and now he paid the price. It was like her effect had packed itself tighter and tighter into a can, building pressure until, with that first sighting of her legs, it burst open with a bang.

Those legs.

*Swinging while she sat on a brick wall. Crossed in front of her as she sat in the sun drying her hair. Slung over his lap as they watched a movie. Wrapped around him, drawing him deeper—*Nostalgia. An idyll. Long gone.

*Struggling to get free, trying to land a blow, then to stand, still shaking—*No. That belonged in the past, too.

Where she should have stayed.

Where she would return as soon as King Jozef stopped whatever game he was running, she got bored and moved on, or Karl could wrap up what needed to be done and be gone himself.

Though that last one could take a year, maybe more.

A year. A year of seeing those legs…

He kept his gaze on the people directly in front of him. Repeating greetings to the guests filing in. Remembering names of those he'd met before. Meeting many more for the first time.

He heard Harmon's laugh. Not loud. Not over the conversations. But burrowing into his consciousness.

He looked up.

He saw her across the room, turning toward someone, which made that skirt swing slightly, revealing both legs for an instant, then showing the back of the dress.

Make that showing where the back of the dress should have been.

His own legs threatened to turn to water.

Another part of him reacted differently. Very differently.

Okay, so he still wanted her.

No big surprise. He could handle that. He wasn't a kid anymore, as they'd both agreed that first day.

He'd seen beautiful women. Women more beautiful than her. Hell, he'd had his share throwing themselves at him since this prince stuff came up. But he hadn't been a monk even before that.

"Karl?" Brad's elbow nudged him at the same time his voice registered enough for Karl to grab onto.

A pleasant couple stood before him, looking momentarily at a loss.

"I get to do the introducing this time," Brad said, covering Karl's lapse. "I happen to know these fine people and would like to introduce you to Gregorj and Malaka Karatok, the parents of Milos from basketball camp. They also stepped in and hosted a national team player and an Ashton University player last year for a dinner in their home."

"It was our pleasure," the woman said, smiling.

"The idea was to have Bariavak's national team players each take an Ashton player home for dinner," Brad said, giving Karl both the time and the clues to help him catch up. "But a couple of the players live up in the mountains and the trip would have taken too long, so volunteers like the Karatoks became host families."

"That was kind of you," Karl said. "And in return your son Milos became basketball mad."

The parents laughed. "He already had a start on that, though it has reached a much higher level," his father added.

"It's paying off, at least to my amateur eyes. He has a nice shooting touch."

Both parents beamed at Karl.

"True," Brad said, "but please don't repeat that to him. I'm trying to drill defense into his head. And now, may I introduce my wife? Katie, these are Milos Karatok's parents..."

As they made the transfer, Karl gave Brad a small nod, signifying thanks and a promise not to fall down on the job again. He couldn't do more than that because if he grimaced a photographer would catch that precise instant. He'd learned that early in this prince gig.

He kept all his attention on the task at hand after that, though aware of Harmon drawing nearer and nearer.

And then she was there.

"Ms. Harmon Reed," intoned the official, apparently coming up blank for a phrase to define her.

She dropped her head, which to an observer might resemble a sign of respect. He knew better, even before she looked up at him through her lashes and he saw the glint in her eyes.

"Ms. Reed. I thought you'd left Bariavak."

"No, you didn't, but good try, Karl."

The official coughed.

Karl wished all he had to worry about was protocol crap.

"With so little here to keep you occupied, it would be understandable and reasonable for you to continue on with your duties elsewhere," he said.

"I'm keeping up with everything just fine here. The wonders of modern communication. As I understand you know from when you're in Wyoming, yet never out of touch with Bariavak and the castle."

"I wouldn't say never. It is to be hoped that you enjoy the reception tonight."

The glint in her eyes flared and she appeared to be fighting a laugh. She'd caught that he'd avoided saying *he* hoped she had a good time. "I'm sure I will, Your Highness."

She flicked a look and a half smile at the official, who showed no sign of seeing it, while still appearing to be mollified.

Smoothly, she moved on to Brad and Katie.

The moment was past, she was past, that damned dress was past.

He couldn't have turned to look at her bare back if he'd wanted to because the next person was there to claim his attention.

And he didn't want to.

He wanted to finish doing his duty and be done with all this damned nonsense once and for all.

Harmon's mistake came after the receiving line had broken up and everyone was circulating.

The receiving line had been interesting.

It had been the first time she'd seen any of them in a situation calling for royal mode. Even as she'd chatted with those around her, she'd had plenty of time to observe them as the long line progressed.

Unsurprisingly, King Jozef was at home in the situation. From all appearances he was a master at saying the right thing, sending each guest out into the party aglow from the king's attention.

Katie was warm and smiling and lovely. Her discomfort and vulnerability appeared to instill a feeling of protectiveness in the guests. Harmon saw a number she'd pegged as tough nuts unbend with Katie in unexpected and genuine ways.

Katie certainly stirred protectiveness in her husband. Brad operated less as a full member of the receiving line than as her combo watchdog and buffer. He disliked the session solely because Katie did.

Karl … Karl was another story.

He handled it beautifully. Not natural—how could anyone, even King Jozef, be completely relaxed and natural?—but focused entirely on each person as he was introduced. Determined to do his duty as expected of him. As he expected of himself.

A duty he hated. Hated every second.

She didn't know how she knew it, because he gave no outward sign. But she had no doubt.

There'd been hints. That first day, how he'd separated who he was from what he called his "circumstances." Her recognition of his reluctance to become the heir to the Bariavak throne.

But this was deeper than reluctance. It was far more than someone failing to revel in a quirk of history and heritage making him a prince.

He was a man who wasn't where he wanted to be.

Karl Wethers, Prince of Gelicia, who could have the crown of Bariavak by simply saying yes, wanted nothing more than to get out.

But King Jozef wasn't going to let him go.

CHAPTER THIRTEEN

With that recognition in Harmon's head, it was like a dim light being introduced into a dark closet. Things she'd heard from citizens, around the castle, from Katie, April, and the others, even from Karl himself, began to take loose shape.

No, even loose shape was too specific. It was a feeling. The beginning of a feeling. About where those undercurrents Karl had mentioned might be most active.

She still couldn't see details in the dark closet, but she sure could tell it wasn't empty.

That focused her more sharply on the players who were here at the reception.

She spotted several ministers she'd heard talked about. Andrej Skala was there as well. Who was that he was talking to? Oh, yes, the top political columnist in Bariavak. One of the people she hadn't gotten in to see. Yet.

The columnist grimaced and jerked his head toward a group by one of the two massive marble fireplaces.

Harmon transferred her attention to that group.

That was when she made her mistake.

She recognized Vatche immediately from photos.

If there'd been a photo of this moment, it could be titled "Prince Vatche and Hangers-On." Not only was he posed in the middle, with all the others focused on him, but every one of them was shorter than the prince, who would need to stretch to reach average height. No way was that a fluke.

But it was trying to figure out who Vatche reminded her of that kept her attention on him overtime.

Ah, that was it … One of the evil stepsisters in the movie Cinderella. Now, which one? She didn't remember character names, but it was definitely the one with less chin. Or no chin in Prince Vatche's case.

That was when she realized that the wide mouth above the absent chin was smiling and the narrow eyes beneath a high hairline were ogling her. He'd picked up on her long look and with stunningly inaccurate self-complacency he'd translated stop into go.

Not bright, Harmon. Not bright at all.

He headed directly for her.

Turning away would be blatant. That didn't bother her much. But some men—and he had the hallmarks of being one—would view it as part of a game. Better to stand her ground and get the rules set.

"We have not been introduced. I—" His smirk as good as said he knew it wasn't necessary to state his name, but was doing it only as a matter of form. "—am Prince Vatche."

She slowly, coolly raised her eyebrows.

The dimming of his self-satisfaction took a little longer to begin than she might have hoped for because, for a long time, he wasn't looking at her eyebrows. He was focused considerably lower. At last his gaze came up and he was starting to get the message when a hand on her arm pivoted her away.

Karl.

Not wearing a happy face.

"Harmon. I want you to meet the Karatoks," he said in a tone that sure didn't sound like he was doing anything he remotely wanted to do.

She shared the mood exactly, since he'd interrupted her ground-rules-setting message to Prince Vatche. She'd probably have to start all over next time.

Karl added perfunctorily, "Excuse us, Vatche."

"But you must not take this enchanting creature away before we have the opportunity to become better acquainted. I do not even know her name.

"Prince Vatche, may I introduce Harmon Reed. Harmon, Prince

Vatche."

"Delighted my dear to meet such a—"

Karl took her arm. "Gotta go, Vatche. His Majesty's orders to circulate."

Unless she wanted to use a self-defense maneuver, she could go with him or she could be dragged.

They were maybe ten feet away when she put the brakes on. "Once again, I had the situation handled. I hope your interference this time doesn't mean you've scheduled me for a side trip to Timbuktu. I can't afford to keep replacing my wardrobe."

"You didn't have to pay."

"Yes, I did."

"You don't want to have anything to do with Vatche."

"My call. Not yours."

His reply grunt was neutral.

Perhaps because they'd reached a pleasant-looking couple who showed signs of being overwhelmed by their fellow guests.

Karl introduced her, explaining their son was in the basketball camp.

Then he excused himself at the first possible moment that qualified as just this side of rude.

So they were making progress.

Katie's air of extreme innocence as she sidled out of the reception room half an hour later caught Harmon's attention.

Intrigued, she followed her. Catching a glimpse of Katie's dress down a hallway, she went that way. After a number of twists and turns—twice Harmon thought she'd lost her—Katie opened a door and disappeared from view before closing the door again.

Harmon came up to the door, knocked lightly, then immediately entered.

Katie started up from a chair, sinking back when she saw Harmon.

"Oh, it's you," Katie said. "Close the door before anyone sees us here."

Only a table lamp was lit. The room had yellow curtains drawn against the night. The furniture was handsome without being loaded with curlicues. It was also ruthlessly neat. Harmon couldn't imagine the speck of dust with enough nerve to stick around.

"Trying to get away from it all?"

Katie looked fierce, but said nothing.

Harmon tried again. "What's the matter?"

"Minister Virba."

"What about him? Did he make a pass at you?"

"A pass?" Her eyes widened, then amusement flooded in. "Well, that put things in perspective. It could have been a whole lot worse."

"What did he do?"

"He kept calling me Princess Josephine-Augusta. Over and over. Growing up, I thought Katie was so boring. I dreamed of an interesting name. Then I had Josephine-Augusta Katrina Mariana Sofia thrown at me. I wanted interesting, not a phone book. And now all I want is be called by my true name, Katie Spencer."

Her face changed when she said that. It made her look less like April yet, paradoxically, because April was such an attractive woman, it made her more appealing.

Katie turned to her. "What about you? Harmon's an interesting name. You must love having a name like that."

"I've hated it my whole life. The Colonel named me after a World War II general. Only thing I can be grateful for is he didn't name me Ernie, because the general's full name was Ernest Nason Harmon."

Katie chuckled. "You're definitely not an Ernie. Your father must have admired him greatly."

"More likely, faced with a baby girl, he used the first name that came to mind."

Katie grinned, but said, "Well, I think it's a lovely name. And it's clear from the way Karl says it that he thinks so, too. I love how he says everything. That slow-talking, western drawl."

"I suspect that feeling's mutual."

"Mutual? That Karl likes my Wisconsin accent?" Her smile was skeptical.

"That he likes everything about you."

Katie chuckled easily. "We're cousins of a sort. Buddies for sure. Nothing else."

Lightly, Harmon disagreed. "Oh, I think he still carries a torch for you."

Katie turned. "Karl? For *me*?"

"Yes. He told me about last year when King Jozef was hoping you two would make a match of it."

"That's true. Grandfather threw us together a lot. It wasn't hard to see what he was up to. But there were a number of obstacles."

"Like your being in love with Brad Spencer."

"Yes." She smiled.

Harmon felt a sudden breathlessness. That smile and what it knew, what it felt…

She had to get a grip on this love-jealousy stuff.

Katie smoothed down the skirt of her dress. "But that wasn't the only obstacle. Karl and I were becoming closer at the same time I was sure there was no hope of a future for Brad and me. Didn't Karl tell you…?"

"What he focused on was that you and Brad were in love, which ended any chance of you and him making a match," she said dryly. "Beyond that, he told me it would have been no trouble for him to fall in love with you. And knowing his tendency for understatement that means he already was at least half in love with you."

"That's…" Katie paused, studying her. She chewed her lip. "You and Karl. He won't say anything and you won't say anything, but it's clear you, uh, knew each other before. That there was a relationship—"

Harmon produced a credible laugh. "Relationship? Not really. We were young. Kids. It was one of those summer things."

"A summer romance. Those can be intense. That sort of, uh, intimacy."

"You mean kissing? We *did* kiss a lot." And more. But she wasn't going to think about that right now. "A lot."

"You said *a lot* twice," Katie said.

"The man can kiss. At least he could then. But that was a long time ago and—"

"Harmon, I think you care about Karl. Now. Not a long time ago."

"You mean when I don't want to kill him?" she said lightly.

"*Really* care about him," Katie pursued, apparently ignoring the issue of homicide. "There's no reason for you to confide in me, but you need to know yourself. Not to hide it under—" She waved a hand. "—what you two do to each other."

"Do to each other?"

"Playing the inside game hard. The jostling for position under the basket."

Harmon wanted to laugh.

Except she had a sudden vision of Brad and Karl, elbows flying, bodies contending for the same space, and the desire to laugh evaporated.

It *was* what she did with Karl. With words instead of elbows. Holding on to her space, trying to keep him out of it.

But it was more than that, because she could move away from him, far away and she'd have all the space she wanted.

Instead, she stayed right there, as Katie said, in that cramped territory under the basket, trying to hold on to her space. And trying to move into his?

"I … I, uh … I don't know what to say," she admitted.

Katie brightened. "Good. So, I'm going to tell you. Karl and I kissed."

"Oh." At least Harmon thought the syllable came out. Absolutely idiotic to react to that. As if the man wouldn't have kissed hundreds of women in the years since she'd seen him. Though there was something about the open heart of this particular woman … No, she wouldn't go there. No love-jealousy. She tried a second time for light interest. "Oh?"

"It was incredibly romantic. A beautiful night—the night of last year's gala. I told you it was also for Ashton's team. Lights twinkling in all the trees. We went down by the stream, where there's a bench. Just over the little bridge in the gardens. Have you seen it? There'd been champagne and dancing. Karl was so handsome with his military posture and so kind with his cowboy easiness. And we kissed."

"Well, sure. That's natural. Would have been a shame to waste that setting and—"

"And there was nothing."

"Nothing?" Harmon felt something inside her ease.

"I was ticked."

Harmon chuckled. How much at Katie and how much from that internal easing?

"I was," Katie insisted. "Karl said it was because we got along too well. Maybe that's a tiny bit of it. Certainly, a lot of it from my side was because I love Brad. But Karl didn't feel any more than I did. Don't look like that. He didn't."

"I'll take your word for it."

"You don't have to take my word for it. You can take Karl's because he told me so."

Harmon produced a chuckle. "He kissed you, then told you he felt nothing? Mr. Smooth."

When Karl had kissed her, he'd rarely said anything. He'd just kissed her again. And again and again. Until the kisses alone had made her so ready, so hot—

But that was long ago.

So very long ago.

"It wasn't like that. It was—"

She interrupted Katie before she could continue the topic of kissing Karl. "Uh, I meant to ask, what is this room?"

"Madame's office."

Harmon stood quickly. "Madame's office? Are you nuts? If she catches us playing hooky from the reception in *her* office, I'm throwing you under the bus and telling her it was all your fault, which it was."

Katie smiled slightly. "She never leaves a reception as long as

Grandfather is there. And no one else dares come in here, so it's the best place to hide out for a bit."

The smile faded as she continued. "Changing the subject won't keep me from telling you this, Harmon. It might sound awful that Karl said he didn't feel anything, but it wasn't. It was so comfortable being able to be completely honest with each other. Probably because our hearts weren't in danger of being broken. Mine wasn't because I was already in love with Brad—and feeling as if my heart were being trampled." She slanted a look at Harmon. "And Karl's wasn't because he carried—carries—a torch for someone who is decidedly *not* me."

CHAPTER FOURTEEN

Lunch at the castle the day after the reception was a command performance.

Karl could have ridden up the mountain in the official car he knew was coming for Harmon. Or he could have offered her a ride in his pickup.

He didn't do either.

He'd spent far too much time last night with that damned dress invading his sleep to spend more time than absolutely necessary with the wearer today.

He met up with Katie and Brad in the hallway outside what they called the family dining room. The king, Madame, Harmon, April, and Hunter were already there.

King Jozef dictated the conversation, drawing out from each of them observations from the previous evening.

Not only was he an expert debriefer, but the king also moved it around enough that everyone had an opportunity to eat.

The overall impression gathered at the reception was of people who were loyal to their king and felt the country was in decent shape, but were uneasy about the future and its uncertainties.

Apparently satisfied with that, King Jozef broadened the conversation. "I looked to introduce you to the columnist for the top magazine in Bariavak, but could not find you, Katie."

"I've met him," she said quickly.

So quickly that Karl looked over at her. She looked guilty. That was weird.

"Was he the man with the Freud-like beard I saw talking with

Prince Vatche?" Harmon asked.

"It *is* Freud-like," April said, delighted.

But that was not the reaction of the king.

"You saw him talking with Vatche?" he demanded of Harmon.

"Oh, yes."

"What did they talk of?"

"No idea. Wasn't close enough to hear anything. But Prince Vatche was doing a lot of smiling."

King Jozef thudded his fist to the table.

"Prince Vatche, Prince Vatche. If my wife were alive now she would kill her brother's wife's son with her own hands for all the irritation he causes to this country."

"What has he done, sir?" Harmon asked.

"He is a little rat starting and fostering outbreaks of the bubonic plague of fear and uncertainty. That is what has happened, as it always happens wherever he goes."

He flung out his hands, as if banishing the nuisance, then drew in a long breath through his nose. He glanced toward Madame, who looked back at him steadily.

More calmly, he said, "What must be done now is to draw those he would infect here, where we can see them and—most important— have them understand that we see and hear them. I had a whisper of his activities and I have already informed Madame that we must assemble as many as possible this evening. With the lack of warning it must be a casual affair, but we shall impress on them the certainty of continuity for Bariavak far into the future with the presence there of our Prince Karl."

"Can't be here tonight, sir."

"You must."

"No." Karl put his napkin on the table. "Got to be at the hotel for a meeting about the ranch with folks back home during business hours there."

"Another day—"

"I set up this meeting based on the schedule your office gave me.

Folks at home worked around that schedule to be available at this time. I'm committed."

With gracious magnanimity the king said, "We could allow you a short time to do it here."

"Won't take a short time. And I have materials set up in my room."

"This ranch you insist on continuing to pursue intrudes in a most—" The king huffed out a breath that fluttered his trimmed mustache. "What possible matters can be of such importance?

"Windmills."

"What nonsense is this? You blow and it circles in a pretty pattern?" He held up his hand as if holding a stick.

"That's a pinwheel, sir," April said.

Karl didn't address that interpolation. "It's not nonsense. Talking water's never nonsense in my part of Wyoming. Windmills have been used for a century to power the water up in the wells. Now, more folks are turning to solar-powered pumps."

"Which are you using?" Harmon got her question in before the king had a chance to say anything.

"A combination, including plain old windmills, what they're calling mechanicals these days. Can't afford to replace everything at once, but we need an overall plan so anything new we bring in works with what's come before and what will come after. Got to balance what we're using, what we're going to use in different spots depending on the depth of the water, what water flow's needed, placement, and weather."

"Weather?" she asked.

He knew she was using her questions to change the course of the conversation. Possibly to divert King Jozef's attention. She'd done something similar a bit ago when Katie had looked so oddly guilty. Now she was doing it to take heat from the king off him.

He didn't need the help. He and the king did this back-and-forth often enough about his ranch. And his future. Still, it was kind of interesting to watch her in action, running interference.

"Wind turbines work when there's good wind, but wind just isn't that reliable. Solar can be most efficient in cold, clear spells, but the days are shorter. Works okay during the long days of summer. But cattle drink year-round. Then there're storage needs for the water and electricity, plus a backup. And there's balancing the cost and how long before it pays back, and—"

"Bah. Enough of this." King Jozef stood. "Go, go to your windmills. I, alone, shall consider the future of my poor country. Harmon, if you would be so kind as to accompany a tired, old man…"

She went to him immediately. "Of course, sir."

"Grandfather?"

"No, no, Katie, I will not take you from your basketball camp. I see already Brad and Hunter look to their watches, and Karl is most eager to be away to prepare for his meeting."

As they and Madame started out of the room—at a good clip for a tired, old man—Harmon looked over her shoulder at him and winked.

He thought he felt Katie's eyes on him. Or maybe it was April's. But when he turned toward them they were looking at each other.

He left right after that.

Only as he got in the pickup for the trip back to the hotel did he realize a grin had been fighting to break through.

Dangerous, Wethers.

The four remaining in the family dining room looked at each other.

Katie spoke first. "How can Karl and Harmon not see how right they are for each other?"

Hunter chuckled. "Talk about the pot calling the kettle black. Want to rewind the clock and look at you and Brad?"

"Would have been interesting to be around right before you and April got together," Brad said speculatively.

Hunter raised a hand in surrender.

April brought the subject back on point. "Somebody should talk to Karl. Make him see he's turning his back on a second chance with her."

"It's his life, his business," Brad said.

"Hunter wants to order around his life and make him be king," Katie shot back.

"Hey," April protested.

Katie turned to Hunter. "I know it's your job and I know it's because it would help the United States. And I appreciate you didn't try to push me, but I wish you'd be as understanding for Karl."

"Between you and Karl, I say let him pressure Karl," Brad said.

"Can't talk about this," Hunter said mildly.

"Oh, of course," Katie said. "I understand. Just don't push Karl."

Grinning, Brad turned to Hunter. "You know they say there are two theories about arguing with a woman."

"What are they?" Hunter asked.

"Doesn't matter. Neither works."

"If you'd remember that, you wouldn't waste time trying," April teased.

They all laughed though Katie returned to seriousness quickly.

"I'm concerned about Karl. It's clear Harmon really hurt him," she said. "It's going to take a while for him to trust her again. I totally understand. It's so hard and you try to talk yourself out of what you're feeling because it hurts with them being blind and stupid until they get hit in the head."

"Hey!" protested Brad. "I was protecting you."

"From what?"

"Me." He put his arm around her shoulders and grinned down at her.

She returned the smile. "Idiot."

"You said it might take a while, Katie, but what if he persuades the king to send Harmon away? You know that's what he's been angling for ever since she arrived. Then there won't be any *while* for them to take. Somebody has to talk to him." April turned to her husband.

He raised his hands, warding off whatever she'd been about to say. "Conflict of interest. I have a professional role in this."

April looked at the person next to him.

"No way in hell," Brad said. "The guy went after Katie last spring while we were married, I'm not going to consult on his love life."

"That's not fair, Brad," Katie protested. "He didn't know we were married and he didn't go after me. Not really."

Brad grumbled something that didn't sound as if he'd been persuaded.

"We're friends," Katie insisted. "Good friends."

"Exactly!" April said. "So you're the perfect person."

CHAPTER FIFTEEN

"No, I'm not coming to South Carolina. I'm just getting started here."

"Doing what?" Ann-Elise asked.

"It's complicated."

"I wish you wouldn't call only when your father isn't here."

"I don't—"

"You have a real blind spot about your father. I hope you're not as blind when it comes to this Prince Karl."

To avoid the second half of that speech, she addressed the first part. "I can respect that he's a good soldier, which always used to be first and last priority for him. I can acknowledge that he's become a good husband to you. But—"

"And a good father to you. Always has been."

"—we don't communicate. Never have. My mother tried and you have tried with no success. That's all there is to it."

"That's not all there is to it. But let's start with this: do you know why you have so much trouble with each other?" She left no time for Harmon to reply. "Because you two are too much alike."

"That's not even funny." Though Harmon did chuckle a little sourly. "I'd have to be one hundred percent Army to be like him. He named me after a World War II general, for heaven's sakes. If that doesn't show the man's priorities—"

"One he has great respect for and believes is vastly underrated and wants the world to know better. One whose soldiers admired him and were loyal to—all things he wanted for his daughter."

"To be a great general. Well, that must have been yet another disappointment to him."

"He's not disappointed in you, Harmon," Ann-Elise said firmly.

She laughed. "Sure we're talking about the same man? You know that would explain a lot, if this were all a case of mistaken identity."

"It's a case of mistakes, but not identity."

He wasn't surprised when he opened his hotel room door to find Harmon there. Not completely.

"Hi. I'm an exile from my room. Thought I'd come update you on the happenings you missed last night."

He watched her taking in the room and his minimal impression on it except for his laptop and hat on the desk.

"Don't you have work to do? I heard you were on the phone with work. There's a lounge downstairs you could use."

She raised her brows at him. He chose to interpret it as wondering how he'd heard she was on the phone, rather than reprimanding him for rudeness.

"Jarta came to clean my room earlier than usual," he said, "because she said you were on the phone and she didn't want to interrupt you."

She made herself comfortable, sitting on the bed, rearranging pillows behind her back. "I was on the phone, but it wasn't work. I just hung up with Ann-Elise."

"Your stepmother." He returned to the desk chair. It wasn't the farthest he could get from the bed, but it would do.

He saw an instant of surprise that he remembered the name. She deflected that surprise and something—he frowned, trying to define it—different, deeper. "The Colonel's wife," she said.

He let that ride. "How is it that you and Ann-Elise get along so well? Did you know her before she and your dad married?"

"No. But she showed the great good sense of insisting that the first time I met her it was the two of us alone. That meant that how we got along—pass or fail—was between the two of us, separate from the Colonel and me."

"Separate from her and your father, too?"

"That didn't matter as much, since she loves him."

"And you?"

She hitched a shoulder. "I suppose most people do, at some level. I make no claim to being an aberration. I'm not nearly as fond of the Colonel, however."

He studied her, recognizing her rising tension.

"But your mother ... you adored her. Francesca."

"I don't know how you think you know the first thi—"

"Sitting in your convertible with the top down, looking at stars." The starlight had caught the silvery trail of tears down her cheeks. The only time he'd seen her cry.

"I never told you or anybody about my mother. I don't talk about her."

"Freezing your face like that doesn't change that you told me. She called you Harry sometimes. She would sing you to sleep, using Harry in place of any other name in the song. You would dress up in costumes, then go to the park or stores and pretend to be from another country or another planet. You played with her more than any kids your own age."

"But ... I don't...

"It was hard to make friends because you moved around so much as a kid. For you. For her. But you had each other. You said how delicate she was."

"She was. As far back as I can remember."

He could hear her voice from the past.

When she got sick, she got even thinner. Those small bones ... I was taller than her by the time I turned thirteen. She died a month later.

"And soft-spoken."

"Yes. Gentle and sweet."

"You said she connected you and your father."

"I said connected?" Then she spoke fast, trying to rub out her question. "She was the only person who did."

"Sounds like Ann-Elise is doing her best."

She gave him a sharp look, but shrugged. Trying to shake it off, but showing her uncertainty to the connoisseur who knew how to look.

"Strange thing is," he said slowly, deliberately, knowing this was going to hit her hard and wondering if any of his saying it was because of that, "for all that you say how much you admired and loved your mother, you've modeled yourself after your father."

Her whole body jerked, then her head came up. "I have *not*. That's crazy." Her eyes narrowed. "You're just trying to land a blow."

He considered that a moment, then shook his head. "Nope. I'm not." He stood. "Think about it, Harmon."

"I'm not going to—"

A sound came from his phone. He glanced at the screen.

"Damn. I've got to take this. You stay right there. Don't make a sound." He moved, angling the phone so she couldn't be seen, as he answered. "Hello."

"That you, Karl?"

"Can't you see it is, Deaver?"

"Don't trust these things."

"What? You think they put a fake picture of me on the screen and make the lips move while an imposter talks to you?"

"I wouldn't put it past them."

"Them who?"

"Those foreigners and kings and such you've got yourself mixed up with."

"Say, maybe you're the imposter. Maybe they got to you and—"

"Now I know you're the real Karl Wethers, giving me grief from sunup to sundown."

Karl chuckled. Deaver Smith cackled. From the corner of his eye, he saw Harmon react with a slight smile.

"Called because no matter what you said last night, you don't have irrigation going in fast enough, Karl. You're not going to have the haying season you need without more water. It's about too late anyhow this year, but if you don't get it in these coming months, you'll be behind next year, too. Greg and me are just holding things steady. You know that. But sometimes holding steady is going backward. Need you back here, Karl."

"I'll get home when I can, but you're going to have to do the best you can. I'll give you a call later, but I've gotta go now."

Deaver protested a bit more but Karl wrapped up the call.

"Back at the ranch … You got problems?" she asked.

"Yeah." No sense denying it, since she'd heard.

"But you won't go back home until you've settled things in Bariavak. I can't do anything with the ranch, but I could help with what you've started here if you'd trust me. I picked up a couple comments last night—"

"Haven't started anything, so no need for help." There'd been something in the way she'd said *home* that caught his attention, but there was no time to consider that when he needed to close the door on the idea that he'd trust her. Because of her penchant for lit dynamite. Nothing personal. "Yours or anyone's."

She ignored that. "You know what he said about holding steady actually being sliding backward—that's your situation here in Bariavak, too, Karl."

"If my situation in Bariavak slid all the way backward to not existing, I'd be more than satisfied."

"I'm not talking about being Prince Karl. I'm talking about what you're trying to accomplish. You and your allies."

He dropped his head, shaking it in bemusement. "Absolutely no idea what you're talking about, Harmon."

"Sure, try to keep things quiet for now. But you can't forever. You can't do this without taking risks and that's going to mean—"

With his head still down, he turned it to get his eyes on her. "*Me. I* need to take risks. *You're* telling *me* to take risks."

"Yes, of course you. You're going to have to go public about—"

"You're telling me to take risks. You. The pot ignoring her own blackness while proclaiming everyone else's."

"Me? I don't have anything to do with this."

"Don't you?"

"Stop with the mysterious soothsayer bit, Wethers." That irritation said he'd hit a nerve. "I don't have any active role in this. Except for this consulting, which you won't let me do."

"I'm not stopping you."

"You're not cooperating."

"Why should I? King Jozef's the one who hired you. Have you wondered why he did that?"

"I'm taking a wild stab here, but because he needed advice on handling all the speculation about Bariavak's future with the media."

He snorted. "You go right ahead and think that. What exactly has he had you do with the media for him since you got here."

She jammed her hands on her hips. "You're saying he *didn't* hire me because he wanted me to consult on media? Hate to tell you, bub, but that's what I've been doing. Including just now when I said you need to take risks. If you'd trust me—"

"I took all the risks I'm going to take with you."

The unexpectedness of that stopped her immediately. If she knew it was just as unexpected for him ... But he wasn't about to tell her.

Even before she spoke, he knew how she would try to handle this.

He didn't know whether to be pleased that he could read her reaction, or if he should start running and not stop until he hit the Wyoming border.

"I never asked you to take a risk on me. I could have gotten out of that mess at the airport. You didn't ne—"

"We're not talking about the airport, as you damn well know. And the hell you didn't ask me to take a risk on you. You asked it with every kiss."

She opened her mouth. Closed it.

As if she'd voiced an objection, he repeated, "With every kiss."

CHAPTER SIXTEEN

With every kiss…

The sensation of his mouth on hers. The scent of him, clean but hot in the summer night. The taste of him, stroking into her mouth, and reaching so much deeper.

She summoned a chuckle. Made herself stand smoothly. "We were kids. I had no idea you would still be—"

"Bull."

His cool calm stopped her more than the word.

"You asked me to take a risk on you and I did. The risk didn't pay off." His mouth twisted. "I didn't realize you weren't taking the same risk. Not until it was too late."

She ignored the last part, hurrying to respond. "That's what risk means. It doesn't always pay off. If you're still holding onto a grudge—"

"No grudge. Not taking risks, either, though. Because I don't trust you, Harmon. Not for a minute."

She knew that. Had known it all along. Understood it.

So why did it feel as if a pit had just opened in her chest?

"Thanks for stopping by with the update, but I have things to do now."

He ushered her out and closed the door behind her.

Firmly.

Back in her own room, it took some time—what did it matter how much? She wasn't watching the clock—but she rallied herself.

She'd had doors closed on her before. When had that stopped her?

Not only had King Jozef hired her, so she was going to do *something*, but Karl needed her skills. No matter what he thought.

And she owed him.

Whether he liked it or not.

Whether she liked it or not.

Karl's voice. Karl's touch in the absolute darkness.

Not that summer, but several years later … and a world away.

She stood, pulling out her phone, making calls as she paced.

The antidote to thinking was working. She'd been nibbling around the edges of this for too long. Time to make real progress.

She finally met with the political columnist—he of the Freudian beard—and picked up a couple more pieces. Unimportant on their own, but they connected others and she began to see a pattern in this puzzle.

Despite Karl Wethers.

He shouldn't meet at the back of the hotel if he was going to laugh so anyone could recognize it was him. At least anyone who crept down the hallway and put her head into the old dumbwaiter shaft that carried the sound of voices, though not the words. Darn it.

The night before the reception she'd heard another laugh. The same one as that first night when she'd heard them in back and had been turned away.

This time, she recognized that laugher, too. Because the king had invited him to lunch.

Andrej Skala, she'd learned, came from a well-respected and close-knit family. His father had been viewed as a business up and comer when he died a decade and a half ago. Andrej's siblings, their spouses, and his wife were all professionals.

More specifically, she had learned he would be at a certain fashionable restaurant downtown for a family celebration of his mother's birthday.

She'd seen him most recently at the reception, of course. Even said hello. But, aware of being watched by the king, she'd left it at that.

Plus the reception was official. A family celebration might provide an opportunity to observe him in a relaxed setting.

Worth a try.

She invited Hunter and April to be her dinner guests there that night. It worked out beautifully, since Katie, Brad, and—most importantly for her purposes—Karl were involved with a basketball camp event the same evening.

She would have gone alone if necessary, but this way she would blend in, when a woman alone might not.

She'd swung by the restaurant earlier to see the setup, guessed the family party would be seated in a large alcove and requested a table with a good view into the alcove. Then all she had to do was be there before Hunter and April to claim the best seat.

She easily divided her attention between her guests and the family group already at dinner.

She knew Andrej Skala, of course. His mother was also clear. From gestures and body language she quickly established which of the women was his wife.

Then another woman in the group caught her attention.

Over their meal, and amid interesting conversation, she watched the interactions among those in the alcove, sorting out more relationships.

She was almost certain one woman was Andrej's oldest sister. Another woman she tabbed as the middle child, with Andrej as youngest. The middle child had a different look, dark and dramatic. Hard to tell if that came from her mother, who was white-haired now. Andrej's coloring was midway between his two sisters.

"What are you so interested in?" Hunter turned to take a look.

When he turned back to their table his expression was neutral. April looked from him to Harmon and also turned.

"Looks like a happy family party. I recognized Andrej Skala," Harmon said. "Remember, King Jozef had him to that lunch with all of us."

"The day after he signed you up," Hunter confirmed. Neutral.

"I believe it was. Now, what shall we have for dessert?"

Hunter gave her a long look before opting for pie. April appeared less suspicious.

Good thing, because Harmon had more digging to do. Digging that would be even more delicate and require more caution than she'd employed so far. Could she pump people already within the castle circle? People like April.

Because Andrej Skala's sister bore a striking resemblance to April and Katie. In fact, she looked exactly the way Harmon could imagine them looking in another decade or so.

In other words, she could be taken for King Jozef's daughter. Or granddaughter.

This would take a whole lot more digging. Very discreet digging.

King Jozef of Bariavak was going to be the death of her.

He'd called her in for a meeting, adroitly questioned her about everything from her room at the hotel to her views on Bariavak to her father's career. And then he'd announced he had to end their conversation because he had another appointment.

Still without giving her the slightest indication of what he wanted her to do.

Fine. She'd keep on following her own lead.

Harmon had barely started down a narrow, corkscrew stairwell left over from the castle's fortification days when Karl came around the last corner, nearly plowing in to her. The brim of his hat did brush her hair.

She tried to step back, caught her heel on the riser above her. He grasped both her arms, keeping her from going down.

The rebound motion brought them against each other for a tantalizing moment. Then his arms extended slightly, establishing a gap.

With the added height of the step, she was face to face with him.

Their eyes met, then she looked down to his mouth.

If he kissed her … The way he used to kiss her. The way they used to kiss each other … All he had to do was bend his elbows more and she'd be drawn up against his chest—

"I was looking for you."

"You were?" She licked her lips.

His eyes followed the motion, but his voice was harsh when he said, "What were you doing at the Hall of Records?"

"What?" She blinked twice. First for the swell that had risen inside her. Second against the deflation from his popping that swell.

"The Hall of Records. This morning."

He didn't release her arms, but now she knew it was no embrace. More like the Big, Bad Wolf growling *The better to shake you with, my dear.*

She widened her eyes. "Is that what they call that building? The old one by the entrance to the university?"

"Don't pretend you don't know."

"It's a beautiful building. Fascinating architecture. I was trying to find out more about the history, which I'm sure I could have if I spoke the Bariavak language. I should take a course—"

"You also could have found out more about the history of the building if you hadn't made a beeline for the records and started snooping around."

"Snooping? By looking into public records? The terms contradict each other, Karl. How can—"

"You were looking up Andrej Skala."

"Among several people. To see how the system worked. To dip into Bariavak's history. Did you know Ruzena's grandfather—"

"You spent the most time and looked at the most documents concerning Andrej Skala."

Damn. She'd hoped the other searches would camouflage the Andrej Skala search, on the off chance anyone noticed. Someone noticed all right, and reported to Karl. She gave a light shrug. "Somebody had to be the longest and the most. Just happened to be Andrej Skala. Did you—"

"Are you trying to dig up dirt on him? You won't find it."

"—know Madame's family has been in Bariavak as far back as

records go? Not dirt, but interesting tidbits. For example, someone else—"

"What the hell are you up to, Harmon?"

She shot back, "What are *you* up to, Karl? If you confided in me I could help you. I know how the media works, I know public opinion—"

"I'll keep that in mind if I ever need those services. Don't often need that sort of thing in Wyoming, but good to know."

Sweet Karl Wethers had picked up a sharp edge he didn't used to have. Was it crazy of her to like it? Was this more of that elbows-flying inside game Katie had spotted?

"I had something closer to your current residence in mind. Bariavak—"

"Mind your own business, Harmon. I mean that literally. Go wherever it is you're supposed to be and mind your business."

"King Jozef—"

"Made a mistake. A monumental mistake trusting you."

He released her abruptly, as if just realizing he still held her arms. Then he was past her, brushing against her side.

She leaned back against the cool wall of stairwell, pulling in a long breath.

Asking him to confide in her—asking again, when she'd already asked before—*that* had gone well.

But she didn't have time to fret about that.

She'd started to tell him about the name above hers on several signup sheets. Someone who'd appeared to be ahead of her in following the breadcrumbs. She hadn't recognized the name, but it was time to find out.

In the hallway beyond the top of the stairwell she heard cautious footsteps. Certainly not Karl. She eased two more steps down so the curve of the wall hid her. The footsteps came to the top of the stairwell, paused, then moved on.

She looked around the curve in time to see the bottom of a man's pant leg and a dress shoe pass.

Definitely not Karl.

CHAPTER SEVENTEEN

Katie steeled herself.

Why hadn't she said April should be the one doing this, since she was the one who thought Karl needed this conversation? Too late to think about that now. When it came down to it, she thought he needed it, too.

His knock sounded at the door of the castle rooms she and Brad occupied when they were in Bariavak. In response to her "Come in" he entered, smiling.

It wasn't one of his best smiles. It certainly didn't hide the worry in his eyes. And deeper than the worry, something else. Unhappiness.

"Got a message you wanted to see me. Something wrong, Princess Katie?" he asked.

When he called her that, it seemed more like a charming nickname than a complication of birth and destiny that made her heart sink.

She invited him to come sit beside her on the loveseat placed for a view of the gardens.

"I've been thinking, Karl—and, please, no jokes about no wonder I look as if I'm in pain."

He smiled. A better one this time. She hadn't seen this smile as much since Harmon had arrived. She'd missed it. But now that she saw it again she realized even his best smiles never reached all the way down. There was always a stillness somewhere in him, around him. It squeezed at her heart.

"I'm sorry, Karl. I'm so sorry."

Surprise replaced the smile. "About what?"

"About all this." She waved at the castle around them. "That my refusing to be heir to the throne has put that burden on you."

"Wanna change your mind?"

"No. But I'm still sorry figuring out the future for Bariavak has landed on you."

He lifted one shoulder. "Along with a number of other people who're working on that figuring out." His mouth went wry. "And there are even more who'd love to take that burden right off all of us."

She grimaced, but would not be detoured into a discussion of Prince Vatche.

"The worst thing would be if you were paying so much attention to the future of Bariavak that you missed opportunities in *your* future."

"Don't worry about that. I've got friends helping with the ranch. It'll survive. For now."

"I don't mean just your ranch, Karl. When you and Harmon knew each other before—"

The smile was gone, though his tone remained light. "Water under the bridge. So long ago it's out in the middle of some ocean somewhere."

"Funny. Harmon said you two had been ships passing in the night. You two have something going on with water metaphors?"

He grunted a would-be chuckle. "Katie, there's no *you two* about Harmon Reed and me."

"But there was. You were in love with Harmon, weren't you? Truly in love."

"I was a kid. It was a long time ago."

Did he realize that sometimes a non-answer was more telling than blurting out yes?

She put her hand on his arm. "I know something about loving someone you think will never love you back. I know that sometimes they do."

"Sometimes they don't. This is a don't. Believe me, Katie—"

"Why? Why is this time a don't?"

"Whatever I felt for her ended a long time ago. Whatever I thought she felt for me never was. All a figment of imagination by a kid from the sticks who hadn't learned his way around yet."

"Karl, this isn't you, sounding so bitter."

"Not bitter. Realistic, like her note said. That's one thing Harmon Reed taught me. To be realistic."

She studied him as he gazed down toward the gardens.

"Of course it's natural if you've had something bad happen in your life to worry about it happening again. And it's natural—even if it's the worst possible thing to do—to push away possibilities that seem like they might lead to a repeat of that pain."

Slowly, Karl's head came up and he looked at her intently. "Go on."

She was getting through to him. She was better at this than she thought.

"You try to protect yourself by pulling back. You think you're protecting yourself that way, making it impossible for there to be a repeat, but, in fact, all you're doing—"

"Is running away."

"Well, that's a little harsh. I mean it's an instinct to avoid getting burned again, even if you're not going to be burned the next time or … Well, you might. Get burned, I mean. No one can guarantee you won't for sure. But you have to take the risk, because the payoff if you don't get burned…" She lost her train of thought for a moment in contemplation of how risking her heart had paid off with Brad. She shook her head to reassemble her points. "That's mixing metaphors and I'm not sure I'm being clear on this, Karl, but with Harmon—"

"Exactly. Mixed metaphors or not, you've hit the nail on the head."

"I'm so glad you—"

"Thank you, Princess Katie. You've helped me see exactly what she's doing."

"*She's* doing?"

"Precisely. With her father, with his wife, and her siblings-to-be."

"What about you, Karl?"

"Yeah," he said slowly. Then slowness was gone. He stood and kissed her on the top of the head. "You're right. I'm going to call her on it if she asks me again to tru—if an opportunity comes up."

He strode out.

"But I meant you, Karl. How you won't give yourself a chance to love Harmon again," Katie said.

He was already gone.

"Madame, may I talk with you please?" Harmon had finally tracked her down with the help of Elisabeta.

"I have a full schedule. The gala—"

"It's important."

The older woman surveyed her.

"Very important, Madame."

"Come to my office."

The room was surprisingly bright and cheerful in the daylight, with the soft yellow curtains drawn all the way back to let every bit of sunlight in. It was as ruthlessly neat, however, during the middle of a work day as it had been the night of the reception.

"Well?" Madame demanded.

She'd been studying décor to delay delivering this warning.

"Let's sit down."

The older woman gave her a sharp look, but sat in a commanding chair behind the desk, leaving Harmon a straight-backed seat across from her that apparently had been designed to prevent lingering.

"Madame, I have obtained information that has led me to a conclusion about Andrej Skala's genealogy."

No response.

"I have looked at records and dates and…" She took in another breath and came out with it. "I believe his father was the biological son you gave up for adoption, making Andrej Skala your grandson."

CHAPTER EIGHTEEN

"You are mistaken." Madame rose. "As I said, I have a full schedule and no time for such—"

"I am not mistaken. You gave birth to Chedomir Skala on November second. There is a record of the birth."

"The only birth record in my name was my son, Georgei Sabdoka."

"This record was earlier, before you married. It was not listed under your maiden name, but rather with the last name Laurentz. There is no family by that name in any Bariavak census or other records, Madame. Not one. Its connection to you is that was your younger brother's first name."

The older woman made a *tch* sound that nicely blended irritation and dismissal.

"There's another connection," Harmon said. "The woman who attended the birth was the same for both your legitimate son and this earlier baby. Rosehilda. She also attended Laurentz's wife when she gave birth. She does not appear in the records as having attending any other births.

Madame remained as composed as ever, but she sat. "It is not proof."

"It's darned interesting circumstantial evidence," Harmon replied.

"What do you intend to do with this discovery you believe you have made?"

"Nothing. Unless—Nothing."

"Unless?"

Karl's face had flashed into her mind. But revealing Andrej Skala's lineage wouldn't help him in any way she could see.

It might, however, harm their efforts.

How would the disparate groups they were trying to coalesce around Andrej Skala react to learning he was descended from the king? That was her real concern.

"It's not my purpose to make any use of it, Madame. But if I could find the information I found and come to the conclusion I came to, so could someone else." No sense alarming the older woman about that name that had shown up too often to be coincidence.

Alarming Madame. Right.

"No one ever has come to such a conclusion," Madame said. "It is absurd."

"Are you sure of that?"

"I am."

"But there are records. Dates that—"

"Coincidences. No one could prove—"

"If someone wanted to badly enough, they could prove it with DNA. I think you know that." The other woman said nothing. Harmon laid her most critical card on the table. "And if certain parties suspect the link, they might use fair means or foul to prove it so they can use it against King Jozef. Since Andrej Skala is also *his* grandson."

Her expression giving nothing away, Madame looked at her a long moment before standing with grace and walking to the window to stare out.

But, perhaps, she had given something away...

That first night Harmon had been at the castle, all of them gathered in the king's sitting room, when King Jozef said he'd had no other children than his dead daughter, Princess Sofia, and the flicker of movement in Madame's reflection...

"He doesn't know, does he?" Harmon said. "You never told him."

"Told him? What was there to tell him? Nothing."

"The king's father had already separated you when you discovered you were pregnant." She was too certain of it to make it a question. "You could have—"

"Nothing you say now could I have done then. As you say, the king's father had separated us. He was to be the king. His wife was selected for him. His duty in one path. Mine in another. The path that had been ours together had ended. It was done. In my loneliness I was foolish. And when I realized the consequences of that foolishness, I did the only thing I could do. It was another time. It was another world."

Harmon had to admire her quick thinking. Acknowledging what the records could prove, that she was the biological mother. At the same time not acknowledging that King Jozef was the father of her child.

In fact, pointing away from the king by saying the child had been the result of a rebound romance. Harmon didn't buy it.

"Did your son ever know? Who his birth parents were."

"There was no one to tell him I was his mother." Madame continued, "Those who received him knew nothing. I went to the woman who had been our housekeeper when I was a child. She took care of everything."

"Did she know who the father was?"

"Never. That was of concern to me alone." Her sternness relented. "And Chedomir's. But he is dead fifteen years now."

"Did you see your son? Meet him?"

"Not when he was young. I ... could not. Later, as a man, he came to the embassy in Washington a number of times. I saw that he was a good man. He lived a good life. A happy life, with a strong family. I do not regret. It was the correct choice."

"But that was when you became curious about his family?"

"I knew he had had a son and two daughters. After he died—" She closed her eyes, barely longer than a blink. "—of a heart ailment, far too young, then I saw more closely his family."

A heart ailment? The same ailment for which His Majesty had had surgery eighteen months ago in the United States?

"So you must have seen his daughter who looks so much like King Jozef," Harmon said with challenge in her voice. "I'm surprised no one's noticed that before."

Surprisingly Madame's lips twitched. "Ah, you noticed that. As have countless others. But no one from Bariavak would find that remarkable," she said dryly. "The old king—Jozef's father—and his father before him were generous with their genes. There are many here who have that resemblance. Only someone from outside would make a leap from that small perch."

"And be right that there is a blood tie," Harmon pointed out. "What about Andrej Skala? Does he know about his father's parentage?"

"How could he know of me when his father didn't know his mother?"

"But didn't you ever want to tell him—them—to claim them as part of your family?"

The other woman gave a thin smile. "They are of my family. The woman I turned to for help gave Chedomir to a family of cousins, distant but linked to both my mother's and my father's families. I have seen them at family gatherings, weddings, funerals through the years. I have seen them, child and grown, and seen that they have a good path in life. I would not impose the drama of a sudden mother then, of a grandmother now. Better as it is."

Harmon looked at her closely. "Especially since appearing mother, grandmother, and now great-grandmother would raise questions about Chedomir's father."

Madame held her silence.

But clinging to secrecy could backfire on them all. The king, Madame, Andrej Skala. Karl.

"Your romance with King Jozef is not exactly a state secret, as you surely know. If you were to be revealed as the mother, the king would be assumed to be the father in a heartbeat. The way the dates line up, it's not much of a leap."

"It was after—"

"That won't wash, Madame. I know when King Jozef's engagement was announced and he was sent out of the country. I know that was the king's doing to separate the two of you, so you clearly weren't running around with someone else—" The older woman's eyes flashed, then it was gone. "—or the king's father would have used *that* to break you up. Besides, the baby would have had to be three, even four months premature for the father to have been the result of a rebound romance after King Jozef left."

Madame did not respond.

"So you were thinking of King Jozef all along. Hiding the birth. Staying away from your son and his family. All to cut the risk of exposing the king politically." Harmon was feeling her way with this. She nodded to herself. "Right. Not just what people might say, but the possibility that an illegitimate son could be used against him, against his legitimate heir, as a rival. You would not do that, not even when that illegitimate son was also yours."

"In such a fantasy as you outline, imagine the role for this supposed rival for the legitimate heir. Even when he was not actually so," Madame said strongly. "But for the gossip, for the rumors, he could be seen as such, and then to be always a weapon, a pawn. Think what use some might try to make of him. What life would that be? Not one for a man of honor."

"But now your grandson is in a position where being King Jozef's grandson might work against him and his goal to turn Bariavak toward democracy. And he doesn't even know it."

"He does not know what cannot be known. No one does. But work against him? Ridiculous. Any man could have only pride to carry the blood of King Jozef of Bariavak."

This woman was smart and tough and as loyal as they came. But her loyalty had left her with a blind spot. She saw the danger to the king, but not to the efforts of Andrej Skala and Karl.

"Madame, that's—"

"I have a meeting. You will not speak of this to anyone. We will not speak of this again."

Karl's voice outside drew Harmon from her laptop to the window in her room.

He was saying something in the native language that had several of the hotel workers gathered around him smiling widely.

She guessed he was commending their preparations for the gala guests who'd already started arriving. The hotel always looked nice, now every bit of glass and brass sparkled. Additional pots of plants were bloomed brightly all around the entry and drive. All the employees, too, seemed to have amped up their usual smiles.

A car swept into the drive and stopped.

Harmon started to turn away.

"Karl!" A woman's voice called his name.

Harmon returned to the window. She decided fresh air would be nice, too, so opened it quietly. She stood at an angle that allowed her to see the people below.

The woman was stepping back from hugging Karl. A man with a sprinkling of gray in his dark hair gave him a back-thumping man hug. Then a twenty-something woman who could only be the daughter of the first woman stepped in for a hug, too.

"But where are Tracy and Sam?" Karl asked.

"Can you believe it? They both came down with the flu during the flight to Chicago," the first woman said. "A double nightmare."

"Jenny's folks came to the rescue, meeting us at O'Hare and taking them home with them," the man said.

"Where they will spoil their grandchildren beyond belief," finished the woman.

They had to be a married couple, Harmon decided. They had their talking rhythm down perfectly.

"Poor kids," the younger woman added, "if they weren't so miserable, they'd be devastated to miss this trip. You know you're going to have to make it up to them soon."

"You're welcome back any time I'm here," Karl said.

"We brought you something from your girl Mercy," the older woman said as she plucked something off Karl's sleeve. "She sends all her love."

Not only did the other two newcomers smile at that, but Karl did, too. A real smile. Relaxed and natural.

His girl Mercy.

"All the way from Wyoming?" He hugged the woman again.

"All the way," she confirmed, chuckling.

His girl Mercy from Wyoming, the place that meant so much to him. So, naturally she was perfect for him.

Except she hadn't bothered to accompany Karl on this or any previous trips to Bariavak—because Harmon would have heard about this Mercy person by now if she'd ever been here. Karl needed support. He needed someone to be in his corner and only his corner. To not want anything from him. To make sure his responsibility-taking, integrity-driven tendencies didn't go into overdrive.

Yet Mercy wasn't here. So, not so perfect Mercy.

Not that it was her business.

"She misses you like crazy," the man said. "But you probably already know that."

Karl's smile widened. "Yup."

That smile. Unlike any she'd seen from Karl since … a long time ago.

Okay, time to back away, close the window as quietly as she'd opened it, quit eavesdropping on Karl and his life…

But before she did, she heard Karl ask, "How's everything at home?"

It stopped her a moment. There was something so deep, so true in his voice when he said *home.*

Mercy and home.

It was clear what truly mattered to Prince Karl of Gelicia.

Karl and his friends were not at the castle that evening for what was, for once, truly a small dinner. Katie and Brad had gone over the mountains for an overnight stay to meet his grandmother, who had been on a tour that had stopped in a neighboring country, and bring her back for the gala.

That left the king, Madame, April, Hunter, and herself.

After dinner, Madame excused herself to attend to still more details. But before she left, she reminded the king of his promise to Katie to walk in the gardens. April immediately said they would accompany him.

Once on the path, April put her arm through the king's, while Harmon hung back.

Hunter gave her a quick look, then sauntered to one of the stone benches that flanked the path.

"I'll wait for you here," Hunter told his wife.

"Me, too," Harmon said. "Wrong shoes."

She sat beside Hunter, who stretched his legs out, looking as comfortable as anyone could on a stone bench.

"What do you want to say to me, Harmon?"

She didn't bother to try to pretend. "It's something to ask."

"Go ahead."

"Has the Department of State considered that solutions other than Karl eventually becoming king could be nearly as beneficial to the interests of the United States?"

"No comment."

"Well, it better, since we both know that if Karl becomes king, he'll fully live up to his commitment to look after the welfare of Bariavak above all other things. That means another solution might be even *more* beneficial to the United States, to the region, and to the people of Bariavak. So the Department of State better stop putting all its eggs in the Karl basket."

He said nothing.

"Is the Department of State—are you—aware of other baskets out there that should be supported and nurtured for the benefit of all and—?"

"Including the benefit that Karl Wethers would go back to being the individual, ranch-owning citizen he wants to be."

"Well, yes, but again, even more beneficial to everybody, with the exception of Prince Vatche."

"The Department of State does not meddle in the affairs of other countries."

She snorted.

His relaxed gaze straight ahead didn't flicker.

"C'mon, Hunter. I know and you know that you try to influence—"

"That's all I'm saying. Except..." He let it die out.

"Except?"

His eyes cut toward her without moving his head. "If you are asking if there has been any thought past Plan A, I'd hope you thought better of me than that."

That was something. What it wasn't was an assurance that Hunter would help Karl and Andrej Skala.

CHAPTER NINETEEN

Without examining her decision, Harmon skipped the receiving line for the gala and headed right into the crowd.

She hadn't talked to Karl since his friends arrived.

Not that that was odd. Everyone associated with the castle had been fully occupied with the preparations.

In fact, it was perfect. Because it had given her plenty of time to catch up on work.

She'd put in lots of hours Thursday and all day Friday. When she'd called Sally this morning, her assistant had said, "Weekend, Harmon. This is a weekend. Unless it's an emergency, get off the phone. Turn off your laptop. Go get ready for your party. Because I'm hanging up now and I have plans right through until Monday morning."

Harmon did hang up, though she didn't turn off her laptop.

But then Ruzena arrived, hours and hours before the time the king's car was scheduled to arrive, and informed Harmon they were going to primp all day.

"Did Sally call you?" she'd demanded.

"Sally?" Ruzena repeated trying to look innocent.

Yeah, Sally had called. But it turned out to be good.

They primped. Harmon got another restaurant recommendation— the one Ruzena had wanted to make until her mother insisted on the mainstream one. And she organized five-year, ten-year, and twenty-year business plans for Ruzena, complete with marketing strategies.

The younger woman had looked almost relieved to send her off to the castle, probably because she'd been a little unsure about the dress until Harmon put it on.

It was spectacularly simple in a blue silk that shimmered toward green with each movement. It followed Harmon's curves without being blatant, had no slit or deep plunge, and might have been even sexier than the dress she'd worn to the reception.

Mirche, Karl's buddy from the hotel, let out a low wolf whistle when the small elevator brought her to the lobby.

Too bad Karl didn't—

She shut that thought off before it could complete. Instead, she arched one eyebrow at Mirche. He grinned and saluted.

Now, standing amid the other gala guests, she was aware from the corner of her eye of Andrej Skala closing in on her.

"Good evening, Ms. Reed. I should like to introduce to you my wife."

His wife was charming, Andrej Skala clearly adored her, and he twinkled as he said, "For the first time, my wife sees value in my position because I can introduce her to you and perhaps find the source of your lovely dress."

"And the one from the reception," added his wife, smiling.

Harmon was delighted to tell her about Ruzena and to encourage her to share the word.

"I shall begin immediately, if you permit, for I see the friend who wagered me that your dresses must have come from Paris and that I shall never attain acceptable fashion unless I, too, shop there."

She left them with her eyes sparkling with anticipation.

"She does not always enjoy these affairs, but you have made this a success for her already. Thank you."

"It is my pleasure. I enjoyed talking with her and I will be delighted if she tries Ruzena and shares her name. I hope Ruzena will be well established before I leave Bariavak."

"Is that imminent?"

She met his gaze. "That is impossible to predict, since there are forces at work that I am not privy to."

"It is a most interesting time for Bariavak," he said noncommittally.

"Very interesting. Sometimes, however, interesting can be tiring."

"True. However, I have received a piece of potentially more restful news. Prince Vatche is going away next week. His office informs us with great punctiliousness that he shall begin a personal holiday to Australia."

"Great place Australia. Did you know it has ten of the most venomous snakes in the world? Certainly the odds could favor Vatche encountering at least one in the wild."

Deadpan, he said, "I understand that even the most venomous snakes do not attack without provocation."

"Can you imagine Prince Vatche crossing the path of any human or snake that he doesn't provoke?"

Andrej Skala laughed. "At any rate it gives us a period of peace."

She felt words piling up at the back of her throat to say that such a period of peace would be the right time for them to advance and solidify their plans.

But her knowledge of those plans was vague at best. If he challenged her and realized she didn't know for certain ... Or, worse, if he thought Karl had told her things he shouldn't have and that made this man not trust Karl...

What she said was, "A period of peace is all to the good."

God, was she getting cautious?

Surely it hadn't been because she'd feel disloyal taking her argument to anyone other than Karl.

Katie was right. Harmon loved Brad's grandmother.

"Call me Andy," said Andrea Colecchi Spencer. "Everybody does."

Harmon bet that was because that was the way Andy wanted it, because it sure sounded like an order to her. Unlike her father's orders when she was growing up, this one drew a smile.

Talking with Andy, Katie, and Brad was like floating along a warm, comfortable stream with minimal undercurrents. They were such nice people.

Maybe Sally was right that she needed balance in her life. Something that brought her in contact more often with simply nice people.

"Karl's buddy from the hotel drove Andy and me up into the mountains earlier today," Brad said.

"Hard to believe anybody can live on those inclines, much less build places like this castle," Andy said. "They're beautiful, that's for sure. But I'll take the wide open cornfields of Illinois, thank you."

"You live in Chicago, Andy. You don't see many cornfields," Brad pointed out.

"I see some. Besides, I noticed today how if you're down in a valley you wouldn't see the sun but for a flash and if you're on a peak you're liable to be blown away."

"Grandfather would tell you that has made Bariavakians a hardy people," Katie said.

"Your grandfather would tell me all sorts of things—" Andy's stern tone was belied by the twinkle in her eyes. "—only half of which I'd even consider believing,"

"Karl's buddy Mirche does tours?" Harmon asked.

"Not usually. He did it as a favor," Brad said.

Looking directly at Harmon, Andy said, "Nice man. He got talking about how he and Karl connected."

Uh-huh. Harmon got it. That was all Andy would say about the topic, unless Harmon paid the toll.

"Oh? How was it that they got connected?"

"Mirche was with UN forces for twenty years. They were in several of the same places around the same time," Brad said.

"Places. Times." Andy dismissed those. She was still watching Harmon. "What mattered was they understood what the other had gone through. They could talk and the other got it without explaining a lot."

"Andy!" exclaimed April, joining them in rush of luxurious fabric, with Hunter right behind.

They all hugged, saying hellos.

April drew in a man who'd followed her and Hunter more slowly.

"And this is Tucker Gates, Karl's friend from Wyoming."

It was the man with threads of gray working into his dark hair who she'd seen mostly from above at the hotel.

She also recognized the name. He'd been foreman of the ranch where Karl worked while taking college classes before joining the Army. Karl had looked up to him. A lot.

April made introductions all around. Harmon couldn't swear Tucker Gates looked at her harder than anyone else, but it seemed that way.

Madame came to them as April finished.

"His Majesty wishes you to join him," she said to Katie. "Your husband and his grandmother as well. Along with Mr. and Mrs. Pierce."

Katie started to protest, but Harmon said, "Don't worry about us. Tucker and I will keep each other company, if that's all right with you?" she asked him.

"Suits me fine. Talk to you all later," he said easily.

A tray-bearing waiter came by as the others left, so they had the handling of glasses to ease over any awkwardness.

"So you've known Prince Karl for a long time?" she asked once they each had a glass.

"Way back. Worked for his family when I was a teenager. When Karl finished high school, Stormy—that's what everybody called Earl, guess it was inevitable with the last name Wethers—got a hold of me and asked if Karl could work on the Double Bar X, where I was foreman. We're close enough to a college to let him take courses there."

"But then he joined the Army. According to his official biography," she added.

He lifted his chin slightly and looked down at her. Karl sometimes did that same thing. Like they were trying to see past ... of course, the brim of a cowboy hat.

"That's right, he did. Took more courses while he was on active duty, then finished up when he left the Army. Keeps on educating himself, too, trying to make his ranch better all the time. Comes in handy for his friends who don't bother with classes, but just take his word for what's a good innovation." He paused, emphasizing the words that followed. "When he sets his mind to something he's not going to be run off."

Not knowing what Karl had—or, more likely, hadn't—told his friends, she took a cautious approach. "That matches my impression while working with him here."

"Suppose it does," he said mildly. Then his face lost all its neutrality as he smiled at the woman approaching them. "This is my wife, Guinevere—"

She extended a hand. "Jenny, please."

"—Peters Gates."

Of course. *Jenny Peters Gates.*

"Karl has talked about when you first arrived at the ranch where he was working," she said. That summer he'd gone on and on about Jenny. How everything changed for the better when she came. Tucker most of all.

"Yes, when Tucker became foreman he made it quite the man cave. Acres and acres and acres of man cave." The older woman chuckled. "With the emphasis on cave. Karl was very sweet to me."

"He was head-over-heels for you," Harmon said, "Major, major crush. Happy to adore you while also being happy you and Tucker were together. I remember he came back to the post after your wedding—"

"Back to the post after our wedding?" Jenny's words caught Harmon before she realized her slip. "You knew Karl when he was in the Army?"

"Yes, she knew him," her husband said. "This is Harmon Reed, Jenny."

No hint of a smile now from the other woman. "*You're...?*"

"Yes." That seemed to cover it, so Harmon added no more.

Jenny Peters Gates drew herself up. "If Karl ever had a crush on me, I would be deeply honored. Because he is one of the best men I know, have ever known, or ever expect to know. He was as a young man when I met him and he is now. A good and honorable and kind man who deserves nothing but the best. Ever. From everyone he encounters."

That also seemed to cover it. So Harmon said nothing.

Jenny turned to her husband. "I'm going to check on Debbie. We'll connect later."

Presumably when Harmon wasn't around.

Then she was gone and silence stretched between the two remaining.

Finally, with a hint of a smile in his eyes, Tucker Gates said, "He might be an Army vet, a ranch owner, and now a prince, but Karl's still one of her chicks."

"And…" Harmon cleared her throat to start again. "And I'm the evil female who hurt her chick."

"Sure looks that way," he said evenly. "He came to see us on leave, not long after, uh, the two of you broke up. Something was bothering him. That was clear as anything, Never told me what, but Jenny has her ways of finding out."

She slanted a look up at him. "You knew from my name when April introduced us who I was, didn't you?"

"Yup." Dimples flickered with the briefest of grins. "I got my ways, too, of finding out things from Jenny."

"But you were okay talking to me." Unlike his wife.

"I figured if Karl could have you here, it wouldn't hurt me to talk to you some. Jenny, on the other hand, will protect Karl against anything. Even himself."

CHAPTER TWENTY

Harmon put down the half-full glass because her hands had the stupidest tendency to shake all of a sudden and holding the glass made it too obvious.

She'd been dressed down and ordered around by executives and taxi drivers. Shouted and screamed at in more languages than she knew. Called names and cursed. Not one of those events had made her shake.

Neither Jenny nor Tucker had used a harsh word or a raised voice. They'd simply conveyed how badly she'd hurt Karl.

She'd had no idea…

No, that wasn't true. She had known he would be deeply hurt by her breaking up with him.

She hadn't cared.

Okay, she'd cared. But it had been the only possible answer.

"The thing is," she said with a smile that made her cheeks ache, "maybe I was doing the same thing in my way—protecting him from my worst instincts. I was so clearly not good enough for him. Everyone saw that except Karl."

"Now, see, if you'd said *that* to Jenny, you might have had her on your side."

Maybe it was his light tone that drew her into saying more. Possibly that western drawl that was similar to … other western drawls.

"That's probably why I didn't say it to her. I prefer not to be encumbered by allies. The need to think about them, keep them happy, avoid dragging them into a fight they don't want." Her tone was as light as his. Faster than his drawl, but relaxed, amused, disarming.

Perfect. "Better to fight alone, be lean and nimble. That's how I've run my business."

"Life, too, I suspect." Neither approving nor critical. More like a scientist looking at a bug.

She wasn't enjoying this. She couldn't get a gauge on him. She kept the smile going. "Of course."

He slowly nodded. "Ah."

"What does that mean?" she snapped, knowing she shouldn't be drawn, knowing she should have let it lie until it died from lack of oxygen.

"Just means it's another bit of confirmation that you're self-destructive."

Another bit. What the hell—And then the end of his sentence hit her.

"*Self-destructive?*" she repeated in astonished ire. "I am not self-destructive. If Karl Wethers said I'm—"

"Not Karl. He said you were your own worst enemy. Self-destructive's all mine. Takes one to know one." He reached up as if for a hat that wasn't there, turned the gesture into an easy half-salute. "Be seeing you."

Fresh air.

That's what she needed. She turned quickly, almost colliding with Prince Vatche.

"The most enchanting Harmon Reed." He tried to capture her hand. Probably aiming to kiss it.

She eluded him and the hand kiss.

"Excuse me, Prince Vatche, I need to—"

"But I shall not excuse you. You appear distressed. Was that disreputable person who was brought here by that … that *cowboy* who so laughably calls himself a prince accosting you? It is as well for you to experience this discomfort now, for you must see now what I have seen from the first moment, that you are too fine to be a part of this,

this cabal of the others. You should come with me to—"

"You're batting a thousand, Prince Vatche. Wrong on every count."

He was too startled to react and she was past him, then out the wide doors to the terrace added by some Eighteenth Century ancestor of King Jozef's. Steps led down from it to lawn and the garden paths.

She was halfway across the terrace when she spotted Karl talking with a cluster of people by the balustrade. Her current path would take her right past him. She stopped and half turned away, feigning fascination with the life-sized nude statue of a woman next to the main set of steps.

After a couple minutes, she would move on. In the opposite direction from whichever way he went. Without being too obvious.

From the corner of her eye, she saw Karl turn his head and spot her. He finished up a conversation, then headed her direction.

He paused long enough to take two champagne flutes from a passing waiter, which would have given her time to slip into the crowd ... if she'd moved. But she couldn't decide which direction she could go without having it look like she was avoiding him.

"Interesting, isn't she?" He handed her a flute.

At least her hands were steady now. "Who?"

"The lady you were staring at. Rumor is that she was the mistress of one of Katie's ancestors."

"Nice for his wife to have her right outside her door."

"Rumor also has it that she started off inside the palace when that was the primary residence. Until she tried to poison the king. She escaped, but the queen had her statue demoted to the castle and put out in the elements. Nice little reminder for the king of what could happen when he strayed, don't you think? Saw you talking with Tucker."

The abrupt change of subject caught her a bit off guard, so she kept it simple. "Yes."

Though now she understood why he was so cordial. He wanted to know about her talk with Tucker.

He turned and frowned down at her. "You don't like Tucker?"

"Like has nothing to do with anything."

"Sure it does."

She ignored that. "He's difficult to read. Purposely opaque."

"*Tucker?* Tucker Gates? Don't think we're talking about the same man. Working for him I always appreciated knowing exactly where I stood. Heck, even when he was thrashing around trying to escape how he felt about Jenny, it was pretty damn clear what was going on with him. Except to him. And ever since they worked things out…" He shook his head. "What was it you were having trouble getting a read on him about?"

She waved her free hand. "Nothing specific. Overall."

His frown eased, but he kept staring at her.

"What?" she demanded.

"Interesting, that's all. You've got to be good at reading people to do your job and everybody says you're good at it—"

"I *am* good at it," she said to his note of doubt.

"—so the only thing I can figure is you're no good at reading Tucker because he's open and honest."

"That's ridiculous."

"Nope. Makes a lot of sense. You're so used to dealing with people lying and spinning and manipulating that when you run into somebody honest, somebody who means what he says, you have no idea how to handle it. Explains a lot."

She did not rise to that bait.

"About you and me, I mean," he added, kindly explaining to someone not bright enough to pick up on his subtlety. Yeah, right. "You don't get me at all because you're not used to dealing with what coming out of someone's mouth being what's in their head."

She rolled her eyes.

"Huh. You know, that's interesting, too. Because you were raised by a man who's not much for lying or spinning or manipulating. You'd think you'd have a handle on that. But, nope."

Goaded, she said, "Speaking of lying, I recommend that you stop lying to the king or—"

"Quiet," he ordered.

Again he caught her off guard. This time because once before, in very different circumstances, he'd issued that order to her in that same low tone.

She'd understood its urgency then. She was inclined to take his word for it now.

He took her elbow in a less than gentle grip and steered her down the steps and along a lighted walkway through the gardens.

"You won't—"

"Not yet," he said.

Silent once more, he led them over a small bridge, then down a path to a bench beside the stream the bridge crossed.

This was the spot Katie had described. The romantic spot where she and Karl had kissed.

Her heart picked up speed.

He released her elbow and faced her. "This is a dead spot. Now you can go ahead and accuse me of lying to the king without it being recorded and potentially leading to me being brought up on charges of treason—"

"You couldn't be brought up on treason—"

"—or something," he concluded. "Hearing you accusing me of lying to him sure wouldn't make the king happy."

She was aware that her heartbeat has returned to normal. Strange, since this argument was apparently just getting started.

"No, it won't make the king happy. He'll be even less happy with the fact of your lies. And he will find out sooner rather than later. So don't try to fool him unless you're sure you can pull it off. Whatever you think you're protecting by doing that will be harmed less by telling him outright than by trying to outmaneuver him."

Karl said nothing.

She wasn't sure if he was absorbing what she was saying or blocking it.

"You won't succeed in outmaneuvering him. He's a master. You're not. I'm not sure *I'm* in his league, but I'm a hell of a lot closer. That's why you should take my help. No, don't bother to say it. I see you won't. Won't even admit to me what you're up to. But at—"

"Not up to anything."

"—least listen to this advice. Don't say anything, just listen. Play to your strengths, Karl. Be who you are."

"If you're back to calling me a kid from the sticks—"

"I'm not. Not completely. But your strengths are that you follow that sort of code. You're forthright, so *be* forthright. You stand up for what you believe in, so quit trying to pretend that's not what you're doing."

"You don't know any—"

"I have a pretty good idea. Though I'd have a clearer idea, which would allow me to really help, Karl, if you would—"

"I was going to say you don't know anything because nothing's happening."

Oh, she knew he had reasons not to trust her, but sometimes hope made an idiot of her, which is why she so seldom indulged it.

"Something is happening and I have a good idea of what. See, this is one of your weaknesses. Underestimating me."

"I never underestimated you. If anyone underestimated you—"

She interrupted before he could tell her she'd underestimated herself. "I have a knack for hearing things. Pieces here and there that can then be put together to know what's going on. It's come in real handy in my life."

It was how she'd known her mother was dying.

Long before the physical changes made it too obvious for her not to ask the question and to get the answer. It was how she'd known Karl hadn't only arranged to introduce her to his parents, which was already way more than she'd been ready for. He'd also bought a ring and planned to propose twelve summers ago.

She swallowed and steamed ahead, "It's come in real handy in my business. And what I have put together is that there are at least four factions with competing agendas for the future of Bariavak's government. Prince Vatche's goal is to have it remain a monarchy with him as king, possibly with an eye to beating back the inroads of democracy. Next—"

"Change *possibly* to *certainly* with an eye to beating back the inroads of democracy. But a blind prairie dog could spot that one."

"Next," she repeated, "a coalition of ministers and government officials want it to shift from an absolute to a constitutional monarchy, but to do so gradually and under their guidance. Presumably preserving their power for as long as possible."

"Again, not hard to—"

"And then there's you and Andrej Skala and a group of younger legislators who want to shift to a representative government with no monarchy, not even a figurehead."

She paused a moment, but he'd gone silent and still. Even now he wouldn't confide in her.

"You want to gain the endorsement of the king and the coalition of ministers and government officials and everyone else except, I'm guessing, Prince Vatche. But you also want to keep it quiet until you've gained enough supporters and momentum that none of the other groups can squash you while you're still growing. But if you stay too quiet, you can't grow. Catch-22."

She challenged him with a look.

He didn't crack, but he did speak. "Under your view, what's the fourth faction?"

"Easiest of all. That's King Jozef. With his granddaughter refusing the crown, he's focused on you. You—Karl Wethers, born an American, veteran of the U.S. Army, and now owner of a ranch in Wyoming—would become King Karl of Bariavak, ruling it well and wisely, as King Jozef has done."

"You forgot the part about the ranch struggling."

She lifted her left shoulder. "Have to leave some things out."

"Yeah? Well, the other thing you left out is the fifth faction. Me. Just me. Not connected with any mythical alliance that's grown out of your imagination. Just a guy who wants to go back to being a Wyoming rancher. Who's not about to be king of Bariavak. No matter what."

"Karl Wethers turning his back on people who need him? No way. You're Don Quixote. Have lance, will travel. You were born to it and heaven knows you were trained to it. You think I don't know what Grif and that merry band of his that you were part of were up to?" That was too close. Far, far too close to the memory she wasn't going to think about. "I knew that summer twelve years ago. Knew where you were headed for your next training."

"You couldn't have known. Your father wouldn't have—"

She laughed. "The Colonel? Tell *me* anything? Much less top secret? No way. But I didn't need him as a source. I knew."

Against her certainty, he shifted his line of attack. "Talk about Don Quixote, what about you? The fixer's fixer. Tilting against big media outlets to protect the lone individual."

"Just trying to improve the odds."

"Don Quixote couldn't have said it better." Then he turned from defense to offense. "You accused me of holding onto a grudge the other day, Harmon. I've realized something. It's not me. It's you holding on."

"Me? I don't bear you any ill-will. We were kids—"

"That's what you keep saying. But you *do* hold a grudge. Oh, not against me. Against your mother."

She sucked in a breath.

"For dying," he said, relentless. "Hurt like hell and you're not about to let that happen again. You're not going to risk having anybody else you love die on you. Somewhere in that brain of yours you've got it all figured out that if you never love anybody else, you'll never lose anybody else. That's why you've been so hard on your father. He has the gall to be mortal, too."

"I don't—That's not—You have no idea what you're talking ab—"

"That's okay, Harmon. You keep telling yourself that, but walking away won't stop it from being the truth."

Only then did she realize she had taken several steps toward the path and away from him.

"Whatever those half-finished sentences were supposed to be," he said. "It's none of my business."

She took two more steps, then forced herself to turn back to him.

"You're right. None of your business. You're also right that whatever you're doing is none of my business. You've made it abundantly clear that you don't want my help. But I'll give you this little piece of advice for free, Karl. If you and Andrej Skala are going to meet in the hotel's kitchen, try not to laugh so much. Not everyone who walks in the front door of the hotel will want to protect you. And you both have distinctive laughs. Not hard to know who's back there cooking up a plot."

CHAPTER TWENTY-ONE

"Are you okay?" Katie asked Harmon in a low voice, while the new Education Ministry Deputy Dalia Beralokza and Brad's grandmother entertained the others by agreeing vehemently with each other about how kids should be raised.

"Me? Of course. What—?"

"I saw Jenny Gates walk away from you. And, after, I saw your face…"

"It was nothing. Really."

"Nothing?" Katie clearly didn't buy that.

"Remember that stinker of a note I sent Karl years ago? Well, she heard it practically in real time. She ho—" She skidded away from the phrase *holds a grudge*. "She hasn't forgiven me any more than Karl has."

"Oh, I think he's making progress there." Katie smiled, clearly satisfied.

So Harmon didn't say the *No, he's not* that wanted to come out.

Besides, she had the unerring sense of being watched.

Discovering a need to twitch at the skirt of her dress, though it actually was lying perfectly, she half turned. Without lifting her face, she looked through her eyelashes and saw Prince Vatche watching her.

A self-satisfied smile added nothing to his charms.

Straightening, she pulled up the image of his face when she practically ran into him after Tucker left her.

Surprise, she'd thought.

Or had it been alarm that he'd been caught near enough to eavesdrop?

And could that mean his self-satisfaction just now meant he

thought he'd found a potential weapon to use against Karl?

Harmon was more surprised than not that Jenny Peters Gates showed up at the park.

The note she'd slid under the other woman's door at dawn had said she'd be waiting here, but she hadn't held out much hope.

So this was good.

Also, good that it was still early enough that they were unlikely to be seen. Which either made her cautious or paranoid.

"Thank you for coming, Jenny."

The other woman leveled a look at her. "Your message said it's to help Karl."

"It is."

"Karl is a great guy."

"He is.

"Someone truly special. To me and to everyone who knows him."

"He is."

"If you break his heart again, I'll … I'll … I don't know what I'll do, but it won't be pleasant."

"I don't have that power, Jenny. I'm not entirely sure I ever did. It was his first serious relationship and—"

"Do not try to wipe it away as a kid's feelings. I know him and it wasn't. You might not be entirely sure that you ever had that power, but I am. He loved you. The kind of love most women dream of. And you tossed him aside without a thought."

Harmon's lips parted, then closed.

She'd done what she'd done. Not her finest hour. But she didn't owe this woman an explanation.

And it wasn't even the worst she'd done. So if she owed anyone an explanation it was…

She snapped off that thought.

"This isn't about the past. It's about Karl now. And his future. I can't go into detail, but there are a lot of things going on. Some he's in the middle of. Some that could have a great impact on him. For good or not, it's still up in the air. You know what he wants his future to be. To run his ranch in Wyoming. It's the place he loves. Where he longs to be. His … home."

The woman's skeptical expression eased a bit. "You know that?"

"Yes. But don't take that as a sign I'm in his confidence." Her chuckle was dry enough to crackle. "I'm not. What I know is despite Karl, not because of him."

"Well, that was honest, anyway."

The older woman openly studied her. Less wary now, which would allow her to look deeper. Harmon fought the urge to duck away from the investigation, to end the scrutiny with fast talking or smart maneuvers. Fought it so hard her nerves twitched with the need to move, to leave, to escape, to forget the whole thing.

At last, Jenny spoke.

"What do you want me to do? I'm not saying I will, but I want to know what it is."

"The most important thing is to mask your dislike for me in public. Especially at the luncheon today." When Katie, Brad, April, Hunter, their guests, and she would join the king, his ministers and other close advisors … and Prince Vatche. "I'm not saying we have to be great friends, I'm not asking that. But don't give anyone seeing us in public the idea that your feelings about me could be a spot to drive a wedge in. Because that could expose Karl … I can't even say to what because I don't know all the details."

Maybe more frustration came out in that than should have.

She cleared her throat before continuing. "But I do know some are keeping a very close eye on Karl, hoping for an opening. I'm trying to help him, despite his best efforts to stop me because he's torn between thinking I might be an enemy and thinking he has to protect me from everything in this or any other universe—"

"Oh!" The other woman's exclamation apparently had been involuntary.

"What?"

For the first time, Jenny Gates smiled at her. "You *do* know Karl."

By Tuesday, things were getting back to normal.

The official functions were over. The gala guests had left. Including Prince Vatche, who had looked both puzzled and disappointed when Jenny Peters Gates had treated Harmon cordially at functions Sunday and Monday.

He'd be off to Australia soon and that, as Andrej Skala had said, would open a period of peace. During which Harmon planned to do a lot of foundation-laying for war.

Step one started when she arrived at the castle that morning.

"Hi, April, I was hoping to see you."

The other woman eyed her. Darn that Hunter Pierce, he'd put her on alert.

Harmon shifted from the direct approach she'd planned. "I hoped you and Katie would come shopping with me again to fill in gaps, then let me take you to lunch tomorrow." Ruzena had told her about the perfect place for what she had in mind.

"If you keep feeding me I'll have to go shopping for myself because I won't fit in any of my clothes."

"Perfect. Then we can shop for you while my budget recovers."

April laughed and accepted the invitation.

Katie was even easier, accepting immediately.

"This is wonderful," Katie said, not for the first time, as they sipped cool drinks at their lunch.

This wasn't so much a restaurant as Ruzena's aunt's back yard. Ruzena's mother had overruled her recommending it for that previous lunch. Ruzena's mother disapproved of her sister-in-law's venture, but Harmon loved it. Ruzena's aunt and Harmon had set the menu yesterday. She cooked and served it, then left them in peace at the lone table in an enclosed courtyard bursting with baskets of blooming flowers.

The shopping had been a success. Each of them finding at least one item that delighted them, even though Harmon had been going more for practicality. The shopping bags were in a line in a corner now.

"This is the sort of place only a native would know about. Ruzena would make a great fixer." Harmon deliberately dropped that mention of her business into the conversation.

She'd long ago learned that giving a confidence—or at least appearing to—was the way to get confidences.

"How did you get started?" Katie asked. "Were you ever a fixer yourself?"

"No. To be good, you have to be devoted to one place, to want to stay there for good. That's the whole idea of the fixer—a native or near enough who can be a bridge for the vagabond reporter or whatever coming in. Me? I'm part of the vagabond class. That's what happens when you're brought up an Army brat."

"I'd hate that," Katie said. "I love spending these months with Grandfather in Bariavak, but Ashton's home to me. Don't you think of one of the places you've been as home?"

"Nope," she said cheerfully.

"Oh, Harmon…"

"I can understand that," April said. "For me, home isn't a place. It's people. My sort of cousin and her husband, Leslie and Grady, basically raised me along with my great-grandmother. Wherever they and a group of their friends who have been aunts and uncles to me gather, that's home. Doesn't matter if it's DC or Chicago or anywhere else. As long as I'm with them."

"Maybe that's what I'm associating Ashton with—the people there. My friends who were all the family I had until Grandfather. And Brad." Katie smiled. "What about you, Harmon, do you have friends who are like family?"

"I had one." She'd wanted this to lead to her confiding some things in them—so they'd reciprocate—but this was closer than she'd ever intended. She added quickly, "But you know how it is. People don't stay in your life forever, right?"

Both April and Katie had their lips parted, prepared to ask questions.

She had no trouble turning aside questions … unless she wanted to stay friends with the questioners. And she did. She wanted to stay friends—friendly—with these two women. But she wasn't prepared to talk about this. She never had.

"Did you—" April started.

The door from the house opened and Ruzena's aunt emerged with a large tray.

Saved by the meal.

By the time it was served, they'd started eating, and all had exclaimed how wonderful the food was, Harmon figured there'd been enough of a break to go back to what she wanted to talk about.

"What a find this place is," she said. "The perfect place for confidential conversations.

"It is," April said dryly.

Katie looked from one to the other of them at that, clearly recognizing the subtext.

"I do want to ask you about something," Harmon said. "Minister Virba."

The other two women seemed to sag a bit at the anticlimax.

Katie asked, "Really? Why?"

"I'm interested in how he operates as Minister of Education."

"Badly," Katie said. "We have to deal with him for the summer camps and he's … difficult."

"Is that because he calls you by your title?"

"That's the least of it. He doesn't seem to care about the kids and he's not very bright."

As if considering a thought that had just occurred to her, Harmon tilted her head. "I wonder if he uses your title because he's one of those ultra pro-monarchy people."

"I think he's ultra pro-Virba," Katie said.

Harmon kept going. "Didn't I hear he was associated with an editor of one of the smaller magazines?"

"The one that's most rabidly pro-monarchy. His brother-in-law is editor." April made her first contribution while watching Harmon closely.

She snapped her fingers. "That's right. It's backing Prince Vatche, isn't it?"

Katie said, "I heard Minister Virba and Vatche had a fight right before he left on vacation."

Both Harmon and April turned to her.

"What? I did. Elisabeta's next-door-neighbor's cousin works at that magazine and told her about it. So it might not be backing Vatche anymore."

"Katie, can you get a list of the staffers and freelancers who work at that paper from Elisabeta's next-door-neighbor's cousin?"

"Probably. Why?"

"I'd appreciate it."

"Why?" April asked.

"It's complicated. If Hunter talks to you about political things—No, I'm not asking you to tell me anything, I'm just saying if he does, he could probably explain it to you better than I could, since I know you'll tell him about this conversation. Don't worry, April. I understood that going in. That's where your allegiance lies."

"Where does your allegiance lie, Harmon?"

What surprised her was that question came from Katie, not April. Though the so-similar faces bore similar expressions.

Ruzena's aunt unknowingly doubled her bonus by saving Harmon again. This time by collecting their plates and bringing coffee and a dessert that reminded her of tiramisu, except with light pastry surrounding the creamy filling rather than in layers.

After their hostess' departure, Katie looked around the empty courtyard, then said, "Before we finish, I have news. You can't tell anyone yet. Promise?"

"Promise," April and Harmon chorused.

"Brad and I are going to have a baby. In about six months."

"Stand up so I can hug you," April ordered. After hugs all around, they settled back. "King Jozef knows?"

"Yes, we told him this morning over breakfast."

"He must have been over the moon."

"He was." Katie related the scene as they started on their desserts.

"Are you going to tell Karl soon?" Harmon slipped in.

"Oh, yes, of course. I wouldn't be surprised if Brad's telling him now."

Amid the continuing congratulations, questions, and dessert, Harmon's brain screamed: *This changes everything.*

CHAPTER TWENTY-TWO

Harmon answered the knock on her door at the hotel almost as soon as it sounded, despite wearing only a shirt.

She'd hung up her slacks to smooth out wrinkles and, standing there by the closet when the knock came, she'd been too impatient to take the time to pull on another pair.

Besides, it was a long shirt. Provided a lot more coverage than a bathing suit. Or the uniforms of waitresses at certain restaurants.

Karl's eyes immediately skimmed down to the shirttail that reached her thighs.

"Where have you been?" she demanded, pretending she didn't feel a skittering of nerve-endings under her skin. "I was trying to get a hold of you everywhere."

His gaze met hers as she stepped back to let him in. There was wariness in it. Despite his clear efforts to mask it, there also was heat.

Heat that made her lungs burn.

Had some level of her brain done the shirt-only on purpose? To see what his reaction would be?

"So I heard. Phone messages, texts, and four people stopped me between getting out of the truck and reaching your door to tell me you want to see me immediately."

When he'd pushed her before—*I'm so sick of wearing these clothes ... Don't let me stop you from taking them off*—she'd retreated. She'd been kidding herself that she'd sidestepped. It had been a retreat and they both knew it. Was this to tell him she wouldn't again?

So what happened if he pushed this time?

"Urgent was the word I used in the messages. *Urgent.* But you took your sweet time." She waved away whatever he'd been about to say. "Never mind. I'll give you grief about that later. What matters now is you have to move your timeline up, Karl."

"What are you talking about?"

"The timeline. Your plan. Andrej Skala. The others. Positioning—"

"I don't know what the hell you are talking about." There was a different kind of heat in his eyes now. "Are you back on that fantasy you were talking about at the gala?"

"—for a transition to democracy. Yes, you do know what I'm talking about. And you know I know, Karl, so quit wasting time trying to stonewall me, because there's no time to waste. That was fine at the gala, but not anymore. Everything has to move up. You know Katie's pregnant, right?"

"How do you know—?"

"You're always asking that. This time I'll tell you. Katie told me. Us. April and me at lunch."

"Brad told me, too. It's great news and—"

"Yeah, it is. But not so great for you and your merry band."

"I thought it was Grif's merry band."

"Now it's yours. Your project. Your plan. Your conspiracy. Like those missions you and Grif went on. Don't bother trying to look confused. I know what you're up to."

"What is it you think you know?"

"Oh, for heaven's sake. I know, okay? I know that you plan to go for a representative form of government for Bariavak with Andrej Skala as the head of it—president or whatever you're calling it. I *know*. Accept it."

He studied her as moments ticked by and her lungs started sucking in fire with the effort to be still and calm under his regard.

"I'm not calling it anything. Bariavak will decide."

She streamed out a breath, fighting a sting behind her eyes.

Forcing him to acknowledge what they both already knew didn't add up to the biggest vote of confidence or "I trust you" statement around. But for the two of them it was a major step.

"And he won't hold that position," he was continuing, "unless the people of Bariavak elect him to it. But that's a long way off. For now, he'll lead representatives in deciding how to make the transition. Rather like the president of the Continental Congress during the Revolutionary War. Without the war."

She nodded. "With Prince Karl putting all his backing behind that movement and doing his best to stop the machinations to get power for themselves by Prince Vatche or certain ministers. Not to mention blocking King Jozef trying to put Prince Karl on the throne."

"Something like that."

She pulled in a long breath. "Karl, there's something else you need to know."

"I said I know about Katie and Brad's baby, so——"

"That's not it. Not completely. It ties in … but this is something that could mess everything up." She pushed her hair back. "*Possibly* it could be turned to a benefit, if it's handled right, you have a lot of luck, and help from a top professional, in other words me. Or it could really, really screw it up."

"After that build-up, tell me fast before I fall over from nerves," he said with a glint of humor.

"Andrej Skala is King Jozef's grandson. His and Madame's."

"What——? You can't know that." The humor was gone.

"I do."

He hadn't. That was clear. But now she saw his mind clicking the pieces into place. "The records building. That's what you were doing. Digging that up."

"Confirming what I suspected. Which anyone else could do in an afternoon, too. In fact, someone else was looking at a lot of the same documents. If Bariavak had tabloids it would have been dug up decades ago."

He swore. Then he zeroed back in on her. "You've talked to them, King Jozef and Madame?"

"Not to the king, no, but to Madame."

"She confirmed it?"

"Not precisely."

His eyes narrowed. "What does that mean?"

"She basically acknowledged that Andrej Skala's father was her son. But she would not say that the king was the father. And she maintains nobody can know for sure."

"But you think you're sure."

"Sure like DNA? No. But pretty darned sure. In my bones. And there's enough in the records to make anyone suspicious. The dates alone are enough. Plus, the same woman attending only the births of Madame's brother Laurentz's wife—God, that last one must have been Hunter under his Bariavak name. Did you know that Hunter's Madame's nephew? That's—Sorry. Of course you know. So this one woman attends only the births of Madame's sister-in-law, Madame's son with her husband, and one other. For a woman who goes by the last name Laurentz, who is nowhere else in the records. And the birth was the same day Chedomir was born."

"Okay, but—"

"That was Chedomir Skala, Andrej's father. Chedomir died fifteen years ago. Of the same heart ailment that King Jozef had surgery for in D.C."

She saw his mind factoring this in, adjusting. "Thank you. I appreciate the heads-up, Harmon."

He sounded almost formal.

"You're welcome. Now you need to work like hell to solidify Andrej Skala's position so it's so strong that it won't matter to anyone that he has royal blood, even if it's not legitimate. And now you think I'm going to shut up and go away and let you and Andrej sort this out, but you're wrong, Karl."

"Harmon." It was a warning.

"Because you're still not taking in all the ramifications. Don't you see how Katie being pregnant complicates all this? Another generation of Bariavak royalty. Katie's refused the crown, but will she—can she— refuse it for her child? It will give the royalists and King Jozef another candidate to rally around. That's why you can't wait until next spring to move on this. King—"

"How the hell do you know—"

"—Jozef already knows about the baby, of—"

"—about next spring?"

"—course, which is bad—does it matter how I know? Anyway the public doesn't know about the baby and won't for a while, so there's still an opportunity to solidify the democracy position if you move fast. You and Andrej Skala and your merry band. Or do you prefer Kitchen Cabinet? That works with you and Andrej meeting in the hotel kitchen. It's what they called President Andrew Jackson's unofficial advisers in contrast to—"

"I know what the Kitchen Cabinet was."

"The point is, you have to move now. Because if you don't, you'll end up sitting on the throne out of that overdeveloped sense of responsibility of yours."

"Why do you care about any of this?"

"I just said. Because you'll end up on the throne out of an overdeveloped sense of responsibility. And you'd be miserable."

"My misery has never seemed to be a concern to you," he said dryly.

"Fine, you're right. I don't care. Be a king for all I care. Marry a princess. Have a bunch of little princes and princesses. Start a dynasty. Or do what we both know you're going to do and that's your damnedest to help Bariavak grow toward democracy. But to do that you have to act *now*."

He looked at her for a long, long moment.

"I'm not even asking you to trust me. You already know these things, Karl. You know about Katie and Brad's baby and you've already figured out what that can do. And you know in your gut that I'm right about Andrej Skala being the king's grandson."

Still he was silent.

"Oh for heaven sakes." She threw up her hands and turned away. But almost immediately, she turned back to him. "Is this still because of how I ended it twelve years ago? Because if what you need in order to listen to me on this is an explanation, you've got it. I knew it wasn't right, but you kept plowing ahead. Making all those plans with your family coming to visit … and after. You had our whole lives planned out—"

"I never—"

"You didn't have to say it, Karl. I knew it. I could see it in your eyes, growing and solidifying, until … So I ended it. To protect you from my worst instincts."

"That way? Then?"

"You wanted me to wait until you deployed?"

"I didn't want you to do it at all." After a pause, he flipped his hand over. Not quite a shrug. "Look, you didn't love me. Okay. Would have been better if you hadn't let me think you did, but I get that, too. You were young. But, damn, your timing sucked."

He moved only his head to look out the window as he continued.

"It wasn't just my family coming. You had no way of knowing, but I'd bought a ring." He made a sound. Not full-fledged amusement but not bad. "I was going to propose. How was that for realistic? Just shows how many knots you had me tied into. Didn't matter that I was nineteen. Didn't matter that you were a major's daughter. Didn't matter I was going to be in a special unit—"

"I knew."

"What?" He turned his head toward her.

"I knew about the ring. I knew you were going to propose."

Slowly he turned the rest of the way so he faced her squarely. She met his look, but his gaze dropped and she knew his peripheral vision had picked up a faint tremor in her hands. Quickly, she put them behind her, presumably grasping the top of the chair back, judging by the fact that it clunked against the desk.

"You knew," he repeated.

"Yes."

"How?"

Her shoulders lifted and dropped, her hands still behind her. "I don't remember where the first couple whispers came from, but then a friend of a friend said she'd seen you picking out a ring at the jewelers."

Now he was silent, absorbing this, no doubt adjusting his view of the past. Darker? Lighter? Or just different.

Her head dropped so he couldn't see her eyes.

"She wouldn't have recognized just any private, you know. But you were so … you. And we caused rather a stir on the post."

"The officer's daughter and the private," he said.

"The bad seed and the straight arrow headed for greatness."

"That's not even funny."

"No, it's not. It's the truth. Why didn't you stay in the Army? You could have been a general. Everybody said so."

"General. Right. I did my duty for our country, but I never was looking to make a career of it. I wanted to be home. In Wyoming. On a ranch. My own ranch."

"Which is where you want to be when this is all over."

"Yes."

"Then you better get to work."

As soon as Karl left, she pulled on slacks, slid into shoes, and called a taxi to take her to the castle.

It beat the alternative of curling up in a ball on the bed for a couple weeks because … Because what? He hadn't turned to her? He hadn't opened up? He hadn't touched her?

Yeah, going to the castle definitely beat the alternative.

Since she usually was driven in an official car, the guards at this door didn't know her. They took their time trying to decide whether or not to admit this uninvited guest. Finally she pulled out the big guns by saying she was here to see Madame Sabdoka.

She was escorted to the woman's office. The would-be knock by the guard barely brushed the door. Harmon leaned forward and knocked hard.

Madame's voice came. "Enter."

Harmon did. The guard skedaddled.

She pulled the door closed herself.

"Having used my name to attain entry to the castle, there is no need to linger here. Go, go wherever it is you intend."

"Madame, I need to talk to you."

The other woman gave her a stern stare that clearly said that once had been more than enough for her. All she said was, "Sit."

Harmon did, then came directly to the point. "Karl is going to tell Andrej Skala that his father was your son—yours and King Jozef's. He might be doing it right now. He has to," she added over the other woman's syllable of objection. "They're trying to accomplish something and this could explode the whole thing."

"They are children, playing at—"

"They're not. They're doing their best for the future of Bariavak."

"His Majesty decides what is best for—"

"He won't be able to when he's dead. I'm sorry to be so blunt, but things are happening fast and … well, I didn't want to risk this exploding in your face, either, Madame. Or the king's. Are you certain that King Jozef has no notion that Andrej is, ah, your grandson?"

"No one ever knew of my son's origins, so no one could know of Andrej's. Put that out of your mind. There is no danger from those who would seek to discredit the king by rumors that he is the grandfather of Andrej Skala."

"What about vice versa?"

The older woman became even more fiercely upright. "If he carries the king's blood it could be only to his credit."

"Not politically," Harmon said bluntly. "Politically it could bite them if Andrej becomes the visible leader of the effort to convert Bariavak to democracy. Being the descendant of the king might not go over well with others in the movement. Another person carrying royal blood to lead Bariavak."

Madame stared at her, expressionless.

"The democracy forces will need to be on top of this. To reveal the connection—"

"No."

"Yes. They will have to. At the right time, in the right way. Or it will explode in their faces. That means you need to let His Majesty know. Now."

"Ah, you come after all," King Jozef said when Karl was ushered into the sitting room attached to his office. "We had a message that you regretted that you could not join us for this tea to quietly celebrate the good news."

Katie and Brad were there, along with April and Hunter. No one else. He'd half expected to see Harmon. But was relieved not to.

"No, sir. I have come to tell you I'm going back to Wyoming immediately. My next trip here won't be until after fall roundup. If you want me then."

"Leave? Impossible. I have far too much for you to do here now. Tonight's dinner and—"

"Sorry, sir. I am going. Look at the bright side, Prince Vatche's out of your hair now that he's on vacation."

"Vatche or no Vatche, it is out of the question. What you do there, we can hire someone to do. What you do here, only you—"

"It's my ranch. My responsibility. To its future, to the people who work for me, to my neighbors who are helping out while I'm gone."

"You have a responsibility here. A responsibility of blood. You must feel that responsibility as the rightful prince of Gelicia and potential heir to my throne."

"Grandfather. That's not fair. Karl has given so much when you know—"

"It's okay, Katie. I can fight my own battles. The pull of that blood must have diluted over the generations, Your Majesty, because I don't feel it. It's not who I am. Do I want the people of Bariavak to have a shot at a better future? Yeah. But they're responsible for that, too. Right now I need to—I want to—" He looked steadily at the king. "—go home."

CHAPTER TWENTY-THREE

Karl hesitated at the top of the stairway. His room was to the left.

His hesitation let the lure of Harmon's door not far down the hotel's narrow hallway to the right draw him. Was he wondering if—hoping—she was wearing just that shirt still?

Jarta would have packed for him by now. All he had to do was pick up his things and go.

Far from Bariavak. Far from her.

The urge to put his hand on her leg and slide up, raising that shirt until she was there and open for him…

Not even what she'd told him had stopped that urge.

The stream of quick phone calls had pushed it back, but hadn't killed it.

Neither had the rushed, risky daylight consultation with Andrej in Mirche's tiny office. It had been a difficult conversation revealing to the man that a secret he'd had no part of creating might inflict a mortal blow for their hopes for his country.

But his response had confirmed for Karl that Andrej was the right man. If they could pull off their hastily revised plan.

And then the trip to the castle.

None of it had killed that urge to touch her, to take her…

Once more.

That old saying that he who hesitates is lost had it exactly right.

He started down the hallway. To the right.

He was lost.

~

He'd come back. Looking five days tireder in just a few hours, but here in her room.

"I've done what I can," he said when she gestured him in and closed the door behind him.

"I could help you, Karl. I could help with this. I'm good at what I do and I could help you negotiate this."

"Harmon, go back to your life. Go back and fix something that can be fixed."

He meant them. That they couldn't be fixed.

She knew that. She'd never thought otherwise. Not even at the deepest level.

"Karl? What happened to the ring you bought?" She hadn't known that was anywhere in her mind, so how had it surfaced as a question now?

"I gave it away. A buddy was broke—he was always broke. Couldn't keep a dime in his pocket—but he'd found the girl he wanted to marry. I gave the ring to him and he gave it to his girl. They have three great kids now and his wife handles all the finances."

She smiled. "That's great. A good luck ring." She felt the smile wobble. "I wish I'd seen it."

"Harmon. Don't cry."

"I'm not crying." She straightened, facing him. "I want you, Karl. I know we can't be fixed, but I want you. For old time's sakes or because the fire's not out, I don't know. But I want you. Now."

She stepped into him, lifted her face and kissed him.

First touch of lips to lips and they were there. Where they'd been all those years ago. Kissing and kissing. Oh, yes, this man could kiss.

He stepped back, breathing hard. Jerked his hands away from her face, but then left them there, near her face and shoulders.

Ready to hold her again? Or to shake her?

His voice came harsh. "If this happens it isn't—it can't be—anything more than sex. Making that clear from the start. So there're no misunderstandings."

"It's clear. No misunderstandings."

"I'm not going to fall in love with you again. Do you understand me? There's too much riding on—I'm not going to fall for you at all a second time. Do you understand that?"

"Yes."

She reached up and tipped his hat backward off his head.

He clasped her wrist, held it lightly as he brought it behind her back, using both their arms to scoop her to him as their mouths met again. Opened.

She arched into him, seeking more. All.

His other hand stroked down her throat, dragging at the material covering her. Two buttons gave way to his urgency. His hand slid inside her bra, pushing that aside, too, and then his mouth was on her.

There was a fierceness in him she hadn't known before. She met it with her own. Each one-handed, they together removed his clothes.

The hands now clasped behind her back, their pressure bringing her tight against him, rocking.

Nearly … nearly…

He released her hand only to draw her slacks and panties down her legs, throw them aside as she stepped out of them, then stroke his hands up.

"Those legs."

He slid a finger inside her and she buckled.

He wrapped his other arm around her. "Not yet," he ordered, turning so he dropped to the bed with her on top of him.

Practically before they'd landed, he was pulling her blouse and bra off together over her head.

Then he rolled them, pressing in to her as her legs opened for him.

He hooked his elbow under her leg, opening her wider, deeper. Stroked into her. Again. And again.

She climaxed fast, calling out. He followed almost immediately.

Panting for breath, they remained joined.

Then the rhythm changed. He was still hard inside her and they weren't panting anymore, but stroking, thrusting.

Her fingers curled into his back.

This was just as fierce, but not as fast. They were sweating, slipping against each other, but not finding quite…

It was aching and straining toward something just beyond … beyond what they'd experienced, beyond what they'd been, beyond who they were.

And then it was there. Heads thrown back, cries from taut throats, shaking and shuddering.

Until they collapsed into each other.

Her free hand curved with the shape of his skull, stroking his head. Until it stilled with sleep.

"Enter."

Therese came in.

It surprised him, both because she rarely came to his office unless summoned and because she'd seem preoccupied during their tea with those he thought of as the young people. Ah, but soon there would be even younger people, and he would be a great-grandfather.

Pleasure erased surprise. "Come in, come in. We shall sit here by the window." He escorted her to the settee positioned to catch the last light of day.

"Is it true? Prince Karl has departed?" she asked.

He glanced at the clock his ancestor had purchased from a Swiss craftsman in the 1400s. "If he has not, it should be at any moment. He claimed an emergency on that ranch of his required his presence in Wyoming. I think we must go to see this place someday."

She looked at him closely. "But you do not think that is the cause of his leaving," she concluded.

"I do not." He added with satisfaction, "I believe several factors contributed to this abrupt departure, chiefly the most charming Ms. Reed."

"I must speak to you openly, Your Majesty, of confidential matters."

Her formality amused him. "Do you not always speak openly to me of confidential matters when we are alone?"

Was she preparing to scold him once more for meddling?

"This concerns … the past—our past—and how it might now affect the future."

He lifted the phone and told his secretary that he was not to be disturbed until further notice.

"What is it, Therese?"

"I have withheld from you—for good reasons—a fact that now I must tell you. Also for good reasons." She drew in a breath. "I bore you a son, Jozef. All those years ago. A son named Chedomir. He was raised by a good family. He became a good man. He died. Too young, too young. He left three children. His son is—"

"Andrej Skala."

"You have known—?" She said no more immediately, absorbing his knowledge. "Why have you never spoken to me of this?"

"Because you never told me."

"You hold me at fault for that?"

"No, no, Therese. How could I? You did always what you felt best. Alone. Always alone. For that I have no words." He lifted her hand and kissed it. "You bore it all. I bore no part of it. I began to wonder many years later, and far, far too late to assist you in any way. With that, I knew it was not my place to force on you a discussion not of your choosing."

He kissed her hand again before adding, "What you tell me now or that you tell me nothing ever is always of your choosing."

Silence.

Then, slowly, she said, "I realized I carried your child six weeks after you informed me that you were to marry royally after your months at the various embassies."

"All those months abroad, with no way for you to contact me. I thought so many times to write to you, but thought to what purpose other than to tear at the wound of our separation? So I left you, instead to carry our child alone. Years later I realized that."

"How? How did you come to know?"

"I met him. Our son. A member of a citizen's committee. He entered the meeting room and I knew him to be your son. More slowly, I saw him to be my son. I learned the date of his birth. Then to count back from his birth, the days and months, to when we were together last. So clear. He was a man by then, already with a family, established in his life. He did well for himself. A successful and upright man. There was nothing I could give him that he had not already attained on his own."

"But Andrej Skala? You helped him?"

He tipped his head from side to side. "A bit here, a bit there. No more than I would do for the son of a friend. Opportunities only. What he made of them was his doing."

"You know he heads those saying to end the monarchy."

"Not so strident as that, my dear," he said with a slight smile. "No storming the castle or demonstrations. They will wait for my departure to the next world, or so I hear."

"Prince Karl—"

"Yes, yes, Karl as well."

"She said that were it known he is your grandson that it could hurt their effort. I say, all the better if it stops their foolish drive to end the monarchy."

"She?"

"Harmon Reed."

"How does she come into this?"

"She came to tell me she had discovered Chedomir's birth. She knew he was my son and she was certain he was yours as well. Ah, I see now you are worried by her. You could send her out of the country. Forbid her to—"

"No, not worried by her. It is interesting the involvement she takes in this." He stroked his beard. "Quite interesting. I shall not banish her, though if it comes to that…"

"I held what she said to me before the gala. But when she came back today and Prince Karl departs so abruptly, I knew I must tell you. If I had told you when she first came to me—"

"Do not concern yourself, Therese. All will be well. Never mind all this now. We shall see it through to what is best for Bariavak. But now, with us here this moment, tell me how it was for you then."

There were tears on both their cheeks when she finished, their hands still locked.

"Ah, Therese. Perhaps I am a weak man. Perhaps I never spoke to you of it because I wanted no part of the heartbreak and sacrifice you have sustained with such dignity these years. For our son. For me."

He put his arms around her.

Harmon knocked on Karl's door again. Harder this time.

He'd been gone from her bed when she woke. That was okay. That was what she'd agreed to.

That didn't mean this was done.

She could accept that their having sex didn't mean there was a future for them, but if he thought he'd had the last word...

Harmon, go back to your life. Go back and fix something that can be fixed.

She wasn't trying to do that. She wasn't. She just wanted to help him and—

"Ms. Reed?"

She spun around. Not easy on legs that still were shaky.

It was Mirche, Karl's crony who'd arranged the pickup for him to drive, who'd given Brad's grandmother the tour, who'd let him use the hotel's kitchen for his nocturnal meetings with Andrej Skala and others.

"I need to get in Karl's room."

"It is empty." He said it almost as if he felt sorry for her.

"I need to get in Karl's room," she repeated.

He paused a moment, then pulled out a key and opened the door.

It was, as he had said, empty. Oh, the furnishings remained, but the sense of Karl was gone. Why was that, she wondered uselessly.

She hadn't been that far behind Karl, yet he was clearly gone.

"What will you do now? Will you go?" Mirche asked her.

"Go? Not until I've finished the job for the king."

"What job is that? It has seemed you were most occupied with agitating with Karl."

Agitating with.

Not a bad description of their relationship. Rather like Katie's inside game.

She turned to him, a sudden suspicion rising. "Mirche, what is it you do in this hotel?"

"I do whatever is needed. I own it."

"It's no accident they've been meeting here, is it. You're part of the merry band with Karl and … others."

"Merry band?"

"Never mind. That's an interesting question you asked. What job I am supposed to do for King Jozef."

"It is. Perhaps it is a job that can no longer be done here in Bariavak."

Now that Karl was gone.

Was that what he was saying?

His expression didn't answer that question.

She quickly turned back to the room. She had it. The reason the room felt so empty.

The cowboy hat was gone.

It wasn't Karl's room without that hat.

He'd taken the hat. He'd left her.

She supposed that was only fair, considering what had happened in their one encounter between that summer twelve years ago and the day she'd walked into the Venice airport VIP lounge.

CHAPTER TWENTY-FOUR

Nine Years Ago

She and Rabiah had been careful. As careful as they possibly could be short of staying holed up in the safe house.

House? More like a safe room. And they'd been out of everything. Including water. They couldn't last there much longer.

They'd discussed whether it was better to go now when they still had some strength or to try to wait it out for the coup attempt to resolve one way or the other and hope it was soon…

They'd decided to go while they still had some strength. Rabiah had even joked that being weak would make Harmon walk less like an American woman. Not so sure, not so determined. So she wouldn't be spotted as easily.

And she wasn't. Not as an American.

But they both were as women. Out at night, slipping through shadows, when the street suddenly closed in with the protestors. Where had they all come from? How could they just appear like that?

It didn't matter. They were all around Rabiah and her. She could pick out a few phrases in the native language about leaving them alone. Most moved on.

But not all. Those who remained wouldn't leave them alone. She saw it in their eyes, their posture as they closed in around them, saying things about teaching them a lesson in the proper way for a woman to act.

And other phrases her rudimentary understanding of the language didn't include.

But the intent was clear enough as these men backed them to the mouth of an alley.

Her sole thought then was that they would survive.

She and Rabiah.

Whatever happened. They had to survive.

She looked around. The alley was lined with covered-up merchandise from what appeared to be small shops. An empty cart for selling vegetables, brooms stacked against a wall, a pyramid of baskets. But it was a dead end. If they were maneuvered into it would there be any coming out?

Another wave of protestors flowed past, more agitated, moving faster. She thought she caught shouts, including the rude name for the local military. But most of her attention was for the men trying now to encircle them. Seven of them.

"Brooms," she said in English, barely a whisper to Rabiah. "Weapons. Alley."

Rabiah shot her a look. Then a short nod.

If they made a fast move, the men would rush them. Probably overpower them. Slowly, slowly they retreated. The men followed, stalking them.

Almost there ... Almost...

"Rabiah," she called. She grabbed brooms, pushed Rabiah toward them, then took a stance closer to the men, who had stopped in surprise.

They recovered quickly, though, lips drawn back from their teeth as they advanced. Harmon paired the brooms, swinging two from the brush end to give the attackers less to grab on to.

Rabiah had one man down. Harmon started high and came down hard against the neck of the man closest to her. As he stumbled back, she pushed back the next one with a jolting jab to his gut.

But two were still coming. And two were on Rabiah.

She kept fighting, but the face-covering made it hard to breathe or see. She lost one broom. The final one was wrenched from her. Her nails caught a face. They drove her to the ground, but she'd hooked her elbow into the solar plexus of the closest one so his own weight drove it into him as he came down on top of her.

Survive. Survive…

She tried to roll. He was too heavy. She tried to kick, the cloth tangled her legs.

Then the long skirt was being pulled up. She got in three good kicks, but they kept coming back, two of them at least. They were trying to pin her arms, her legs.

She couldn't see, could barely breathe.

Survive. Survive…

She heard a grunt even though she didn't think she'd connected with that last kick.

And then the weight was gone. There were faint sounds. A fight? But…

Government troops? Could they have found them? But she and Rabiah were not likely to fare better at their hands. She had to get free of this thing. Be able to see, to breathe, to fight. To have a chance. To—

She was being hauled up to her feet, the motion making her dizzy inside the blindness of this hood.

Then a voice she knew. Barely audible. Unmistakable.

"Quiet."

She pulled at the covering again. Wanting to see. Needing to see … him.

"Keep it on, Harmon."

"Karl." She whispered it.

The fabric shifted and she could see through the mesh inset in the hood.

She'd said something else and he'd replied, but she couldn't re-member what. She'd been too absorbed in trying to make out his face amid the shadows, his equipment, and the barrier of the mesh. All colluding to separate them.

He ushered her to Rabiah, who was held up by two more dark figures. Harmon took her shaking friend into her arms.

Karl said something too low for her to hear to the other two, who disappeared. He nudged her and Rabiah into the darkest corner of the alley.

"Stay here. No movement. No sound. Understand?"

"Yes."

"We'll be right back. We'll get you out." He added, and she knew he wasn't speaking to her now, but into the com system, "We're bringing her home, sir."

Then he followed the other two into darkness.

That was when she'd made a liar of him.

She hadn't been there when he and his comrades returned.

He hadn't brought her home.

CHAPTER TWENTY-FIVE

The trip home to Wyoming was a mess, with a delay in Frankfurt, then thunderstorms popping up all over the country like fireworks on the Fourth of July. Karl was rerouted to Toronto and then to Seattle. They couldn't get him into Cody, where his truck was, because another cell of storms was sitting over it. So he accepted a flight into Casper. He'd need a one-way rental car, but at least he was in the right state.

And for once his ability to sleep deserted him.

Maybe King Jozef had a point about using the royal jet.

He came out of the secured area feeling like a piece of overcooked pasta—limp, pallid, and unfit for consumption. He looked around for the rental car counter.

"Wethers."

His posture recognized the voice before his brain did, because it came to attention as he pivoted. "Sir."

"At ease," said the smiling man in the cowboy hat. "Good to see you, Karl."

"Colonel Griffin." Exhaustion brought old habits to the surface. "Grif. It's good to see you, too. Taking a flight out today?"

"Nope. Here to pick you up."

"Me? How the hell—How did you know I'd be here and why—"

"We'll talk about that on the way. Let's get your bags. You're coming to stay at Far Hills Ranch a night or two."

"But—"

"Ellyn's orders," Grif said of his wife. "No arguing with them."

In the colonel's pickup, heading north out of Casper on I-25, with the air fresh after recent rain, Karl started to feel human again.

He opened a second bottle of water from the cooler in the back seat, having chugged the first.

"Okay, Grif. I can take it now. How'd you know I was coming into Casper?"

"Colonel Reed."

"What? How'd he—" He bit it off.

"You have had a brutal trip if you can't figure that out. Harmon called him. Brooks told me. I called her directly for more details. Ellyn heard and there you are."

It was a succinct recap of what must have been interesting conversations. But it was the first one he couldn't get his mind past. Harmon had called her father.

"Got anything you want to tell me about, Wethers?"

"No, sir."

Grif shot him a look. "Not what's been going on in Bariavak?"

No. Definitely no.

"With the king," Grif added.

Oh. That. "He's not a man who gives up easily."

"So I understand. And with cause from what I hear of this Prince Vatche who wants the crown bad. Can't imagine State's ready to give up on you being king there, either. Would suit them down to the ground to have an American on the throne."

"If I were on the throne I wouldn't be an American any more. I'd be the king of Bariavak." He swore. "I know people think I'm crazy, but I don't want to be king of anywhere except the Wethers ranch."

"You could walk away."

He said nothing.

Grif looked over at him. "Okay, no you can't. So what are you going to do?"

Slowly, Karl began to talk.

Grif asked a good question here and there but mostly listened.

As the truck turned into the road under a sign announcing Far Hills Ranch, Karl wound down, too, "There are so many ifs and maybes to get through that we can't hope to pin things down yet. Need to let some of the possibilities sort out."

"I can see that." Then his former CO asked, "What are you going to do about Harmon?"

Karl let the question hang until they had passed the house where Grif's cousin Kendra and her family lived and reached Ridge House, where Grif, Ellyn, and their kids lived. Farther down this road was the home ranch, where a sturdy two-story white house that had been the center of Far Hills Ranch and of the Susland family for generations.

"Nothing to do with me," he said at last.

Ellyn came out of the back door with a welcoming smile.

"Keep trying to tell yourself that, Karl," Grif said. "Course you'll be a bigger damned fool than I ever took you for if you buy it, but keep trying."

Karl was barely out of the truck when Ellyn gave him a warm hug. She stepped back from it, looking at him, then frowned across the pickup hood at her husband. "You grilled him during the drive, didn't you?"

"It's called a debrief."

"Well, he looks like he's been debriefed right into the ground. No, don't take his things out. It's too noisy and crowded here with the kids and everything. I called Marti, and she agrees Karl should stay at the main ranch. She and Robert and the girls are in D.C. Won't get here until next month. Kendra and Daniel and their kids are in D.C., too, celebrating the Delligattis' anniversary—they'll be sorry to have missed you—and I called Luke," she added of the Far Hills foreman, "so he won't mistake you for an intruder at the home ranch and put buckshot into you."

"We offer all the comforts at Far Hills Ranch," Grif said dryly.

Karl chuckled.

Ellyn continued, "Our kids are all set here, so we'll get back in the truck and take Karl up there right now. The order of business is to feed him well tonight and let him sleep as long as he wants. We'll have time tomorrow to catch up."

"You are an angel of mercy, Ellyn. If I can take a shower in there somewhere, I'd raise your rank to archangel."

"That can be arranged."

Grif kissed his wife's temple. "A well-deserved promotion."

Ellyn cooked him a steak and the fixings while he showered in the bathroom attached to the guestroom she'd shown him. Then, true to her word, she hustled herself and Grif out and let him sleep.

One thing to say about his airline misery marathon, he was too tired to feel jet-lagged.

As agreed last night, he called when he woke the next morning.

"Perfect timing," Grif said. "We were just deciding whether to start breakfast here or wait for you to eat up there. We'll be right there."

He was in jeans, an untucked shirt marked by too-long-packed wrinkles, and barefoot, starting the coffee, when Grif came up to the back screen door and held it open for Ellyn. Then he kept holding it open as a pregnant woman Karl had never seen before came in, followed by a man he had seen before.

"Karl, of course you remember Lieutenant Colonel Reed," Ellyn said lightly, as if she hadn't just pole-axed him. "And this is his wife, Ann-Elise."

He came to attention, but stopped himself from saluting. "Colonel. Ma'am."

"Wethers."

"Oh, for heavens sakes," said the pregnant woman who had to be Ann-Elise. He could see why Harmon liked her. "It's Brooks and Karl. And if you ma'am me again, I'll treat you to a case of hormone horrors."

To his surprise, Lieutenant Colonel Brooks Reed grinned and held out his hand. "It's good to see you, Karl."

Karl hesitated an instant, their previous meeting still a wound. Then he returned the handshake.

"It'll be even better for all of us to see each other once the coffee's poured and everybody's fed," Ellyn said.

She doled out tasks that kept everyone busy and working together. So by the time they sat down to a breakfast that added fresh strawberries, pancakes with all the trimmings, sausage, and hash browns to bacon and eggs, awkwardness was past. Only Grif had the gall to ask, "What? No chicken-fried steak?"

Ellyn whapped him with the cloth she'd had slung over one shoulder. "Not unless you're going to pass up what's here in order to cook your own."

"No way. Brooks and Karl would have it all consumed before I was half done cooking."

"Don't count out the pregnant woman," Ann-Elise said with a grin. "Twins means I'm eating for three."

But it seemed like she and Ellyn did more talking than eating, while the men devoted themselves to their plates.

When they were all sitting back and sipping from coffee mugs, Grif said, "So I told you Harmon had called Brooks—"

"Actually, Ann-Elise," Harmon's father said.

Karl thought he caught sadness in the even tone.

"—and he told me about your flights from Bariavak, Karl. What I didn't mention was that he and Ann-Elise were visiting with us."

"My last soiree before the babies come."

"Harmon told me about the twins. Congratulations." He looked at her husband. "Both of you."

"Harmon told you," Brooks repeated.

"Of course she did," Ann-Elise said. "You've got this strange idea she goes through the world pretending you don't exist. She doesn't."

"Seemed like she spent most of her teens doing just that."

"Nonsense. She spent those years rebelling against you. You don't rebel against what doesn't exist. So, how is she, Karl?"

He swallowed a sip of coffee faster than he should have. "Fine."

"Interesting that she's spent so much time in Bariavak," Ann-Elise said, her eyes on him.

"King Jozef had a job for her."

"Uh-huh. I hear you two were involved. Romantically."

From the corner of his eye he saw both Brooks and Grif give faintly apologetic shrugs. But he stayed focused on Ann-Elise. It always paid to keep an eye on your most dangerous opponent.

"When we were kids. Long time ago." How many times had he said that lately? A million? Sure seemed like at least that many people knew his business.

Ann-Elise tipped her head back to regard him from half-closed lids. "Doesn't sound to me like what's been going on in Bariavak has been for old-times' sake."

"Harmon—?" He bit it off. Too late.

She gave a slow, satisfied smile. "Harmon's working as hard as you are at pretending nothing's going on."

He willed his face blank.

Her smile remained.

Grif groaned. "Give it up, Karl. You're not even fooling me. Sometimes when you fall that hard, that deep when you're young you never get over it." He looked at his wife. Ellyn smiled at him and put her hand out. Grif took it in his. "No use fighting it. You're going to lose the fight. And if you're as fortunate as I've been, losing that fight will be the best thing you ever do in your life."

Ann-Elise rested a hand on Karl's shoulder. "You should listen to Grif. After he told Brooks he was an idiot for not snapping me up sooner, I made him put it in our marriage vows that I could always have Grif on speed dial."

"Just trying to save my friends from being as stupid as I was," Grif said, grinning at his wife.

She smiled back. "Stupid and stubborn and slow and—"

"All right, all right."

CHAPTER TWENTY-SIX

Grif insisted on driving him to Cody, where he would pick up the truck he'd left at the airport.

They were taking his oldest, Meg, to give her highway driving experience. That suited Karl. It would prevent private conversation.

Brooks walked next to him to the truck. "You know Ann-Elise was kidding about having it put in our marriage vows that she could have Grif on speed dial."

He grinned slightly. "Figured."

"She wasn't kidding about anything else."

He'd figured that, too. "Yes, sir."

"I know Harmon was rough on you back when you, uh, first got together. That it was a bad breakup and it was all on her. I don't pretend to know what's happening between you two now. But if you have the chance to hurt her, to even the score, I'm asking you not to do it. For her sake, yeah, because I don't want to see her hurt. But for yours, too, Karl. It would make you a different kind of man from who you've always been."

Karl slowed up as he turned off the highway onto his land. He often did that when he returned from a trip to take a good, long look, picking up signs of what needed doing, what was running along fine.

Also because he wanted to savor that lift in his heart.

His land.

This time, though, all his attention zeroed in on a tableau in the vaguely circle-ish graveled area that connected the house, the barn, the equipment shed, the trailer where he'd lived before the house was rehabbed, and other outbuildings.

Deaver and Greg Peters, Jenny's son from her first marriage, along with the old horse Deaver rode most often and the ranch dog all stood lined up, as if barricading the way to the house's back door. The two humans had their arms crossed over their chests. The dog's body language said she would have done the same if she could have. The horse was nodding off.

The rest of them were staring at a blue car parked smack in the middle of the graveled area with the driver's door opened toward the trio. The car blocked his view of the occupant. But he had a feeling…

His foot came down hard on the accelerator. Only because he wanted to sort this out as soon as possible. He pulled in and was out of the truck before anybody moved.

And then all hell broke loose. Most of the hell came from the baying, howling, piercing throat of the dog who broke ranks with the humans to dash toward him. Deaver and Greg contributed, trying to shout over the dog.

Only Harmon Reed said nothing, though she wasn't quiet. She clamped her hands over her ears and laughed.

"What are you doing here?" he demanded of her.

"That's what I said," Deaver shouted in triumph. "Who is she and what's she doing here?"

"Well, she told us her name and said she was going to wait for you. But since we'd never heard of her…"

At least that's what Karl thought Greg said.

He shook his head, then held up a hand to the others as he bent to greet the dog, rubbing behind her ears in the way that turned her howls and bays to bliss. Still loud, but happy now.

"Enough," he ordered. He took his hands away. She eyed him, decided he meant it, quieted down, and sat on his boot, leaning up against his leg. "Good girl, Mercy."

"*That's* Mercy?" Harmon had her hands off her ears, but held up, as if in readiness to resume their protective duty.

"You know this woman, Karl?" Deaver accused. "She came high-tailing in here, nearly gave Rooster a heart attack."

The horse, contentedly munching in the grass at the base of the fence around the house's small yard, belied that diagnosis.

Deaver continued suspiciously, "Did you *invite* her here?"

"No."

Now it was her turn to cross her arms over her chest.

It had an entirely different effect than when Deaver and Greg did it.

"You said I should see your ranch," she disputed.

"Women on ranches." Deaver spit off to the side. "Just ain't right."

"You like Mom well enough," Greg said.

"That's different."

Karl wasn't interested in Deaver's explanation for why Jenny Peters Gates was the exception that reinforced his rule. But there'd been a certain distracted quality to Greg's objection that tugged at his attention.

He looked away from the fabric pulled snug against Harmon's breasts … and saw the kid was appreciating the same view. "Don't you two have something to do?"

Deaver snapped his mouth closed—he'd been in mid-sentence. Then opened it again. "You're refusing the hired help even a crust of bread to keep body and soul together and driving us back out to work until—"

"You're trying to tell me you haven't had lunch yet?"

"We just finished—late, 'cause we'd been working and working—when this one came high-tailing in like—"

"Like you already told me. Since you've had lunch, you can get on with whatever you planned to do the rest of today."

"Since you're back, you might have different instructions from what Deaver planned," suggested Greg.

Karl wasn't fooled. The kid wanted to extend the time he could be looking at Harmon.

"We'll talk about where things are after I've looked around. For now, back to whatever you'd planned."

Deaver started away, grumbling. Three strides off, he turned. "Are you coming, boy?"

"Uh, yeah. Pleasure to meet you, ma'am," he said with a smile and a tip of his hat.

She smiled back. "You, too." When the truck doors slammed, one-two, she added. "He's going to be a charmer."

"Why did you come here, Harmon?"

"I could say Mirche sent me." She tipped her head. "Or maybe King Jozef when he hired me for a job he refused to define."

"Harmon." He was in no mood for nonsense. Mirche or King Jozef his ass.

"First, I wanted to be sure you got here okay. You do look tired and since you can sleep any time or place that means the trip was even worse—"

"Phones work in Wyoming."

"Second, I wanted to be available for when the you-know-what hits the fan with what's happening in Bariavak."

"It's not going to any time soon, when it does it's going to happen in Bariavak, and, again, phones work in Wyoming."

"Third, us."

He waited, but she didn't say any more.

"What about it?" *It*, not *us*. A hell of a lot safer.

"I don't know."

He couldn't—he didn't—doubt the sincerity of that admission.

"You don't either," she added. "So I'm staying. Until … Well, I don't know that, either. I came for all three of those reasons. I'm staying for the last two. I guess until I do know. Or you do."

He put his hands on his hips, looked out to the horizon where the hills lifted rapidly toward mountains. "Light'll go and I want to see the place."

"Go ahead. I'll still be here."

He started to cut her a look, thought better of it and went back to the horizon. "There are only three bedrooms in the house and they're all taken."

He waited, but she didn't respond to his implicit statement that she wasn't sharing his.

He swore, but only inside his head. Aloud, the words were "You can stay in the trailer."

"Fine."

"It's not fancy."

"Fine."

"It's bachelor fare here."

"Fine."

"You'll have to carry your own bags. Do—"

"Only brought carryon."

"—your own laundry. And there's not much shopping."

"Fine."

"There is internet," he added grudgingly.

"I figured, since you're in touch with Bariavak so much."

"Right." He pulled in a breath. "I'm going out now. You're on your own."

"Fine."

He started off.

"Karl."

Reluctantly, he stopped and turned back to her.

She gestured at the animal who'd immediately taken advantage of his standing still to lean against his leg again. "How'd she get the name Mercy?"

"That was Deaver. First time she went into her routine, he said, 'Lord have Mercy.' And that was that."

Her laughter followed him as he continued toward the ranch truck suited for the tour he and Mercy were about to take.

If only the heat it brought hadn't stuck around, too. It gummed up his mental gears like hot honey in a truck engine.

CHAPTER TWENTY-SEVEN

Even dusk had about given up when he returned from seeing as much of the ranch as he could.

Lights were on in the house, making the deep shadows on the porch darker than usual. But his truck's headlights swept across it, picking out a wrapped-up figure in the chair.

Only one person it could be.

So why did his damned heartbeat pick up?

He came up the steps, maybe making more noise than necessary. Only because he enjoyed the feel of these old work boots he'd found in the truck.

"Did the troops pass inspection, General?" Harmon asked out of the dark.

"Cows don't salute worth spit."

Her low chuckle was as bad as her laugh.

Then she turned serious. "Karl, why did you run back here to Wyoming? I mean, I know what happened between us wouldn't have budged you from Bariavak—far more likely to have me deported—if you thought staying was the right thing. Which I would have thought it would be so you'd be on the ground there, behind the scenes getting things moving. So why leave?"

"You told me to."

"I did not. I said—Oh. Really?"

"Yup."

"This is part of the plan?"

"Yup. What you're looking at here is the timeline accelerating."

"Explain."

"Andrej needs to solidify his position. Needs to draw together the smaller groups who don't know yet that they all want the same big thing because they're focusing on how their preferred methods differ."

"So, Prince Karl is the preferred method for some? And Andrej can't operate as well with you there casting him into a shadow. Okay, I see that. Too bad you can't just persuade King Jozef that Andrej is the option he wants."

He said nothing.

"Oh," she said slowly, "you think you *can* persuade him of that."

"Not me. I'm way over here on the other side of the world."

"Is that part of it? Hoping out of sight will make you out of mind with him? I don't know, Karl. The king doesn't show any sign of budging from viewing you as his top option."

"He'll have to," he said grimly. Then, more upbeat, he continued, "The plan for a transition from a monarchy to representative government is a good one."

"I don't doubt that, but—"

"You settled in the trailer?"

He could practically see her weighing whether to accept his change of subject.

"Yes, thank you," she said at last. "Deaver said you called him and told him to make sure I have what I need. I suspect he didn't want me thinking it was his idea."

"Probably. Did he give you any supper?"

"We made sandwiches."

"He made you make your own, didn't he?"

That damned chuckled again. "I figured I was better off making my own. Besides, Greg helped me find all the fixings."

Crush confirmed.

"What about you?" she asked. "You're going to get something to eat now?"

"Yeah."

That seemed to cover it. He had his hand on the doorknob when her voice came again.

"You only have one chair on your porch? Most people have at least two."

"Only need one. For me."

"That's not very sociable."

"You noticed that, huh?"

She laughed again.

This was not good.

Karl woke up sharply. All senses on alert. Adrenaline firing through him.

It was a dream. A memory.

It always started with Grif's voice saying, "Harmon Reed's in the middle of that coup attempt."

They all knew about it. Hell, they'd made black humor jokes about it being the worst kind of coup attempt because the two sides were evenly matched. No such thing as a quick, bloodless coup in those circumstances.

Evenly matched fights dragged on, while the casualty count rose.

Grif had taken him off base for this talk so he'd known something was up even before Grif's first words.

"No one's heard from her. There's reason to think—Brooks is worried. I trust his instincts. This as unofficial as it comes. A potential career-ender if—"

"I'm in."

Three of them had gone in. It had taken Grif to keep Brooks Reed from being a fourth. But Reed had been the voice in their ear. Calm, professional, desperate.

A civilian Grif knew had tracked her phone in ways that weren't supposed to be possible and definitely weren't legal.

Trouble was, it seemed she'd disabled it—they hoped to God that's why they'd lost the signal—so they couldn't pinpoint her now. Still, the history got them not only the name of the native woman she'd been visiting, a friend of hers from college now working as a journalist, but also three locations they'd been staying.

They had five hours and forty-two minutes to find her and get back to the meet coordinates.

The first two locations were busts.

The third was empty, but hadn't been for long. Supplies had been used up.

The women were either moving somewhere else—no idea where. Or resupplying and would return here—no idea when.

Grif said there was intelligence of clashes between the rebels and government forces.

Karl made the calculation to go to where the nearest clash was reported.

If Harmon and her friend were in another location, there wasn't time to find out where it was. They couldn't be of any help to them.

If Harmon and her friend were in the process of resupplying and returning to this location, waiting here to see if they showed up before the deadline wouldn't be of any help to them.

The most likely way they could help was to go to where the greatest likelihood of danger was.

"A shot in the dark," one of the others muttered.

But still a shot.

They had to stay in the shadows, paralleling the movement of the skirmishes.

He might have missed the scuffle in the alley amid all the other noise if he hadn't heard a man in pain cursing a woman and swearing she would pay for what she'd done.

Harmon.

He knew it.

His discreet gesture directed them all down the alley. The other two went to aid the smaller figure who was in even deeper trouble. He went to Harmon, not questioning how he knew it was her.

As he moved in, he could just make out her struggles. Her legs trying to get free of the enclosing fabric, try to get kicks in. Desperate.

He pulled the first guy off, more focused on speed than permanency. The second one, he dealt with.

His comrades had the other woman's attackers cleared and were helping her.

Harmon came up, gasping, gulping in air, fighting to get clear of the enveloping covering.

"Quiet." He said, low, "Keep it on, Harmon."

She didn't go still or take a second to absorb.

Her head whipped around to him. From under the fabric, he heard, so soft, "Karl."

A statement. Not a question.

He adjusted the headpiece so she could see out. He caught a faint gleam of her eyes.

"What are you doing here?"

"Same to you, but that discussion'll keep for later," he'd said.

There were three bodies in the alley. Four figures heading toward the street. If they reached their friends, brought back reinforcements, told their story…

He jerked his head for the others to start after them. He gave Harmon the necessary instructions. Told her father they'd bring her home, then joined the others.

One was caught inside the alley. Another two were dispatched by the government forces, who were pushing past the alley.

The final one became difficult. He'd gotten out of the alley ahead of them and ahead of the government forces. He might have disappeared forever, except for two things. He was bleeding and he was using a broom as a crutch.

Still, they had to circle wide to avoid being taken for rebels by the government troops.

One of his comrades got to him first.

The return trip required equal caution.

They returned to the alley with just enough time to reach the coordinates.

Harmon was gone. The other woman was gone.

His comrades looked for them in other cubbyholes in the alley.

Karl stood without moving, knowing she wasn't there.

He remembered telling Lt. Col. Reed that she had left the location.

Remembered the silence.

Remembered saying he'd stay on the ground, keep looking, be prepared when they located her again. The other two shaking their heads in clear "Bad Idea" mode.

Remembered Reed saying, "Permission denied."

Remembered saying he was staying anyway.

Remembered Grif coming on. "Stick with the plan. That's a direct order, Wethers."

"Not official. Can't order me, sir."

"The hell I can't. If I have to have you shot in the foot and dragged to the meet I will."

Though no shot was fired, the rest blurred, in memory and in dreams.

Until Karl stood in front of Harmon's father and said, "I failed, sir. I'm sorry."

That moment never blurred.

CHAPTER TWENTY-EIGHT

The solution to Harmon must have been sitting at the edge of his brain just waiting for him to wake up enough to recognize it.

Well, solution might be too strong. Perhaps a way to neutralize some of her impact.

Waking up wasn't as easy as usual. Jet lag was gone, so he couldn't put the blame there. More likely the thoughts of Harmon that had dogged him into the house, through dinner—while listening to Harmon charm Greg out on the porch—as he unpacked and showered, and then into his bed.

His discipline to fall asleep when and where he could tangled with those thoughts far longer than he was used to. At last he defeated them and fell asleep.

They had their revenge in his dreams.

Deaver grunted at him as he came into the kitchen. Karl couldn't remember the last time he hadn't beaten Deaver to the coffee pot. In a reversal of roles, he accepted the mug poured for him and sat at the table, spooning cooling eggs onto a plate.

"You look like hell," the older man said.

He didn't bother to answer. The eggs helped some. The coffee more. On his second cup, the mists parted enough to let him see the solution.

That didn't please Deaver, either.

"What're you looking so happy for? I coulda sworn you weren't happy to see that gal. Not anymore'n me and Greg and Mercy were."

Deaver better re-count, because Greg's allegiance had slid sharply toward Harmon.

"I've got a notion to invite a couple of people I saw recently to come for a visit."

"*What?* More visitors? Did you go off your rocker for good being over in that foreign place with the weird name? I swear, ever since you took up with those—A couple? Whaddya mean a couple? Like two men?"

"A man and a woman."

Deaver slapped his palm on the table. "I knew it. I just knew. And—"

"The woman's pregnant. With twins."

"Pregnant! There is nothing crazier on this earth than a woman who's pregnant. You have gone completely off your rocker. I'm telling you this, Karl Wethers, I've known you boy and man, but if you're going to go around inviting females until they're three-deep all over the place, I'm going back to the Double Bar X."

"Where Jenny and Debbie and even Tracy will spoil you the way you like, you mean?"

"Sam's there. Tucker's back, too, now he's done gallivanting around Europe after you," Deaver grumbled.

"Up to you if you want to go," he said. "If you stay you'll have to bunk in with Greg."

That drew another spate of grumbling.

But he knew Deaver was too curious to take off now.

He wanted to see what happened next.

So did Karl.

If she thought she would needle him, she was about to discover that the needles used around a ranch weren't those flimsy little things you got stuck with in a doctor's office. They were substantial weapons with points sharp enough and long enough to get through tough hides. Like hers.

Harmon slept better than she'd expected.

She'd been unsettled—no, not unsettled, considering the places she'd been that would be ridiculous. Just *aware*. Yeah, aware of the vastness above her.

They weren't kidding about Big Sky country. Okay she knew that was Montana, but they were only twenty miles or so from the border, and it fit.

She was still on Bariavak time, so she should have fallen into the bed—surprisingly, a double rather than the single she'd expected—and been asleep the minute Karl left for his homecoming tour. Or certainly after Deaver dropped a set of linens on a counter, then Greg showed her the charms—loosely speaking—of the trailer.

Instead, that awareness had driven her back to the main house. She'd sat in that chair, wrapped in a blanket she'd snagged from the trailer.

After Karl went in Greg had come out for a while, then she said she needed to get to bed.

She fell immediately and deeply asleep.

Waking only when she heard a truck pass the trailer and opened her eyes to bright daylight.

The shower stall made it impossible to shave her legs without sticking first one then the other out, propping her foot on the toilet seat. The water pressure wasn't anything to write home about. The mirror was permanently fogged.

Yet she was in a remarkably good mood when she reached the unoccupied kitchen and found a note that said, "Help yourself to food." She did.

She sat on the porch with her laptop and ordered a few necessities online to supplement what she'd brought, with an emphasis on jeans and t-shirts. Checked in with Sally. Made three other business calls and wrote a half-dozen emails.

All the while she was aware of the mountains over the top of her screen, tempting her to stare at them instead of it. She resisted.

She thought one or more of the guys would be back for lunch, but as the clock neared two she made a sandwich and ate a peach.

She called Sally again.

"Nothing new. Why're you calling again?"

"Just checking in."

"Uh-huh."

"And … I feel kind of weird."

"What kind of weird?"

"Like nothing's happening."

"That's called relaxing, boss. Some people do it sometimes."

"Ha-ha-ha. Very funny."

"I wasn't being funny. You run full-out all the time. You've got that candle blazing from both ends *and* the middle. There's going to be nothing left of you pretty soon."

Harmon got off the phone quickly then.

She decided to take a walk.

A brown horse with plenty of gray on his face ambled over to the fence that divided his corral and the road she was following. When he realized she was going to keep going, he twitched his tail and resumed grazing.

"Sorry, no treats here, buddy. Maybe next time."

The roadway made for tough footing in her light flats—she'd need boots if she took this walk again.

Finally, she quit resisting and stared at the mountains hogging the horizon.

The mountains were as jagged as those in Bariavak. But the effect was entirely different because the space before and above them—that sky again, now bright blue with white streamers of clouds—made it seem as if they had more elbow room to do their thing.

She'd seen them, of course, when she landed and as she drove, but they'd mostly provided the western arrow on the compass as she'd focused on getting here. Last night, sitting on the porch, they'd been the dark ballast for the sunset's pyrotechnics. Until they became the looming, dense silhouette cutting up into the star-spangled fabric of sky.

But now she could make out individual mountains, groupings, ranges. How the tree line meandered in a duet with the snowline.

She never walked far without stopping to look at them, because their expression changed, practically with each step she took.

She was leaning against a wood fence, contemplating cloud patterns as the wind skittered or plodded or swept them across the faces of the mountains and deep into the wrinkles between them.

A pickup crested the closest hill, a full-grown hill that had made her decide it was a good time for a rest before she tackled it.

The pickup stopped.

Karl.

She was sure before she had any reason to be. She was also right.

He braked and climbed out, pausing to look along the road before jumping the ditch she'd laboriously climbed down, then up to reach the fence.

"You okay?" he asked.

"Fine."

"Fine?"

"Good."

"I read somewhere that the shorter a response you get from a woman the more trouble you're in."

"Where? Cosmo?"

He shook his head. "I only get Cosmo for the pictures."

She tried not to, she truly tried … She laughed. Damn him.

He gave her an odd look. And he spoke faster than usual when he asked, "What are you doing here?"

"Looking at the views. Thinking." She had no idea why she'd volunteered that part.

"About?"

She opened her mouth to say cloud patterns. What came out was, "Rabiah."

They both went still.

It had to be something in the air. The clean, clear air with so much space for it to occupy. It was like it stripped the brakes on her tongue.

He broke the silence. "That was the woman you were with when…"

"Yeah."

"And the friend who needed your help. The reason you started being a fixer's fixer."

Surprised, she looked at him. He was gazing straight out to the mountains.

"Yeah. She was."

She waited for him to ask why, what happened, how the pieces fit together.

He said nothing.

"We'd met in college," she heard herself saying. "Maybe we gravitated toward each other because we were both outsiders. The Army brat who'd been all over but belonged nowhere. The brilliant woman from a culture where too few people value that combination. She worked in D.C. a few years. I was there, too. Working in communications, helping organizations get their stories across. I was pretty good at it. She was brilliant. But the tug of her family, of *home*…"

"She went back."

"She went back," she confirmed. "But she couldn't forget who she was and what she did when she was here. She'd just become a fixer when the coup attempt…"

Memories from that night rose like fog between them.

She answered what she knew he was thinking. "I didn't mean to make a liar of you to my father, Karl. Rabiah—"

"We'd have taken her, too."

"I know that. She knew, too. I'd told her about … She knew. But if you took her out of her country that way, she couldn't be a fixer because she wouldn't have access, being associated with Americans. So, she wouldn't do it. And I couldn't leave her to try to get to the safe house on her own."

She looked back to the mountains.

"After the coup failed," she continued, "Rabiah started working with this big-time correspondent. She made him look so good, so much better than he was."

"You didn't like him."

"He was full of himself and a blowhard. She told me she loved him. That damned British accent. I told her that if she wrote down what he said and read it, she'd fall out of love with him in a heartbeat. She didn't think it was funny. She said I was pushing her away, that she'd wanted me to be happy for her. I couldn't. That was that."

"What happened?"

A nice, vague question she could answer the way she wanted.

What came out was the ragged truth.

"He used her up. Professionally and personally. He got big-deal status and a boatload of money. She got pregnant and disgraced. He left—her, the country—and never looked back. He's such a self-absorbed ass that he's used my company and he hasn't even made the connection of my name and Rabiah's friend."

"He's used your compa—?" He broke that off with a nod. "Ah. You charge him double."

Grimly, she said, "I charge his network double. *Him* I charge quadruple. And the only fixers I'll give him are men who have daughters, and I tell them the whole story first. The extra money goes to Rabiah's little sister, who's at university in England."

He frowned. "What about your friend?"

Not so vague. Yet she could still sidestep. She could avoid...

"She drowned herself two months after he left."

He put his hand over hers where it rested on the top fence rail.

That's all.

No dramatic gesture. No words trying to convey how thoroughly he understood her feelings about something she still didn't understand herself. Just his large, working hand over hers.

She squeezed her eyes closed. Made herself breathe steadily.

"I cut her off when she most needed someone. If she'd still felt she could confide in me—"

"He's the bad guy, Harmon. Not you. Don't get your roles mixed up."

Her heart did something strange in her chest ... Count on Karl to set things straight.

"Early on, I wanted to kill him. I wanted to kill her parents. I wanted to kill that whole society." She'd never said these things aloud before. "I thought about it. Seriously thought about each of those. Had ideas of how … I had to pull myself back. To stop thinking about my anger."

"How'd you do that?"

Something about his tone reminded her that he'd seen war. He'd seen friends killed. He seemed—he *was*—so sane, so steady, but that didn't mean he didn't hurt.

She turned her hand, so they were palm to palm.

"I thought about what she would want."

He dropped his head in a single nod. "That works."

"It did. Eventually."

"What would she want?"

"What she would want most of all would be that it never happened again. Not to another fixer. Not to another woman. Not—" She had to pull in another breath. "—to her little sister."

"The one at university."

"Yeah."

"You're paying for her education, aren't you?" He didn't even wait for her confirmation. "But she doesn't know it. She doesn't know *you.* You don't think she'd want to know about her sister from you? Yet you've kept your distance and—"

His phone rang.

She jolted back, away from the fence, away from the moment, away from confidences, away from him. He extended a hand toward her, but she gestured him to stop, to answer his phone.

He did both.

"Hello…. Yeah … Okay. That's good … No, not yet … Uh-huh … See you soon."

She stood limply, staring unthinkingly at the faint path her trip across the ditch had left.

He disconnected. "You ready?"

"For what?" she asked without looking up.

"Thought you'd want a ride back to the house. Unless you're not done walking."

She looked at the hill she'd wondered about. She could keep going, see what was over it, while he drove back to the house. The two of them heading in opposite directions.

"Yeah, thanks. A ride would be good."

CHAPTER TWENTY-NINE

There was a car with Wyoming plates in the central, graveled area.

Karl showed no surprise or curiosity. Could be a neighbor of course, but she'd have expected a pickup. Or a friend of a different kind. Because there was no guarantee Mercy was the only female in his life … except for the way he'd made love to her in Bariavak.

As they pulled in, several people came out of the house onto the porch. Deaver and Greg. Then—

"No."

She hadn't realized she'd said it aloud until he said, "Yup."

Slowly, she turned her head to look at him.

He leaned forward, resting his arms on top of the steering wheel. "Aren't you going to get out and say hello to your daddy and step-momma? They're going to stay here a while."

She'd been surer of herself meeting King Jozef and all his top ministers than she was saying hello to her father and his wife. Especially her father.

Ann-Elise rolled past any stilted awkwardness by drawing her into a hug and saying how great it was to see her.

"Wasn't this a wonderful idea?" Ann-Elise said. "You could never come to South Carolina and I won't be able to travel much longer, but we were close—by Wyoming standards—and Brooks was able to extend our trip, so here we are."

"Uh, yeah, great," Harmon said. "But … There are only three bedrooms."

"Are there? How interesting."

Ann-Elise said that with enough emphasis that Karl quickly said, "Harmon's staying in the trailer."

"It'll be fine, ma'am. You'll have your own bedroom. Deaver will get the other bed in my room," Greg said.

Karl saw Harmon recognize that he could have made room for her in the house that way, but had chosen not to.

Then he became aware of Ann-Elise watching him.

When they made eye contact, she smiled. She looked … pleased. He had no idea why.

All she said was, "Anything to eat for the pregnant lady?"

Deaver might have groaned.

With the added buffer of her father and Ann-Elise, the next two days settled toward a do-able routine.

He worked. Harmon worked and apparently took long walks and accepted delivery of packages. They were part of a group at meals, card-playing one night and dominoes the other.

Ann-Elise stayed around the home ranch, drawing, including what she called a study of Deaver's head, which had it growing bigger by the minute. Brooks joined him and Greg out working. With Greg along there was no chance for private conversation, Thank God.

The third day was shaping up the same as they finished breakfast, except Deaver had been relieved from modeling duty.

Harmon had been on a business call and came in as the men were preparing to leave.

"Have a good day."

She walked past his chair, letting her hand trail ever so lightly across his shoulders. He felt it down to his toes, though it wasn't his toes he had to worry about. Quickly, he stood and went out the door as if he'd forgotten an appointment.

He'd forgotten something all right, but it was his good sense.

Only when he went to pull the truck door closed did he realize

Mercy hadn't followed him.

Ann-Elise sat in the solitary porch chair, sketching, as usual, while Harmon occupied the top step with her back against the railing, rubbing Mercy's ears.

"I was thinking about you overnight while the twins made their presence felt."

"You can feel them kicking?"

"Not yet. I just hope when they start neither is as tough on their mom as you were on your dad."

"Yeah, boy, I was a badass." She pushed her hair back. "I broke some of his unending rules, big deal. I wasn't on drugs. I didn't drink myself into stupid. I wasn't in jail. Well, except for that one time, and if the cop had had a sense of humor…"

"I wonder what that cop would say about you?" After Harmon chuckled, Ann-Elise added, "I can only hope these two love me as much as you loved Francesca."

Harmon went serious. "I'm sure they will. And whatever else there is between my father and me, I have never questioned that he loved my mother."

"You both loved her, absolutely. You also both turned to her because she'd go along with you."

Harmon opened her mouth to dispute that hotly. Then a memory came. A moment. Her mom sitting on one side of the table that was just a little longer than it was wide, while she and her father sat at the ends. Her mom's arms reached out, to make contact with each of them, looking from one to the other. They both looked at her.

She'd always thought of her mother as the link. Had she also been a buffer? A buffer that prevented them from banging against each other, but might it also have kept them apart?

Harmon became aware Ann-Elise was watching her. She cleared her throat, searching for something innocuous. "I do wish she hadn't gone along with him on naming me."

"It could have been worse, Harmon. You could have been Ike."

She sputtered. "Nah, he's never been that big a fan. With these two, maybe he'll go for a matched set, like Colin and Powell."

"I should be so lucky."

"Or one of the newer—"

Ann-Elise shook her head. "He's strictly old school. I think he's angling for Norman and Schwartzkopf right now."

They laughed together.

After a moment, she added, "Look at Mercy tipping her head back and forth. It's like she's saying, 'What are you two cackling about?' "

Harmon was still chuckling when Ann-Elise said, "You know, that's quite the breakthrough."

"With your drawing?"

"With Mercy."

"What about Mercy?"

"She watched you touch Karl this morning."

"I didn't—"

"And she watched his reaction."

"—touch him any—"

"And then she followed you out here and sat by *your* side."

"—particular way."

She had. She knew she had. And she knew he hadn't responded at all.

Other than getting away as fast as possible.

Ann-Elise tipped her head, directing Harmon where to look.

Harmon looked down at the dog who was, indeed, sitting at her side. Mercy rolled her head back. Probably to see what the holdup was with the ear-rubbing. But it also had the effect of making eye contact. She looked into those melting caramel-brown eyes and could almost swear she saw understanding in them.

"She's accepted you as a fellow Karl-lover."

She should have disputed it. Should have said it was ridiculous. What she said was, "Good heavens."

"Of course she wouldn't accept you at all if Karl didn't have feelings for you."

She snorted. "His kind of feelings should make his dog bite me."

"His kind of feelings are more likely to lead him to bite you … in the best way possible."

"Ann-Elise, I know you pride yourself on reading situations, but you have this one wrong. He—"

"Didn't want you sleeping under the same roof with him."

"Exactly. See? He could have made room in the house for me the same way he did for you two, but instead, he sent me to the trailer. As far away as he could get me."

"As far away as he could get you while still keeping you on his ranch. What was to stop the man from telling you to get lost? And the reason he doesn't want you sleeping under the same roof with him is he's not at all sure he can withstand the temptation."

"That's…" Her hot denial lost steam fast. "I don't think…"

"Why did you stay in Bariavak?"

"King Jozef asked me to."

"Why did you come to Wyoming?"

"It's part of the job."

Ann-Elise flipped over another page on her sketch pad, giving a momentary glimpse of mountains beyond a porch railing. She immediately began on the next sheet.

"You keep telling yourself that, hon. You know what I find most interesting about your name?" she added.

Harmon blinked. "What?"

Ann-Elise said, "I asked if you know what I find most interesting about your name." She didn't wait for a reply. "You haven't changed it."

"Changed it?"

"Why not? Lots of people do. It's a hassle, but for someone as determined as you are that wouldn't stop you. If you wanted to change it. But you haven't."

CHAPTER THIRTY

Karl braked hard, carrying more speed than he should have and spewing gravel and dust.

Harmon was with Ann-Elise on the porch. He got out, but only to stand beside the open door. "C'mon, Harmon. We're going for a ride."

"Where? Why?"

"Will you quit asking questions and get in the truck?"

Harmon had stood, but she wasn't coming down the steps. Instead, she put her hands on her hips. "You think that's the way to get me to cooperate?"

"Oh, I can't wait to see if it is the way to get you to cooperate," Ann-Elise said.

He and Harmon united for an instant in glaring at her, then Harmon turned it back on him. "Just tell me what—"

"Harmon, Harmon, Harmon," Ann-Elise said with the thickest southern accent he'd heard from her. "Can't you see he's not going to spill the beans here, in front of me? If you want to know why he wants you to go for a ride, you're going to have to take the ride. Sort of a metaphor for love and live and—"

"Oh, for heavens sakes." Harmon clomped down the steps and got in the truck.

"You can thank me later, Karl," Ann-Elise called out as he got behind the wheel.

Would he thank her?

Hell if he knew. He wasn't even sure why he'd decided to talk to Harmon, except she was the only one around who knew the situation in Bariavak.

He could call Bariavak, but ... well, who knew how secure that was.

They had turned from the drive to the road when Harmon spoke.

"As much as I enjoy the scenery and scintillating conversation—"

"I got a call from Bariavak."

"Who?"

"Katie."

"Katie has you this wound up?"

No, she did. He wasn't saying that. "She said you asked her to find out something for her."

"I did? Oh, right. Staff members and freelancers for a magazine."

"She emailed it to you." She pulled out her phone. "What's that about?"

"I started to tell you a couple times. When I was looking at the records that pointed toward Madame giving birth to the king's son, I saw someone else had signed in for those records and—Yes. Got Katie's list and ... Here she is. Listed on the magazine staff as Associate Editor. Same last name as the editor—."

"His wife, Minister Virba's sister."

She swore. "If they're aligned with Vatche—."

"They're not anymore. Big blow up just before he left for Australia. Nobody knew why. This explains it. If Vatche wanted to go public, Virba and the others in that crowd never would. They're just this side of thinking the king's a god."

She huffed out in relief. "Crisis averted."

"Don't count your chickens yet. Katie said more. The king knows Andrej is his grandson."

"How?"

"Madame. He's told Katie and Brad, too."

"What's worrying you?"

He cut a look toward her, then back to the road. "He hasn't talked to Andrej yet. You'd think that would be one of the first things he'd do."

He'd been making excuses about why he was talking to her. He'd wanted to tell her, to hear her thinking. He'd wanted to see her. Be with her.

Damn it.

"Not necessarily. His best move could be—"

"Move? This isn't a game for you to play. Something for Harmon Reed to have fun with."

"I'm not pl—"

"These are people's lives. A lot of people's lives. Not just the ones you saw in the castle, the government, the leaders, but every person in Bariavak. Every one of those kids in the basketball camp and their parents and grandparents and sisters and brothers. And when it comes down to it, the lives of the children they'll eventually have, too."

A short silence met that speech.

"I know that, Karl. I don't consider it a game. Any of it." That was all she said.

The person she was when she said it, though, was the one who had told him how she had become a fixer's fixer. The one who had lost her friend. Who still mourned her, while devoting herself to making life better for any who followed.

I don't consider it a game. Any of it.

And that scared him even more.

Because if she didn't consider it a game there was more at stake.

Maybe too much.

And it had nothing to do with Bariavak.

They'd reached the spot along the fence where she'd told him about Rabiah's death.

He tromped on the gas to accelerate up the rise.

"That doesn't mean strategies can't help with what you and Andrej and others are trying—*Oh.*"

Now that he'd hit the crest, he braked to a stop, twisting toward her, preparing to slam her, argue with her, anything to gain some space.

She had her hands layered over her chest, her eyes glistened with tears, her lips parted.

"What?" he demanded.

It took a couple beats, then she said quietly, "It's … amazing."

He followed the direction of her gaze to … the view.

The road turned and ran along a ridgeline until it reached a point where going west didn't mean dropping off a cliff the way it did here. The thing was, that cliff-dropping opened a view of a downward sweep of grazing land, leading to a swoop of trees following the creek. Those set the scene for the main event. Layers of ascending mountains to the horizon of snow-topped peaks' jagged intersection with bright blue sky with lazy puffs of clouds.

"Yeah," he said.

"It's … it's home. Your home," she said rapidly.

"That's not exactly a headline, Harmon."

"Not to you."

"I wanted to know what was over this hill. I almost did it—walked over it myself. But you offered me the ride back to the house, then the Colonel and Ann-Elise were there and I'm so sorry I didn't meet your family, your father. And…"

Was there such a thing as verbal whiplash? He had no idea what she was talking about. He probably hadn't been this deep in the weeds when it came to her since before she dumped him twelve years ago. No, maybe even more deeply into the weeds, because he'd known something was up then.

What the hell was she talking about?

"And what?" He prodded, because maybe more words would help. They couldn't hurt.

Then his own thought hit him like a horse's kick in the gut.

He'd known something was up.

Before the note. He hadn't been caught completely off-guard, the way he'd told himself all this time.

He had known something was up.

Yet he hadn't asked her about it. Hadn't even asked himself about it.

He'd hidden from the truth she'd been telegraphing. He'd laid it all on her.

"And I would have missed coming over that hill with you and seeing this with you. Seeing your home."

He looked at her then. She was smiling, but her eyes were shiny with tears.

He asked, "Is this making sense to you?"

"Yes. A lot of sense. Maybe more sense than I've made in a long time."

"I'll take your word for it."

"Good. Thank you." She patted his arm.

That should have been harmless.

It wasn't.

He felt it like she'd electrified the hairs on his arms, sending sensation through them into his skin, where it met the sensation she'd already applied by touching his skin. Unified, the multiplied sensation sizzled through him.

"Gotta get going," he said gruffly.

"Sure."

That was the last thing she said for a hefty stretch. She seemed in deep thought when he glanced toward her. Two, maybe three times.

Maybe three times that.

Harmon's advice had been to tell King Jozef everything and begin their plans toward democracy for Bariavak immediately.

"But I know you won't," she'd said fatalistically.

"He's not ready."

"King Jozef—"

"Andrej. He's still working on getting the factions in line."

"He needs to work faster. I can feel the tempo accelerating. He—you—will be behind the eight ball if you don't get this going."

"I'll tell him you said so."

"Do," she said cordially, as if she hadn't recognized his sarcasm.

Harmon's odd mood continued through dinner and after, when they pulled out a decrepit box of Trivial Pursuit and played in teams of two—Brooks and Ann-Elise, Harmon and Greg, Deaver and him.

It wasn't a bad mood, because she joined in the spirit of the game, debating with Greg over answers, celebrating when they got one right, teasing the others that she knew the right answer to their questions.

"This isn't fair. All this stuff is before I was born," Greg groaned at one point.

"Sure it's fair," Deaver said. "It all evens out, because anybody old enough to have lived then doesn't have any memory left."

Harmon laughed as much as the rest. But it was as if a haze of distraction surrounded her.

The game broke up and everyone headed for bed.

Karl stayed in his chair an extra beat, then said, "Wait up, Harmon. I want to check that the corral water tank was shut off tight."

Deaver snorted his view on the possibility that the water tank hadn't been shut off properly. Karl was aware of looks from the others as he snagged his hat and followed her out, but Harmon, still in that haze, hardly seemed to notice until they were practically at the trailer steps and she stopped.

Abruptly, she spoke. "Karl, what do you know about Harmon?"

"Not a solitary th—."

"General Harmon," she clarified. "Not me."

" 'Old Gravel Voice.' That was his nickname."

"Great."

"Patton thought highly of him. So did his men. Especially his men. School of thought says he's the most underrated World War II general. His units were key in North Africa, Italy, and the Battle of the Bulge."

She gave him a look that he thought meant *That didn't help a bit.*

"Ah. Well. Guess I should read up on him," she said.

"Yeah, you should. Ask me why."

"Because my father named me after him and maybe it will help me understand him better."

He faced her. "Quit answering yourself and ask *me* why, Harmon."

She turned toward him, too. "Why, Karl?"

"Because he put the welfare of his men—and the war effort—before his advancement. Because he took on tough decisions without flinching. I can see a father wanting his child to grow into that kind of name."

She stared off over his shoulder for what felt like a long time. Finally, she put her hand on her forehead and pushed her hair back.

"I'm sorry, Karl."

He knew his hat blocked her view of much of his face yet she seemed to read his question, though he doubted she knew that part of his question was where that gentleness had come from.

"I treated you badly. You didn't deserve that. And being young was no excuse. I knew what I was doing. I deliberately tried to make you fall in love with me."

He took the hat off, combed his fingers through his hair, and settled the hat back in place. Perhaps the brim was a touch lower.

"And succeeded."

She released a breath that sounded like a sigh. "I was cruel."

"Cruel's a mighty strong word. Whatever it was that you were it wasn't that way until the end."

She looked away from him. "I'm sorry."

"What have you done with the real Harmon Reed?"

"Funny. You could say 'Apology accepted.' "

"Apology accepted."

"Thank you." She seemed to shake off some of her solemn mood. "All of this is worthwhile since it's brought us back on good terms."

"I wouldn't go that far," he said dryly.

"Hey."

He grinned at her. He watched her gaze go to his mouth.

She grinned back. He looked at her mouth.

And then they were kissing.

CHAPTER THIRTY-ONE

Karl had learned a lot.

She'd thought so in Bariavak, though it could have been a result of the fierceness.

There was fierceness now, too, but somewhat mellowed, as they stumbled up the stairs to the trailer together, banged into the countertop, ricocheted back into each other, then fell onto the bed.

They removed clothing without sacrificing buttons or fabric. Though where things landed was anyone's guess.

And then the fierceness flared again.

Until she was so far past ready that she groaned, "Now, Karl. Now."

He was there. Right there. But he didn't move into her.

"You're not running again."

"Run? I'm not running anywhere."

"You ran away—"

"You're the one who left Bariavak."

"You ran away from me. Because you were scared of how you felt. Of loving me. Not going to deny that?"

She shifted down the bed abruptly, opening herself to him. He bowed his back, holding off from her but at the same time putting his mouth over her nipple and drawing on it.

Control was one thing. But this was too much of a good thing.

Hands on him, she tried to draw him in to her.

"You loved me. Kids that we were, you loved me, dammit. But you kicked me to the curb—"

"I didn't kick—"

"—because you were afraid of loving me."

"That's—I didn't—"

"Pushing me away."

"I'm not pushing you now. I want you. Now." She moved against him. "Karl … please."

He paused, she felt the fight in him. Then he let her pull him inside.

She stretched, rolled over, reached for him. He wasn't in the bed.

But he wasn't gone. Not this time. Because he was home.

Harmon opened her eyes, already knowing he was sitting on the bench that doubled as a night stand. He was fully dressed, his hat hooked on his knee.

"Good morning," she said with a smile. It had certainly been a good night.

"We're not doing that anymore."

She sat up, drawing the sheet with her, flimsy protection against his tone and words. "Why not?"

"Because it's not good enough. Just sex."

It wasn't just sex.

The cry came from deep inside, but she didn't let it out.

"I want marriage, kids, a future until we're a hundred years old. Just like we talked about that summer."

"You talked about."

He looked down, unhooked his hat and put it on with deliberation. "Right. I talked about. That's what I want, Harmon. I'm making it clear. Those are the only terms I can give you for going on. So if you can't, just say it. But this time, do it to my face. None of that protecting me from your worst instincts crap. Don't be a coward and—"

"I am not a coward."

"The hell you're not. You've pushed your dad away ever since your mom died, just in case something happened to him—"

"Like that was a long shot, with the Army being his life," she snapped reflexively.

"—not risking loving him, thinking that way it wouldn't hurt to lose him. Pushing me away that summer. And even your friend Rabiah. And now you pay for her sister's education, but you have nothing to do with her. Not risking getting close. Might as well write her a note telling her to be realistic, too. Admit it. You were scared. You *are* scared."

Words tumbled out before she could stop them. "I couldn't risk losing you, having you die the way—" She sucked in air, defeating a sob. "I couldn't ... I still can't."

He stood. "You're stronger than you think, Harmon. But if you're not willing to test it, you'll never prove it to yourself."

Harmon saw Ann-Elise in her usual spot in the porch chair and started toward her.

Then she saw her father sitting on the top step, leaning back against the post and Ann-Elise's knees.

She stopped.

She stayed there a moment, then started forward again with deliberation.

After good-mornings, she sat on the top step. She cleared her throat. "Tell me about General Harmon."

"Your grandfather fought under him during World War II," her father said. "Admired him greatly. Made it through the Bulge with him. They stopped the furthest penetration by the Germans. Turned the tide."

She faced him. "I didn't know that."

He told her more, filling in the details of those tough decisions Karl had mentioned.

When he'd finished, Harmon gave a slow, deep nod. "I'll try not to dishonor the name."

"You never have."

Her eyes stung fast and sharp. "The things I did when I was a kid—"

"You were a kid," he said.

"Someone said—Karl said I gave you a hard time."

"You did."

"Turned a cold shoulder to you, treated you like you were a sadistic dictator."

"Mostly when you didn't get your way." The corners of his eyes crinkled, though the rest of his face remained solemn.

"And that I hurt you every chance I got."

He was silent a moment. "I guess kids that age lash out a lot. Pulling back from their parents and starting to be more of a separate person."

"Ann-Elise, was that you?" she asked without turning around.

"That was me," she said.

"She tells me I have that to look forward to two more times." He smiled. Then it faded. "On top of that, though, you were grieving your mom."

"So I did hurt you."

"You're my daughter, Harmon. I love you. I can take hurt."

"I'm sorry." She stood. "I am sorry."

"Harmon, wait a minute. There's something you should know. About Karl."

She sat.

His eyes narrowed. For the first time she realized it was concentration, not condemnation.

"What?"

"When you were caught in that coup attempt—"

"You sent him after me," she interrupted. "I know."

He made a short, level slice with one hand, both dismissing and silencing that. Telling her it had been a secret mission or way, way off the books.

"He wanted to stay. Find you the second time. Bring you home. Even though it would have meant going AWOL. Took tough talk from Grif and a sucker-punch from one of the other guys to get him out of there."

"Because he'd promised you."

He eyed her a moment. "Ever wondered why he didn't make a career of the Army? He could have, you know. Would have done damned well."

She didn't know why he was changing the subject, but she knew the answer to this one. "Because he missed Wyoming, the ranch. Because they're home to him."

"I'm sure that's part of it."

"He *told* me that's why."

"As I said, I'm sure that's part of it."

"So what do you think another part of it is?"

"Ten days later, when word came that you were safe, I went to each of those men who'd gone in. Grif came along. Told them you were out, Rabiah was with her family. Karl last. Told him he'd done everything right, that nobody could have asked more.

"He looked up at me and said, 'You could have, sir. You could have asked me to keep my word by bringing her home safe.' And then—"

"I know he blames—"

"Wait, Harmon." He dropped the hand he'd raised to silence her. "I sat beside him and said I was grateful for what he did and for what he'd wanted to do. He said he should have stayed. Just flat like that. No question he meant it.

"Grif told him that's why he hadn't let me go. Because I would have put you above the mission. Grif said that's why the Army operated the way it does, why it had to operate that way. And that he'd understand that, even appreciate it as he rose through the ranks.

"Karl said he understood it and appreciated it, but he wasn't ever again going to let the Army stand between him and his doing everything in his power for someone he loved."

She stared at him. Trying to absorb, to understand.

To understand both these men.

And herself.

"Tell me about when Mom died."

She heard Ann-Elise suck in a breath. Her father frowned harder. "What?"

"Tell me about when Mom died. After she died. How you ... reacted. How I did."

"I, uh ... It was rough. At first, there were so many people, so much to do. Then with the transfer—"

"Transfer?" Ann-Elise demanded. "Are you telling me you transferred right after Francesca's death? You didn't tell them hell no, I won't go?"

Harmon's eyes met her father's for an instant in shared recognition that Ann-Elise hadn't yet fully grasped Army life.

"It wasn't so bad," Harmon said. "Gave us something to do. And being somewhere without so many reminders of Mom."

"I bet the two of you were just fine with it because it let you ignore all your feelings." Ann-Elise huffed. "I can see it now. You go through all the motions, move somewhere else, start your lives there, all while you're still numb with grief. And then, as the numbness finally wears off you look around at each other and—say the first thing that comes into your mind—what was your reaction, Harmon?"

"I think I—"

"No thinking. Just answer. You looked at your father across the dinner table and thought—"

"I don't know him." Her eyes widened as she looked at her father and added more slowly, "He doesn't know me. He's a stranger."

"Good. Now, Brooks. First thing—"

"I have to protect her. From the world. Prepare her for the world. Everything. All up to me."

Ann-Elise stroked the back of her husband's head.

There was such sweet soothing in the gesture. Harmon could practically feel Ann-Elise's empathy for the struggling single father he'd been.

Harmon felt that twinge again, that love-jealousy twinge, but it felt different this time. Almost ... like it included a new recognition.

She suddenly remembered watching Karl in the receiving line at the reception—and opting not to participate at the gala. She knew he hated it. She didn't want to add to the time he needed to fulfill that duty, even by one person. Because she didn't want him suffer. Because her father wasn't the only one to feel protective.

Because she loved Karl Wethers.

No. No, that was crazy.

To think she loved someone just because she couldn't stand to watch him suffer.

To think she loved someone because seeing him where he so clearly belonged brought her to tears.

To think she loved someone because she would do whatever she had to so he could remain here, where he belonged.

Ann-Elise's voice brought her back to now. "So there's Harmon thinking you're a stranger, that you don't know her and she doesn't know you, and what's the first thing you did, Brooks?"

"I don't know. Tried to talk to her—"

"Gave orders," Harmon said. "A whole list of shalls and shall nots."

"I ... I remember that," he said slowly. "I had to make myself be firm, to discipline you. It was the hardest thing I've ever done. All I wanted was to wrap my arms around you, give you everything you wanted or thought you wanted, to smooth every bump in the road for you with my bare hands. The one shred of reason I held on to after your mother died was to not spoil you. To raise you to be strong. That was the way I could best protect you, to give you the strength you'd need out in the world. But first I had to protect you from my worst instincts. Because—What?"

Harmon swallowed to get her voice started. "Protect me from your worst instincts. Did you say that to me when I was a kid?"

He frowned. Clearly lost over why this could matter, but trying to find the answer.

"I might have. I thought it often enough."

She pressed the heels of her hands to her forehead. "I hate it when he's right." She hiccupped between a laugh and a cry. "I have to talk to him. Right away. First."

"Excuse me?"

She stood. "Karl. Being right. Right about me, about him, about … everything. I am like you, Dad."

Her father got that granite look.

Oh, God. Of course, of course, of course. This was what Karl meant about her frozen look. She'd known what it felt like on the inside—the surprise and the determination not to show it. But she'd never imagined that's what it looked like from the outside. She'd never realized that granite look of her father's could be from what she felt when—

"What's wrong?" she demanded of Ann-Elise, who had tears dripping over her perfect cheekbones and down to the increased bustline of her dress.

"Bad."

At least that's what Harmon thought she said. Hard to tell from her thickened voice.

After getting a look at his wife's teary face, her father started up, but Ann-Elise gestured him to sit.

"Of course you think it's bad that I want to talk to Karl first, because you always put the Colonel first, but—"

"Not *bad. Dad.*" Despite the tears those words came through clearly. A great voice for commanding twins. "You called your father Dad."

She looked from Ann-Elise to her father and back. "I guess I did. But—"

"You never do. You never call him *dad*. It's the first time I've ever heard you call him that."

"Is it?" She did the one-to-the-other look again, but this time snagged on her father. His eyes were shiny.

"It—" He cleared his throat. "—is."

"Oh."

"Oh, for heaven's sakes, stand up, Harmon." Ann-Elise started to stand. Her husband leapt to his feet to help. With surprising grace, she evaded his hold, got behind him and pushed. "The two of you are hopeless. Hug each other. Now."

Harmon would never know if her father's arms flew wide because he wanted to hug her, because he was obeying his wife's commander-of-twins tone, or because he was trying to regain balance after that shove. But whatever sent his arms wide, Brooks Reed was the force that closed them around her, drawing her tight. Harmon hugged him back.

She felt him kiss her head and knew her eyes had gone shiny, too.

"We'll do better from here on out," he said.

"We will." She backed up enough to kiss him on the cheek.

Ann-Elise released a gusty sigh. "Finally. *Finally*."

Her father still had one arm around her shoulders, but loosed the other one to encircle his wife. For an instant the three of them stood there together, a trio of shiny-eyed, grinning idiots. It felt great.

But only for an instant.

"Karl," she said.

"Yes, go find Karl," Ann-Elise agreed. "I don't want either of you to get the bends from too much sudden immersion in truth and emotion."

Harmon made a face at her, then took off, but not before she caught a glimpse of her father pulling his wife into his arms.

CHAPTER THIRTY-TWO

Mercy loped over to her as soon as she left the steps. Oh, good, that probably meant Karl was somewhere around the home ranch.

"Where is he, Mercy?" she asked the dog.

The dog trotted to an empty space in the graveled circle and gave an indignant yip-howl.

Karl had taken the truck somewhere and hadn't taken Mercy. Where…?

Oh. Right. He'd said yesterday that he was going to spray weeds today and didn't want the dog exposed to the chemicals. She went to the battered ranch truck and got in. Mercy started to follow. Harmon had to hold her off. "Sorry, girl. The boss man said you couldn't come."

As Harmon pulled away, the dog expressed her betrayal and outrage in no uncertain terms. Between that and the noise of the truck engine, she almost missed her phone ringing. Even when she heard it, she intended to ignore it.

Until she recognized the ringtone.

Daylight still lasted long enough this time of year to let a man work himself into a sorry state.

Despite the chemicals he had the feeling he'd had a worse day than the weeds.

He was hungry. He was hot. He was dirty. He was frustrated. He was tired. He was heart sore. And his dog not only didn't greet him with her usual joy, she didn't bother to raise her head from where she was lying across the top step of the trailer.

Okay. Yeah. He got it. Even his dog had transferred allegiance to Harmon.

And then there was the major piece of his misery. He hadn't managed to work himself hard or long enough to get out of the state of wanting Harmon Reed.

Wanting her in his bed. Wanting her in his life.

Maybe a few more decades.

Ann-Elise was in the porch chair, Brooks sitting on the step, with one arm over her knees. Very cozy, very happy.

That didn't improve his mood any.

He nodded, grunted a greeting, and prepared to pass them.

"Where's Harmon?" Ann-Elise's question had something in it that raised his head.

"Don't know."

"She didn't find you?"

"No."

"Oh." That seemed to relieve some worry the woman had. Her frown smoothed, then a new one formed. "But then where is she?"

"I have no idea." He took another step toward the door.

"No, Karl," she said. "Really. Where is she? She left right after lunch to find you. We haven't seen her since. We've been out here— what? A couple hours?"

"Two hours and twenty-four minutes," Brooks said.

"Come to think of it, Mercy was at the door to the trailer when we came out and hasn't budged since."

Karl swept a look around the familiar area. "Her rental car's gone."

Those are the only terms I can give you for going on.

He'd known she was scared. He'd understood this morning what he hadn't understood a dozen years ago. But he'd pushed anyway.

"She left here to look for you. You say she never found you. Something's off about this." Ann-Elise stood. "I'm going to go look in the trailer."

Ann-Elise and Brooks headed for the trailer.

He should go in, take a shower, get something to eat.

If Harmon had gone—over the next hill or for good—he couldn't take back what he'd said, because he couldn't change what he wanted from her. What he needed. What he knew *she* needed, damn it.

He followed them to the trailer.

He reached the open door in time to hear Ann-Elise say, "It's addressed to Karl. We're not going to read it unless he says we can. Ah, Karl, good. Harmon left you a note."

He stopped.

Ann-Elise held the note out to him.

So if you can't, just say it. But this time, do it to my face.

Last time Harmon used an envelope. This time it was just a folded piece of paper with his name on the outside.

Ann-Elise waggled the paper.

He took it.

Karl, I had to go to London to deal with a situation for work. I will be back. Harmon. P.S. I will be back.

"Will" in the P.S. was underlined three times.

Without comment, Karl handed the note back to Ann-Elise. She and Brooks read it together.

"This isn't right. May I have your phone?" Ann-Elise held her hand out to her husband. He supplied it. After a moment she said, "Voicemail" to them. Then into the mouthpiece, "Harmon, it's Ann-Elise. Call us as soon as you get this, please. No matter what time it is."

The only thing to do now was wait to hear back from her.

He showered, ate, and went to bed. Ann-Elise's uneasiness must have infected him, though, because he couldn't sleep. He sat up and checked the time.

He couldn't call them now. It wasn't yet dawn in Bariavak.

When he started calling, he woke Mirche first. He had heard no news that might have stirred Harmon.

With Andrej, he was more direct. "Is anything happening that being in London could affect?"

He was silent for a long time. "Nothing."

That should satisfy him. It all pointed to her being in London doing something for her work just as her note had said.

He pulled out his bag, started packing. He called another number.

Katie greeted him with enthusiasm. "How wonderful to hear your voice. We miss you. How are you? How are … things?"

"You mean Harmon?"

She chuckled. "Yes, of course that's what I mean. I'm so happy she went there. If you two would talk—"

"We talk."

"And be honest with each other."

"We have." Which might have sent her on the run, despite what her note said.

"Without digging your elbows into each other under the basket."

"Doing what?"

"You heard me. Playing the rough inside game. Staking out your territory and using your body to keep the other one out of it."

He had a flash of the night before last. "Definitely not that last part."

"That's great, great. So how *are* you and Harmon doing?"

"I don't know."

"That's an improvement. You have to take the leap, Karl. But being with the right person is worth any risk—"

"Why should I risk it? She got me to fall for her before. She didn't care." He was still packing.

"How can you think that, Karl? She remembered word for word what she'd written years ago. Is that someone who doesn't care? She was running away from—"

"Seems to be a habit of hers."

"From caring too much about you," she said over his interruption. "If you'd just be honest with her about how you feel and ask how she feels—"

He had. Sort of.

"Maybe I would if I knew where she was. Do you know, Katie?"

"What do you mean? She's there in Wyoming with you, isn't she?" There was something in her voice. Katie Spencer was one lousy liar.

"No, she's not. She left a note saying she had to go to London."

Katie let the silence go a beat too long. "London? That must be something for her work."

"Uh-huh. That's what her note said, too."

"See? So it all makes sense—"

"I don't believe the note or you, Cousin Katie."

"I … I don't know why you'd say that."

"What's she up to, Katie?"

"I have no idea—Brad, no—"

A rustle, then her husband's voice came on the line. "Karl? It's Brad. Katie's promised somebody not to say anything. She won't even tell me. But she's worried." Katie's protests in the background died out.

"Worried about Harmon?" Karl's throat constricted.

"I don't know. All I know is it's something involving Vatche."

Tucker was getting out of his truck, with the dust raised by his tires still showing behind, when Karl came out the back door with his bag in one hand and an apple in the other.

Tucker. He'd totally forgotten.

"Sorry," he said shortly. "I gotta go to the airport. You and Deaver look over the stock. I'm okay with any bull you want to use. And I'll use Fortescue. Tell Jenny we'll reschedule dinner for when I get back."

He'd finished packing while he was on the phone getting the earliest connections to London. There'd been no word from Harmon, no response to Ann-Elise's message.

"Okay," his friend said slowly. "This sudden departure have something to do with Harmon's trip? Sure hope that storm that's all over the news doesn't mess it up."

"It won't, since it's in the Pacific." Karl opened the driver's door of his own truck and tossed bag and apple across to the passenger seat.

Tucker nodded, standing beside the truck. "Yeah, it is. But how do you think she's going to get to Australia?"

Karl froze. "*Australia?*"

Tucker frowned. "Yeah, that's what Tracy's best friend's mother, who works part-time at the airport, said last night when we dropped off Tracy for a sleepover. She said she was so jealous and Harmon promised to bring her back Tim-Tams, the cookies they have there."

Australia. Where Prince Vatche was vacationing.

This could explain Katie's reaction.

"Sorry, Tucker. I've gotta go." He was in the truck, starting the engine.

"Anything I can do?" Tucker asked through the open window.

"Yeah. Keep an eye on the place. I'm imposing on our friend-ship—"

"No problem. You know, if you want to take on being a prince for real, we could work out something."

"Thanks, but no thanks. Right now I need to make sure my efforts to *not* take on this prince stuff full-time don't go to hell."

And to make sure Harmon was okay.

CHAPTER THIRTY-THREE

Port Campbell National Park, Australia

"Enjoying the scenery?" the low male voice asked from beside Harmon as she leaned on the safety railing, ostensibly staring at the churning Southern Ocean below.

A lot closer beside her than she'd been aware of anyone being.

"Listen, buddy—" Her ears caught up with her mouth. She pivoted toward him. "Ka—?"

She didn't finish the name because his head jerked in warning toward where Prince Vatche's party was admiring the view.

"What are you doing here?" she demanded in a low voice.

"What are *you* doing here?" he shot back.

She studied his face under a hooded jacket. His beard stubble glinted red in the morning sun. His eyes were as sharp as ever. Damn the man. He'd probably slept through the entire flight. She'd barely slept at all.

"I've always wanted to see the Great Ocean Road." She knew it wouldn't fly, but she gave it a shot.

"You've got lousy taste in touring companions. Is that why you're staying so far away from … my, oh, my, is that Prince Vatche? That would explain why you're traveling in separate vehicles, too, I suppose. But then why come here with him at all?"

She grimaced. "Fine. You got me. How did you find out I was tailing—? No, never mind that. What are you planning to do? You're not going to let—" She jerked her head back toward Prince Vatche's party still standing at the farthest overlook. "—know that you're here. I'm here. We're here. You can't, Karl. He's up to something and—"

"Later. They're coming back." He slung an arm high around her shoulders and brought his head close to hers. As long as they kept facing each other, no one passing behind could see their faces.

The trouble was, she had to keep looking at Karl. And she was having a hard time reading his expression.

"Quite remarkable," she heard Vatche say as he passed behind them. His bored tone belied his words.

Other voices confirmed his observation in a variety of accents. None Australian. Good. If the Australian media thought he or his statement-to-be were hot topics, they'd be all over him.

The group cleared where she and Karl stood. She started to follow. Karl's arm around her shoulders tightened, drawing her in the opposite direction—toward the overlook.

"I have to follow him. Let go."

He didn't. "It'd be a shame to come all this way and miss seeing this."

"I'll lose them."

"No, we won't."

She looked up at the change of pronoun. He didn't meet her eyes. Still, she stopped resisting.

He directed them to the spot with the best view of the iconic scene, standing close together against the whipping wind.

"I'm still partial to Wyoming," he said with more drawl than usual, "but there's no denying this is damned fine scenery. The Twelve Apostles they call it. Even though—"

"I know, I know. One fell into the ocean in 2005. The guide told me. The guide I need to get back to so I can stay close enough to Vatche to see where he goes next."

"My tour guide told me the same thing. Must be something all the tour guides say. He also said there were only eight to start and the water keeps working on them. Will you look at those waves? It's like they think if they hit the rock hard enough they'll break through."

"Eventually they will. You have a tour guide?"

"Didn't want to try driving on the opposite side of the road, not without more sleep than I've had. So I enlisted a—"

"How did you get here so fast?"

"—tour guide. Nonstop to Melbourne, then a hop close to here. But what you should be asking about is my tour guide. Did you know the Great Ocean Road was started as a way to give veterans returning from World War I work? That's the part closer to Melbourne."

She put the heels of her hands to her forehead. "This is crazy. Completely crazy, Karl. Vatche is hatching something. The magazine refusing to publish hasn't stopped him. Did you know he tried to get a sample of the king's DNA?"

He nodded. "And Andrej's. He'd tried the same lame trick with Katie. No, don't get that look. She didn't break her promise not to tell me anything. But none of his attempts have worked."

"Which is making him all the more desperate. My source in his household heard him screaming he would discredit the king, you, everybody. He plans to tell the world Andrej is the king's grandson. Getting his spin set in everyone's mind, so it can never be completely wiped out. I have people tracking down where and when—."

"Good. I have people working, too. You didn't think I came halfway around the world just to make sure you were okay, did you?"

There was challenge in his words and tone, but something completely different in his eyes. What...?

You didn't think I came halfway around the world just to make sure you were okay, did you?

She had come halfway around the world to make sure *he* would be okay, but he didn't know that.

Unless he did…

"So while our people work away in Melbourne, we can enjoy the Great Ocean Road," he said. "Wonder if the Gibson Steps will be next on Vatche's itinerary. Besides, I'm betting my tour guide could beat up your tour guide. Especially since I have two of them."

"Two?"

"Yup. In two vehicles. Did I ever tell you we had some joint actions with the Aussies? Pays to have Army buddies all over. You ready to go find your tour guide and explain how he's picked up another passenger?"

"Yeah. No—wait." She did a slow, deliberate three-sixty, taking in the sky, the ocean, the stubborn earth, the against-all-odds vegetation. "You're right. It would be a shame to come all this way and miss this."

He took her face between his hands and kissed her, slow and deep.

There was plenty more spectacular scenery. Craggy caves that had sheltered shipwreck survivors in Loch Ard Gorge, sweeps of seascapes, lighthouses snuggled in to neighborhoods, forests closing up around the highway during inland forays. Koalas, kangaroos, wallabies, birds both brilliant and songful, in the wild or rubbing shoulders with towns.

Those sights were caught in snatches because Vatche didn't linger.

With Karl communicating with the drivers of the vehicles he'd brought, they switched around which tailed Vatche, minimizing the chances of being spotted.

In between, they both were on their phones. She had her favorite Australian fixer, Trevor, dig into exactly what Vatche planned. Karl's pals worked the hotel where Vatche and his entourage were staying. As information came in, she and Karl disseminated it to the others.

By early evening, heading back to Melbourne, they were both jet-lagging ... and her tour driver's jaw was sagging.

"Twenty years and never seen the Great Ocean Road like this before," the guide said as he pulled up to the hotel Trevor had told them to come to.

Karl leaned over and tipped him with a wad of cash.

"We appreciate all you've done today and we'd appreciate it more if you don't share this with anyone."

Taking the wad, the driver shook his head. "Nobody'd believe me. They'd take it as one of my tall tales. Serves me right, I s'pose, to finally have a real tale. But I'll console myself, indeed I will." He hefted the cash and gave them a salute.

The hotel was another kind of gorgeous scenery, but they barely glimpsed it as they took the elevator to the room number Trevor had told them.

He, a young fixer named Gracie, and a couple of Karl's guys were already there in a suite that overlooked Fitzroy Gardens. When the driver who'd followed Vatche on the last leg arrived, Karl stood and everyone's focus sharpened.

"Trevor, sounds like you have the best overview. Want to explain to everyone?"

"Prince Vatche has reserved a meeting room in this hotel for one o'clock tomorrow for a news conference. They arranged today's tour of the Great Ocean Road to keep from being plagued by pesky reporters trying to get a pre-statement scoop."

"Have pesky reporters plagued him?" Harmon asked.

"Nope. His people have been trying to drum up interest, it's been scarce on the ground."

"Good," Harmon said. "If you hold a news conference and no news comes…"

"Let's try to keep it that way," Karl said.

Several of his guys nodded. One said, "We'll be there tomorrow. Which room?"

Trevor told them. "They booked an anteroom beside it. That's where speakers wait to be introduced."

"Harmon and I will take that," Karl said.

"Gracie, do what you can to direct any media who do show up elsewhere," Harmon said. "Tell them the room got switched, change signs, anything like that."

They worked out details, then the others left, until it was only Karl, Harmon, and Trevor.

"Do you know what he wants to announce?" Trevor asked. "And why Australia?"

"We have a good idea," Harmon said. With the room mostly empty there was no way not to notice the huge, luxurious bed in a prime spot. "As for Australia, he already had a vacation set here."

Karl shook his head. "He wanted to be as far from King Jozef as possible when he pulled his stunt."

"I suppose there's some interest in Bariavak, what with lost princesses and found princes. Now if they knew you were here…" Trevor tipped his head toward Karl. "But Vatche? Couldn't sell an umbrella in a rainstorm. Better shove off now. Tomorrow."

When the door closed behind him, Karl took a long drink of water, set it down, then turned to her.

"Why didn't you tell me about this in Wyoming. Why did you leave disinformation about London and come here to handle it alone."

"I could handle it," she said.

"That wasn't the question."

"Fine. You want to know why I didn't tell you? Because you kept shutting me out. I'm done asking you to trust me and having you refuse. I know you had reason, Karl. But what matters now is I *can* help. This is too important—"

"Why do you care?"

"What?"

"You heard me. Quit trying to buy time. You said out at the Twelve Apostles that Vatche could be trying to discredit King Jozef, Andrej, me. But why do you care?"

She walked to the window. Stared out without seeing the gardens below, then spun around and came back to him.

"If he discredits the king and Andrej Skala, you will step in like you always do to try to rescue everybody and their brother. You will put yourself on the line. You will devote yourself to fixing other people's problems. You will sacrifice being on your ranch, which is where you want to be, where anyone with eyes can see is where you ought to be, and you'll do that whole must-do-what's-right dance. And you'll be miserable. *That's* why I care. That's why I care about you trusting me. That's why I care about all of it. Because I love you."

She stared at him challengingly, while she pulled in much-needed breath. He didn't respond.

"I love you, Karl Wethers. Probably did when you were nineteen and with my luck probably have loved you ever since. Okay?"

"Yeah. Okay."

She blinked at the deadpan response, then jammed her hands on her hips. "Is that all you have to say?"

"Pretty much. For now. You might have noticed we don't have all that much time on our hands, what with settling the future of a country. So, yeah, that's about all I have to say for now. Later on we'll figure out how you can make a ranch in Wyoming headquarters for your work—which has a whole lot to do with rescuing people, putting yourself on the line, and devoting yourself to fixing other people's problems. But we won't get into that now."

"Oh, we won't, won't we? Why is that?"

"Because it'll wait until after we finish the second thing we need to do, which is to spike Vatche's guns tomorrow."

"The second thing, I'd say that's the first—"

"Nope. The first is to make good use of this bed."

She couldn't help it. She looked at the bed.

Then she looked at him.

"Karl..."

"I love you, too, Harmon. Surely did when I was nineteen and probably have ever since. Now, are you going to get in that bed?"

Oh, yes, she was.

They were back in the large bed.

They'd made love. And again. Showered together, returned to the bed.

She wrapped her legs around him, drawing him in.

He resisted, the veins and tendons in his arms showing the strain.

"Not again," she groaned.

"You're done running away, Harmon Reed. Not ever again. You're done avoiding the biggest risk."

"It *is* a risk. A huge risk and I'm gambling on you, Karl Wethers. Scares me half to death. And, yes, before you say it, that might be—

is—a carryover from Mom's death. I'm trying. With Dad, with Ann-Elise and the babies-to-be. And most of all with you. Because I do love you. So if you die on me before we're a hundred, I will find you in the afterlife and make you miserable for eternity."

He grinned. "I can live with that." Then his expression changed as he stroked deep inside her.

CHAPTER THIRTY-FOUR

Harmon was as confident as ever.

On the outside.

Inside, she was mush.

Some of that might be from the night spent with Karl. At least he was as tired as she was because he hadn't had any time for sleep, either. Odd how you could be so sleepy and yet find better things to do than sleep.

Some of it certainly was from fear.

If this didn't go right there was still the danger of Karl feeling he had to step up, step in, rescue. He'd be so miserable as the heir, as king…

Karl paused with his hand around the doorknob of the anteroom. He looked at her. "Here we go." He leaned over and kissed her. Brief, hard, possessive.

He opened the door and they stepped in. As they did, she caught a glimpse of Trevor's big grin.

But that was only for a second. Because the face she was concentrating on was Vatche's.

She was to keep track of Vatche. Karl and Trevor were making sure his entourage didn't try to pull anything.

"What is this?" Vatche said. "We are not to be disturbed. We left strict orders that—You. *You!*"

He'd spotted Karl. Harmon moved between them, but there was no need, because Vatche had recoiled two steps. Still talking, but retreating.

"You cannot be here. Go away. Immediately. I command it."

"You can't command in Australia, mate," Trevor said.

"Or anywhere," Harmon said.

"I shall be the next king of Bariavak. When the world knows that King Jozef has schemed to set his bastard to rule the people of Bariavak, they will rise up and—"

"Not rule," Karl said. "Govern."

"—turn to a true monarch. You will see. You will all see, most of all Jozef, who invites me to the castle merely to laugh at me. But after I speak today, he will laugh no more!"

"You're not speaking today, Vatche," Harmon said.

"I am! You cannot stop me. I speak to claim my throne, and those gathered shall tell the world."

Holding out an arm as if to ward them off, though no one had advanced, Prince Vatche flung open the door to the meeting room, the impetus carrying him a couple yards in.

It was empty.

Completely and spectacularly empty.

Harmon followed Vatche into the room, where row upon row of chairs lined up, waiting for … no one. Gracie and Karl's buddies had done an even better job than she'd hoped.

"You fools! Incompetent, stupid, fools," Vatche screamed toward the people still in the anteroom.

Was it her imagination or were there fewer than when they'd entered? None were trying to get past Trevor, blocking the doorway, to join their prince.

"All you had to do was get them here," Vatche screamed. "One thing only and you fail. I am cursed to be surrounded by fools."

He shifted into a torrent of curse words in an impressively wide-ranging number of languages.

Karl came up beside her, watching as Vatche stumbled toward the lectern, his mouth gaped, then closed, gaped then closed. Now he looked less like one of the evil stepsisters from Cinderella and more like a fish. Not one of the cute ones.

Breathing hard, he showed signs of trying to regain his composure.

He assumed the wide-legged stance of a diminished Henry VIII.

"The internet. My people will go on the internet. That is the direct way to the people. The modern way. They will reveal how Jozef—"

"That's His Majesty to you, Vatche," Karl growled.

"—has deceived his country. How he—"

"What people, Vatche?" Harmon asked.

"—schemed to make his bastard—What?"

"What people are going to spread the word on the internet?"

She gestured to the anteroom. Trevor obligingly stepped aside, showing the entourage had evaporated.

Prince Vatche dropped to the floor, crying.

The king agreed to meet with Andrej Skala while Karl and she joined in through a secure connection from Australia.

Harmon explained Prince Vatche's plan and how they had stopped it.

The king appeared remarkably unsurprised that Vatche had known of the connection between the king and Andrej Skala. But he did look grim. "He shall not return here. Ever."

"You can keep him out, sir, but he could still make trouble from outside Bariavak."

"He shall not," the king said decisively. "That shall be resolved once and for all. He will remain in Australia."

"They don't want him," Harmon said.

The king gave a wave of his hand. "We shall resolve that as well."

"Yes, sir," Karl said. "But it is Bariavak's future we must resolve now. You have known for more than a year that Katie will not take the throne. That I will not take the throne. What does that leave?"

"It leaves the people of Bariavak," Andrej said strongly. "We are your people. People you know. And you know we will govern ourselves well. We know it. We deserve it, as all peoples do. We will not push you from your throne, Your Majesty. But after your lifetime, the people of Bariavak require the right—the inalienable right—to govern themselves."

Karl picked it up. "You need to do this, sir. You need to lead your people to the bridge to democracy. And you need to do it now."

"Yes."

Stunned silence extended from Bariavak to Melbourne.

"Yes, you know you need to be the one or, yes, you'll do it, Your Majesty?" Harmon asked.

He looked at her through the screen. "You are wise to insist on clarity, Harmon Reed. Yes, I will support the transition to democracy. So, indeed, my answer is yes to both."

Karl cleared his voice. "Andrej, tell His Majesty the plans as they stand."

For an instant she saw hesitation on Andrej's face. Then it was gone. Respect for his king remained, perhaps the beginning of a connection to the man who was his grandfather, but he was sure and powerful as he explained the plan to end the reign of the royal house of Bariavak.

Harmon and Karl escorted Vatche on a ten-hour commercial flight to Hong Kong.

One of the king's jets met them there, having transported a legal team, accompanied by security force members, who would see to Vatche's future, including relinquishing even his remote claim to the throne.

The king made it clear the allowance he had bestowed on Vatche from his personal coffers, out of respect for his wife's memory, would end if Vatche did not choose a country in a different continent and remain there.

The royal jet, complete with a fully-equipped shower, took Harmon and Karl back to Bariavak. Ruzena came on board with clothes when they landed in Bariavak. An official car took them directly to the castle, where a live broadcast had already started from the reception room.

They were escorted through a side door into seats behind Madame, Katie and Brad. Hunter and April were farther back.

King Jozef sat on a dais to one side of the microphones, with top ministers behind him. On the other side of the microphone sat a line of officials backing Andrej, who was concluding his address. Karl and Harmon had read a draft of it and given their comments during the flight.

The applause was thunderous.

Andrej then introduced the king.

He looked older, standing there alone behind the microphones. Yet so dignified and solid.

"You have heard the dreams for Bariavak that this coalition of leaders from so many aspects of our country has formed. You have heard the step-by-step plan they have presented to you. Now you shall hear what I, King Jozef of Bariavak, have to say."

It seemed as if Harmon could feel the country hold its collective breath.

She slid her hand into Karl's. He clasped it. Protective, while also accepting her protection.

"I have thought long about the future of our beloved country. My dear granddaughter says with certainty that she shall not be queen, that she wishes democracy to replace the monarchy. Prince Karl, who could be king if he so wished, says the same. Many of my people have expressed this desire as well. Among you some have worked hard and have worked well to begin the process toward this.

"I commit now, to you the people I have served my entire life—"

Harmon's eyes stung. If the people of Bariavak knew the sacrifices he and Madame had made, they might begin to understand how truly they both had put duty first.

"—that I shall work with a congress representing the people of Bariavak to establish a transition from the complete monarchy we have known to a democracy we shall form together. We shall create a constitution and a government that shall sustain and protect our people going forward as our mountains have for centuries past. This will not be easy. Those peoples who have been given democracy have so seldom treasured it. It will be that we, all the people of Bariavak, must earn it through careful, measured approaches and through learning the vital skills of democracy—to listen openly to those of different opinion, to compromise because no one is infallible. We must all work hard."

He added a phrase in Bariavak's language. She heard it echoed by his listeners here, could imagine it traveling throughout the small country. It had the ring of "God bless, Bariavak."

"Bariavak now faces the future, led by the royal blood." There was deep satisfaction in King Jozef's voice when they finally settled in his private sitting room.

It was those Karl had come to think of as the king's family— Madame, Katie and Brad, April and Hunter, him and Harmon— though only one had the tie of blood.

He turned to the king. "You knew about all of it all along."

"All—so broad." A twinkle appeared at the back of the king's eyes.

"You certainly knew Andrej was your grandson."

"You have heard Madame say she told me only recently."

Madame immediately backed him. "That is so."

"There's Madame telling you and there's you knowing. Two different things," April said.

"Ah. Perhaps."

"Is this what you always wanted, Grandfather?" Katie asked.

"No." The single syllable seemed to cover possibilities long eliminated. His daughter as queen to succeed him, his granddaughter raised to eventually become queen herself. "It is, however, a tolerable alternative."

"But you wanted the monarchy to continue, you could have made Andrej a prince and…" She was frowning when she let that die. "That doesn't feel right."

King Jozef lifted her hand and kissed it. "My dear granddaughter, I think you will find that your friend Prince Karl has a theory."

"Suspicion more than a theory. You've planned for democracy. You, along with your subjects, saw the unsatisfying candidates to succeed you and knew that would not do. I'd say you started formulating this plan before you went to D.C. Was Hunter your first candidate to bring democracy to Bariavak?"

King Jozef looked remarkably noncommittal. Hunter made a sound of protest.

Karl continued, "He was the first not to cooperate with you. Though you did get him to corral me. Just out of curiosity, how long had you known about me?"

The king tilted his head. "Since you were born. Your great-grandfather's rebellious ways made an impression on my father and his father. It was thought prudent to know the whereabouts of the Princes of Gelicia."

Karl gave a grim smile. "Should have known. But then something happened that you hadn't planned for—you found Katie. At first, you thought the monarchy would continue after all. But she not only said no, she openly espoused democracy. You could not dismiss her as you would almost anyone else, yet you were not ready for an open movement toward democracy, because you wanted to mold it."

"To strengthen it," demurred King Jozef. "You have no idea how disorganized those who wanted democracy were for so long. It was disheartening at times. But I would not give in to despair."

"You saw promise in Andrej and you kept plotting."

"Planning for my country's future."

"It was delicate. To never associate Andrej too closely with me or my government, yet to open doors to see if he had the ability and will to go through them. The boy has done well," King Jozef said with satisfaction, looking at Madame.

"That is why you refused to have him as your private secretary," Madame said.

"Yes. That was most difficult, to deny you when you asked that for your relative in that so proper, so formal letter. But I could not say that

I knew what you alone had the right to tell me. So I had only to continue."

"Which," Karl picked up, "included using me as a stalking horse for the democracy forces to unite against."

"Never that," the king protested.

"No, that was Prince Vatche," April said. "I wondered why you had him around when you couldn't stand him. *He* was the stalking horse."

The king beamed at her.

"So we come back to the fact that you made this happen," Karl said.

"No. You made it happen. You and Andrej and many others. I contributed by arranging that you and Andrej and others of your thinking might cross paths. What you did together was of your own making."

Karl frowned. Harmon knew he still didn't see his true role. She did.

"You brought Karl in because you needed someone ethical and strong and inclined to fight for other people—even when they don't deserve it—who would not try to secure power or position for himself, but instead would rouse the pro-democracy forces, light a fire under Andrej Skala, and show him this was a winnable fight."

"He is most admirable at lighting a fire," King Jozef said with an impish expression.

Katie, Brad, and April chuckled, Hunter gave an unconvincing cough, and Madame's expression relaxed toward a smile.

"You took advantage of his overdeveloped sense of duty," Harmon accused. "He's been pulled away from the home he loves. He's had to be in this role he's hated. And he's had to work three times as hard at his ranch to be at your beck and call. That's—"

"Harmon," Hunter said before she could add the decidedly undiplomatic *despicable.*

King Jozef appeared unfazed. "I have, indeed, taken advantage of his nature. I shall hope he will forgive me. I have no such hope for the forgiveness of the woman who loves him."

That tied up her tongue while looks ricocheted around the room before they all seemed to land on her. There hadn't been a chance to say anything to the others about their changed status. There hadn't even been time for them to talk about it.

Karl saved her. "What I want to know is what you would have done if I'd said yes, I'd be heir to the throne."

From impish, the king's expression turned serious. "I would have thanked the heavens for bringing such a man to Bariavak and left the pro-democracy forces to find their own way if they could."

Okay, fine. King Jozef was partially forgiven.

"And Harmon? How did she fit into your plan?" Karl asked.

"Ah, there I shall claim accolades for recognizing I could not let her fly away after you failed to talk to her on the flight from Venice."

"What?" Karl demanded. "What difference did that make? I was tired. I slept."

But Harmon's eyes slowly widened. "Of course. Why didn't I see that?"

"See what? There wasn't anything to see." No one paid any attention to Karl's protest.

"Because, my dear, you were laboring under the same handicap as he. The same pain of still being in love and not recognizing it." He took one of her hands and reached for Karl's, drawing them together. Their hands clasped. "Someday, Harmon will tell you all. She has been a most wonderful improvisation."

Madame made a sound.

They all looked at her.

"Do not believe what the fox says to the chickens. He despaired that you and you—" She jerked her head first at Harmon, then at Karl. "—would ever find your way. If you had not yet, he still would be maneuvering and ordering and manipulating. I fear for what will occupy him now that you are awake to what you feel."

After a slight pause, Brad started laughing.

"What?" Katie demanded.

At last, he got out, "God help Andrej Skala's kids when they're old enough for the king to start matchmaking for them."

EPILOGUE

Ten weeks later

The pageantry dazzled. But it was the symbolism that had Katie and April in tears as they sat side by side with their husbands and Madame in the royal box at the legislature building in Bariavak.

This was the opening day of the constitutional convention that would provide the road map for Bariavak's future.

A procession had brought them here, with citizens lining the route, cheering and waving flags.

King Jozef would be involved in major discussions, though citizens' votes would be the final arbiter. For now, he was opening the session. Hunter, who had known the language as a child, and Katie, who had studied it since learning her lineage, translated quietly for their spouses.

At the end of his brief speech, King Jozef handed a wooden box to Andrej Skala.

Under Harmon's supervision, their relationship had been revealed through the top political columnist. Shortly after, she let drop the few elements of their lifelong romance that the king and Madame approved. Their human story swamped any discontent or concern over the political aspect.

Andrej opened the box to disclose a beautifully simple gavel. A gracious symbol of the change taking place.

"Karl and Harmon should be here," April said.

"Karl didn't want to distract. Besides, I think he was afraid of what Hunter would say on behalf of the State Department." Brad grinned as he looked down the row to the other man.

"I'm here as an individual, who wouldn't say anything Karl needed to fear. As for State, he already knows they begrudgingly acknowledge this is a close second to having him on the throne."

"More important," Katie said, "I think he and Harmon are very happy right where they are."

The Wethers Ranch, Wyoming

Harmon was on the phone when he came in.

He could tell by the tone of her "mmm-hmms" that the call was important. So he just leaned in to kiss her.

She parted her lips. There was no refusing that invitation. He stroked deep into her mouth, felt her exploration of his.

When they had to come up for air—and a "mmm-hmm" by her into the phone—he started to back up. She fisted her hand in his shirt and brought him back to her, reaching up to kiss him again.

"I'm hot and sweaty," he whispered into her free ear.

"Yes, you are," she whispered back.

He kissed her again, quick and hard. "Shower."

When he came out, shirt hanging loose and open, she eyed him, but she was still occupied on the phone.

He tipped his head to indicate he was going outside, and sat on the still solitary porch chair.

She dropped her phone in a pocket. He drew her down to sit on his lap. "News?"

"The best. A girl and a boy. It's not unusual for it to be this early with twins. Everybody's healthy. They're over the moon. Ann-Elise says she hears rumors that her ankles have been resurrected, but she's too tired to make sure. The name battle goes on. We're expected to come visit this winter."

He nodded. "Great news. And I won't mind a trip to South Carolina in mid-winter."

"How about you? What do you hear from Bariavak? Progress?"

"Only for a snail. I must be the only man in the world who can't schedule his wedding because some country on the other side of the world is trying to write a constitution."

"Hey, count yourself lucky. You won the battle about the wedding being here."

He snorted. "No way was King Jozef pushing us into a royal wedding in Bariavak."

"He wasn't the only one wanting the wedding there."

"His security people are just going to have to figure out how to make it work in Wyoming."

"Sally wanted the wedding in Bariavak, too. And her mother. I think they had a Cinderella fantasy going."

"They'll have to make do with Wyoming. I'll tell Sally that next time—"

"Hey, don't make waves with Sally. Remember, she schedules my travel. She might decide she can't find any connections that will get me back home."

He kissed her deeply. Did she even know she referred to the ranch as home?

"Good point. Maybe we can sell Sally—and her mother—on a cowboy fantasy. Wouldn't get that in Bariavak. Or we could elope. Look how well that's turned out for Ann-Elise and your father."

"True. But they wouldn't have had to answer to King Jozef, Madame, Katie and Brad, April and Hunter—"

"Hunter wouldn't mind."

"—he's more sentimental than you think. And you didn't let me finish. Sally and her mom. Ann-Elise and Dad." He kissed her on the nose for calling her father Dad. "Not to mention the future president of Bariavak and Mirche, who's entertaining certain cowgirl fantasies of his own. Last but not least, Ruzena, who has already designed a dozen amazing dresses. I have no idea how I'll pick, but she's well on her way to a bridal line. Wouldn't want to deny her that. Besides, we can keep ourselves entertained before the wedding."

He shifted her slightly, sliding one hand along her hip then under her pulled-out shirt. Since that day in her hotel room, he'd developed a thing for discovering her from under the hem of a shirt. Though he preferred it when that was all she was wearing. "True."

"Mmm." But she stilled his hand. "Where is everyone?"

"Greg went to Billings to see a movie."

"What movie's worth that trip?"

"Not the movie. The girl who works at the theater."

"Ah. And Deaver went, too?"

"It was his idea."

She chuckled and released his hand. Then she produced a different sound as he stroked higher.

"Sun's still up," she pointed out. But as a protest it lacked conviction since she opened her top two buttons.

"Not for long. And Rooster won't mind."

"True and true. It's going to get cool as soon as the sun sets."

"I'll keep you warm." His hand cupped her breast as her blouse opened.

"Oh, yes, you will."

Some time later, with the cool and the dark drawing around them, their heat held them still and sated.

"Told you I only need one chair," he said.

When her chuckle faded, she said softly, "I never forgot you, Karl. I wanted to. I tried to. I pretended I had. But I never did. You were always the prince I'd run away from but couldn't forget."

He kissed her temple. "Welcome home."

Thank you for reading Karl and Harmon's story!

In this Wedding Series finale, you revisit characters you've come to love in *The Christmas Princess, The Surprise Princess* and *At the Heart's Command,* another Wyoming veteran's story from the **A Place Called Home** series. For more connected small-town romance, explore the **Wyoming Wildflowers** series, **Seasons in a Small Town** and **Bardville, Wyoming.**

And for you Wedding Series readers, I have a special incentive. If you join my readers list at www.patriciamclinn.com/lp-su-tsk, you'll receive an exclusive offer to download a free short story. *The Soldier's Kiss,* a prequel to *The Forgotten Prince,* introduces Harmon and shares how her father, Lt. Col. Brooks Reed, discovers his true love, artist Ann-Elise Jerakenko … with help from a cat.

April, Hunter, Jozef, Madame and friends ask if you'll help spread the word about them and The Wedding Series. You have the power to do that in two quick ways:

Recommend the book and the series to your friends and/or the whole wide world on social media. Shouting from rooftops is particularly appreciated.

Review the book. Take a few minutes to write an honest review and it can make a huge difference. As you likely know, it's the single best way for your fellow readers to find books they'll enjoy, too.

To me—as an author and a reader—the goal is always to find a good author-reader match. By sharing your reading experience through recommendations and reviews, you become a vital matchmaker. ☺

For news about upcoming books, as well as other titles and news, join Patricia McLinn's Readers List and receive her twice-monthly free newsletter.
www.patriciamclinn.com/readers-list

The Wedding Series

Prelude to a Wedding

She's all work and no play. He's an expert at fun. Their romance could be the biggest game of all.

Wedding Party

As one couple ties the knot, the best man hopes to find love with the bridesmaid.

Grady's Wedding

Marriage can be catching. Will the last bachelor take the leap?

The Runaway Bride

Escaping a bridal disaster in Illinois, her life takes a wild, wild turn in the West.

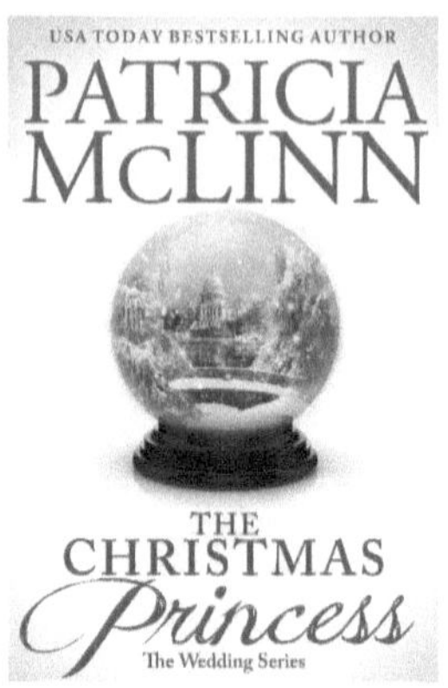

The Christmas Princess

A princess for a few weeks … a prince for a lifetime.

Hoops (prequel to The Surprise Princess)

Can the coach and the professor play on the same team?

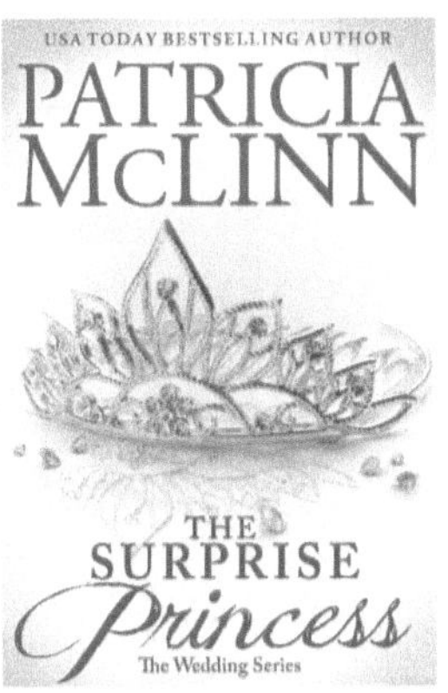

The Surprise Princess

She's an ordinary young woman living an ordinary life in small-town Wisconsin … isn't she?

Not a Family Man (prequel to The Forgotten Prince)

City girl Jenny, the ranch's attractive new owner, spells trouble for foreman Tucker.

Praise for The Wedding Series

"A wonderful series that will make you laugh and cry. Each page is filled with love that will eventually come to the people who so need it. A must read!"—*5-star review*

"McLinn is an expert at revealing the layers enveloping her characters. With each reveal, sometimes exquisitely subtle, we are pulled in deeper to be active participants in the emotionally charged, yet heart-melting romance."—*USA Today*

"Love this series … so many twists and turns that take you all over the world!"—*5-star review*

"Fun and serious all at the same time. Love how the friends intertwine and add new along the way. It was refreshing to read the different stories and having them all come together. Really enjoyed this series!"—*5-star review*

"Perfect. The characters were multi-dimensional and played off each other in warm, thoughtful, loving ways. Each couple faced a different situation and overcame their obstacles together and with the insightful comments of their friends. … Heart-warming."—*5-star review*

"Full of warmth, understanding of human nature, and great characters. They are connected, following the lives of college friends, and by the time you are finished, you feel as if you are a part of their extended circle. A dash of sex here, but not to the point that it overshadows the well thought out storylines. Definitely a feel good experience."—*5-star review*

Also by Patricia McLinn

Marry Me Series

Wedding of the Century

The Unexpected Wedding Guest

A Most Unlikely Wedding

Baby Blues and Wedding Bells

Seasons in a Small Town series

What Are Friends For? (Spring)

The Right Brother (Summer)

Falling for Her (Autumn)

Warm Front (Winter)

Wyoming Wildflowers Series

A Place Called Home Series

Bardville, Wyoming Series

Explore a complete list of all Patricia's books
patriciamclinn.com/patricias-books

Or get a printable booklist
patriciamclinn.com/patricias-books/printable-booklist

Patricia's eBookstore (buy digital books online directly from Patricia)
patriciamclinn.com/patricias-books/ebookstore

About the Author

USA Today bestselling author Patricia McLinn spent more than 20 years as an editor at The Washington Post after stints as a sports writer (Rockford, Ill.) and assistant sports editor (Charlotte, N.C.). She received BA and MSJ degrees from Northwestern University.

McLinn is the author of more than 50 published novels, which are cited by readers and reviewers for wit and vivid characterization. Her books include mysteries, romantic suspense, contemporary romance, historical romance and women's fiction. They have topped bestseller lists and won numerous awards.

She has spoken about writing from Melbourne, Australia, to Washington, D.C., including being a guest speaker at the Smithsonian Institution.

Now living in northern Kentucky, McLinn loves to hear from readers through her website, Facebook and Twitter.

Visit with Patricia:

Website: patriciamclinn.com

Facebook: facebook.com/PatriciaMcLinn

Twitter: @PatriciaMcLinn

Pinterest: pinterest.com/patriciamclinn

Instagram: instagram.com/patriciamclinnauthor